Knights of
the End

Book One

J.D. Cowan

Acknowledgments

Thanks to mom and dad, Jagi, Tovio, Dawn, Randy, and everyone else I missed.

Prologue

Teddy MacIsaac stood atop the junkpile, victorious. In his hands shone a golden coin with a perfect circumference flashing against the afternoon sun. This was his treasure; this was what he would use to save the world.

The coin twinkled as he inspected both sides. No markings had been embedded on the flawless treasure. It fit perfectly in the palm of his hand. It *spoke* to him.

He was only a fourteen-year-old eighth grader, but Teddy knew greatness when he saw it. This was more than greatness. This was a gift from the heavens.

He climbed down the mountain of trash. His left arm shielded him from the light of the sun as he descended. His boots crunched into old Styrofoam and rotten food. He brushed himself off as he reached the trash strewn road at the bottom of the hill. Despite the shower he would undoubtedly need, his trek through the junkyard was still worth it. His nose would hate him forever, though.

It was almost unbelievable. The dreams had told him that unimaginable riches awaited him in the trash. He had searched that junkyard for over a year because of those dreams, and, in every moment he spent there, he knew he would find it. He never lost the faith.

Wind blew his strawberry blonde hair back. He brushed it clean.

He patted down his old green jacket to make sure no trash clung to him, and slid the coin into his pocket. Walking through the trash was worth it, even if he stunk like rotten milk and the taste of copper filled his mouth.

He removed his boots and put them into his backpack just like he did every day. There was nothing important in there, anyway. Just school books.

As he changed back into his red sneakers, a heat traveled through him and up his spine. Gooseflesh sprung up all over.

He stood up.

"*Theodore MacIsaac*," a voice spoke into his mind. "*Press your hands together, and heed the call.*"

Skepticism overtook him but momentarily. He *knew* the words. He didn't know how he knew them, but they echoed through his mind like a Prayer of Devotion that old warriors chanted before they charged into battle. Visions of lonely nights he'd spent over the last year flashed through him, and the familiar voice soothed his fears. This was his chance. He wouldn't waver now.

Teddy clasped the coin between his pressed together palms like a prayer or a stance in a martial arts movie. Heat shot into his hands and through his body.

"I beg you," he said, "bestow on me the glory!"

A flash of light overtook existence. Nothing remained

but dabs of black against a white canvas. He was gone and then he was back again within a second, standing alone in the junkyard.

He blinked. "What did I just do?"

Teddy checked himself over. His old blue jeans and black shirt were still there, as was the rest of him.

But the coin was gone.

"No. No, no, no, no!"

He patted his pockets. He searched the garbage covered road around him. The coin had vanished.

He debated putting on his boots again and going back out into the trash. It was getting late, but this was a treasure worth more than being grounded. He wouldn't go home empty-handed. Not after finally learning the dreams were real.

"I think MacIsaac came out here," Stieg Johns said.

"I thought I heard someone yelling over there."

Teddy froze. They'd found him. He cocked his ears and listened for the voices again.

"What would he be doing in the junkyard, anyway? Do all you eighth grade losers have brain damage or something?"

Teddy followed the sounds of the voices south down the narrow path between junk piles. He circled around as they drew near, making sure to keep their view obscured of his presence. Sure enough, his first inclination was right. They rounded the bend, joking away with each other. Teddy recognized the group of five teenagers. They were led by Stieg Johns and Corey Hoffman.

"You just don't know MacIsaac, Corey," Stieg said, in his

best suck-up voice. "I've known the loser for years. Never throws a punch, runs from everything, still plays make believe in the woods. Hanging out at a junkyard is the exact sort of thing he would do. Besides, the garbage guy in the truck outside said he spotted a short kid with blonde hair hanging out here almost all summer. Who else would it be?"

Stieg Johns wore a non-threatening bowl-cut hairdo, a thick jacket two sizes too big for his average size, and had the face of a horse. If he didn't latch on to Hoffman's gang, he would have been even lower on the food chain than Teddy was.

There was a time that Stieg Johns was Teddy's friend. That was before seventh grade started. Things changed. Teddy didn't put much stock in friends anymore. They all ended up like Stieg.

"He *is* a freak," Hoffman said, gazing around the piles of waste. "Man, it reeks here. Can't stand it. Let's just get him tomorrow. I know a guy that can make this much easier."

Hoffman was burly, most of which was fat. He wore a thick black jacket and perfectly stylized spiky hair to complete his appearance as a thug. He'd been held back a year, which was fairly obvious to anyone who spoke with him for more than three seconds. It didn't change the fact that he was the second most feared kid at school. Corey Hoffman was no wuss.

Stieg shrugged. "If you say so."

"I do, Johns. Just because freaks hang out here, doesn't mean I'm gonna. I've got places to be. Now, shut up and let's get out of here."

Teddy didn't stick around to watch them leave. He

sprinted over to the fence by the exit while they were still talking. He knew this place too well by now.

Without pause, he scurried over the fence. As he landed on the other side, a pang of regret knocked into him.

He didn't want to be like Stieg. He didn't want to fall in line and hand over his life to the first fat thug that sneered at him. He wanted real friends, and he wanted to be needed.

Teddy wanted to be a hero. He wanted to save the world. He wanted to be the monster-slaying hero from all those games they played as kids. Evil rises, Good slays it. No matter where the monsters struck, and no matter who the innocent was, there would always be a hero to make things right. That is how the world works. That is how it is supposed to be.

Teddy was going to be that hero.

Someday.

He leaned against the fence. His palms itched when he glared at them. He still stunk of sour milk. The whole situation was pathetic.

Teddy was no hero. He was still playing pretend.

And that wasn't good enough anymore.

Finally, after wasting enough time, he decided to head home. His mom would kill him if he wasted anymore time.

The world was not what it had been when he was a kid. Was this the way things were supposed to be? Would it continue like this forever? A voice in the back of his head answered with one definitive statement.

"*No.*"

Heat built up inside Teddy MacIsaac's body. If he didn't know better, it was like he was ready to explode.

Chapter 1
Welcome to the New World

Teddy ran home through the forest and down the trail. His sneakers kicked up loose blades of grass and pebbles. Heavy breaths pumped through his lungs, as his backpack swung off-kilter from shoulder to shoulder behind him. A smile crept across his small face.

The forest was a second home. Teddy spent his time here outside of school and home, running about and playing games as kids do. The crisp smell of maples, the rough feel of pine needles, and the chirping of the robins, all were as natural as the pillow on his bed, or the old book sticking out of the back pocket of his torn jeans. The world was how it should be.

But there wasn't any time to play around. The sun had begun to set, and he was late getting home.

He shuffled across the open meadows, and onto the abandoned train tracks, making better time than he usually did. It was like a spare battery had juiced him up. He'd always been short and a bit puny, but now he felt like he could punch a moving train from its tracks, or run full-tilt across water. Teddy felt like a hero from one of his books. He was a kid again.

But he wasn't a kid anymore. He knew saving the world was impossible. Even a fourteen year old like him could take a look around and see the brokenness everywhere. Murder and suicide on the rise, apathy as plentiful as oxygen, and the loss of Justice and Truth had shaken his faith in the human race. When he was a kid, it was all so simple.

It was simple, until everyone grew up and forgot what it meant for the Good Guy to win. Only he was left, all his old friends had moved on and left him, and he was beginning to lose the faith. Everything he stood for could have been a lie.

Nothing had changed from that morning to make him feel any different; nothing, that is, except for the coin he had found in the junkyard. It was a game-changer.

A voice in his head, a prickling of skin, and the scent of spring breeze, all shot through him when he thought of his purpose in this giant mess of a world. It formed the picture of a coin in his mind. The more he thought about it, the clearer it came to him. He'd spent the better part of his summer vacation and seventh grade year searching for that treasure: a treasure he almost didn't believe existed anymore. He didn't want to believe it was only a dream.

And then when he finally found it there in the middle of nowhere, shining like a beacon into his soul, it slipped between his fingers. It had vanished and gone.

Teddy ran up the tracks. He whipped along the fence to the neighboring houses. On his right was more forest and wild brush that he would have loved to explore; he jumped the fence to his left instead. He wasn't risking getting grounded.

As he landed on the opposite side of the fence, a familiar voice called out to him from across the yard. He looked up to meet the gaze of Mrs. Werner staring at him from her back porch.

"Still think you're some sort of hero, Mr. MacIsaac?"

Teddy smiled. "If I was, I wouldn't need to take this shortcut, ma'am. Besides, I haven't played those sorts of games in years."

"But you still play in the woods."

Teddy did spend most of his time in the woods. He loved the scent of pine blowing across his face, and the sound of grass bending under his shoes. That would never change.

"I'm not playing. Just remembering the good old days."

Mrs. Werner was a retired teacher who lived alone. He had known her for years. Teddy had never had her as a teacher, but he could imagine how scary it would be to have her. Most days she spent out on her back porch. She would stare out into the endless woods on the other side of the tracks. But despite her toughness, Teddy had always thought of her as a good friend. Friends were getting rarer every day.

"I still remember when you started playing those games," she said. "You, Matty Sova, Stieg Johns, and a couple of the neighborhood boys would run through the woods all day. Darryl envied you boys for having such fun. Where are they these days? I haven't seen them around in a dog's age."

He felt an eyebrow twitch. "We're not really friends anymore."

"That's a shame. Darryl did like to watch you boys play."

"They were good times. But I'm sure he's thinking about better things now, ma'am."

She nodded. "Why are you so late coming back, anyway? Beth is going to be blowing steam out of her ears if you don't get a move on."

"I know." He shuffled his backpack and bounded forward. "Thanks for letting me cut through your yard like this, by the way. It really saves time. My mom doesn't really like that I take the long way back, but I just really love the forest, you know?"

Mrs. Werner smiled as only the old know how: with wisdom and grace. "Darryl used to babysit for you. I feel like I'd be letting him down if I didn't let his young friend catch a break. It also doesn't help that you're a sweet boy. Who can say no to you?"

Teddy waved it away. "Come on, ma'am. Just 'cuz I'm short doesn't make me a kid."

"I kid. But you have to stop reading those comics and old adventure books. I see one in your back pocket from here. They're not good for you. These days with all those earthquakes and roving gangs, I'd feel better if your head weren't in the clouds all the time."

Teddy had heard about the gangs. They mostly stuck to the big places like New Sun City. As for the earthquakes, there was not much he could do. The mall in the center of town had been taken out by one months ago. They also got two earthquakes a week, usually. Just another sign the world was ending.

"Don't worry about me. I'm on the straight and narrow. Besides, we've been lucky enough to not have an earthquake since August. They'll probably get back to fixing up the old mall soon enough, I bet. Can't leave it falling apart forever, right?"

"They could leave it to rot for all I care."

"I'm just saying that you don't need to worry about me, ma'am."

"Darryl would be worrying about you, so I will worry in his place."

Teddy didn't like to think about Darryl much. When he was a kid, Darryl was his babysitter. He gave Teddy his first adventure book: a tale about pirates looking for treasure in the sky. Those were the good memories.

But then he graduated High School, and moved to New Sun City. Teddy didn't hear about him again until after he was murdered a year ago, and he didn't see him again until the funeral in McLeod. They'd never found his killer. The only clue they got were Darryl's final words. He gasped out a description about a fat man made of stone with a ring piercing on his right ear. That wasn't much to go on, so it was never followed up on.

Mrs. Werner was alone now, and Teddy wouldn't let her be alone more than she had to.

"Have you eaten lunch today, Mr. MacIsaac?"

He scratched the back of his head. "I, uh, lost it on my way to school "

She reached into a solid white bowl on the table beside her chair. She'd always kept one for when Teddy came by. There were apples inside. Mrs. Werner tossed him one.

He caught it with his left hand. The apple was a Cortland.

"Get moving, Theodore. The world might be getting worse, but it doesn't mean you should forget to eat right."

"You got it."

The way back home from Mrs. Werner's backyard was a breeze. He sprinted down the streets. Orange and red leaves tumbled from the branches of birches in the yards. Fall was definitely here.

McLeod wasn't a big town, but it wasn't the smallest around, either. It had a private and public school for elementary students, it also had one high school which spanned from seventh grade up to twelfth. The only other school was a town over in Riverview, but there was no way his mom would have gone for that. Unfortunately, most of his old friends did.

Instead, Teddy went to Harding High School, or as he liked to call it, *Hell On Earth*. His old friends had chosen to go to the junior high in Riverview, or had moved away. His lack of friends was due to coincidence and circumstance. Or so he liked to believe.

Afternoons were lazy on the outskirts of town where Teddy lived. Birds sang and dogs barked streets away. The adults were still at work and the kids were long since home and watching television. He enjoyed the quiet. That was part of the reason he liked the forest, after all.

Finally, he made the turn down St. Bona Street. It was good to be home.

His house was a two-story home with a tanned yellow paintjob, black shutters on the large window to the living room, and the gate to the backyard left ajar. The latter meant his brothers were home.

In the driveway sat his father's truck. A dark blue number that was older than Teddy was, it still drove beautifully.

His father sat in the truck, leaning back in his seat. The old man looked exhausted.

Teddy knocked on the window. His dad flinched in his seat. Teddy enjoyed sneaking up on him.

He rolled the window down, shaking his head.

"Late again, Theodore?"

"What are you doing home so early? The restaurant can't function without its boss."

Jonas MacIsaac scratched his beard. He sat back in his seat. The old man liked to think, and had a tendency to overdo it at times. There was also a chance he forgot he was supposed to go inside.

"No," he said, "we've been having problems getting the younger guys to come in for their shifts. No work ethic in these kids. That reminds me of something I wanted to ask you."

Teddy grinned. "Ask me? I thought you didn't want me working there."

"You can't even get home on time without getting lost in the woods. You think I'm going to trust you to be punctual? No, I wanted to ask you if you knew a boy named Rochester

Carson. He goes to Harding in the ninth grade."

To say that Teddy *knew* Rock Carson was a stretch. It would be more accurate to say that he knew the jerk's reputation. Rock Carson was the toughest kid at Harding. Even scarier than Corey Hoffman and his band of idiots, Rock Carson was a crude jerk who kept to himself. He was also a mountain of a kid.

Teddy only knew the stories. He had never spoken to Carson before, and he had never seen the thug outside of school. He considered that a particularly good blessing.

"I know *of* him," Teddy said. "Why?"

"He came asking for a job. Said he wanted to save up enough money to head to New Sun City. Didn't say much else. Even though I didn't hire him, he insisted on calling me *Boss*. A strange boy. Sort of like you."

Teddy smiled politely. "Yeah, sure. Anyway, what are you doing out here? If mom's going to bite my head off for being be late to dinner, then she's gonna incinerate you with her heat vision."

"Beth can be a bit scary, true." He stared at the dashboard. "Actually, I was just listening to the radio before you showed up."

"Anything about the earthquakes? It's late September and we haven't one in ages."

"No, this was something else. I can't keep thinking of that one story about the bank robbers in New Sun City." He waited for his son to shrug before he continued. "The prison break from back in March."

"Dad, that's ancient history. Those guys are long gone."

"The media might not say it, but I've heard the rumors about what those three scumbags did to escape. One released the prisoners, causing a riot, and disappeared during it. The second ran along the roof to the outside wall, breaking through the guard stations, and escaped. The third one apparently just jumped over the prison wall and vanished. None of them have been seen since."

Teddy tried not to roll his eyes. His dad tended to get paranoid the news. Though it was hard to blame him these days.

"I know what you're thinking, Theodore. It isn't that I believe the rumors. The problem I have, is that it has been almost half a year since, and not only have none of the three ever been found, but there has been no official statement about what really happened. No explosives were found, no weapons, no anything out of the ordinary. So, how did they escape?"

"Why even think about it, Dad?"

The truth was that Teddy found it impossible, too. But he'd read about stranger things. Maybe there was some truth to it. Teddy only doubted that it involved magic powers.

"I know. Bethany is going to kill us if I keep her waiting." He sniffed the air. "And why do you stink of garbage?"

"Long story," Teddy said, rubbing his heated forehead. "I'm not feeling too good."

And he wasn't. Every moment since leaving Mrs. Werner's backyard had left his arms and legs aching more and more. His head throbbed. Sweat stuck to him under his clothes. Heat rose inside him.

"Well, head on in. I'll let your mother know you're here. Just don't let her see you stinking like this."

Teddy sidled into the back door. His brothers were attempting homework in the living room with his sister. They were unusually quiet. He heard his mother talking by the front door to his father. That was his cue. He dropped off his shoes, backpack, and coat, at the backdoor. No one noticed him climbing the stairs. He would thank his dad later.

The shower was great. The sour milk and trash stench melted from him with the hot water. It was like being bathed in the Water of the Gods. But the jackhammer in his head tore on.

A fresh set of clothes sat awaiting him on the sink. No one was there. He didn't hear anyone come in.

"Mom," he said, with a sigh. He dried off and changed.

In the mirror was a face even paler than usual. His brown pupils dilated, and his breaths fell heavy. Teddy looked like a corpse.

He shuffled downstairs, hoping no one would notice. He sat down at the crowded dinner table. Everyone glanced at him.

"You look like you're about to keel over," Donny said, laughing.

"Nice seeing you, too."

"Enough," Mrs. MacIsaac said. "Let's say Grace before we begin."

Dinner was the same as always on a Monday. Grilled chicken and lima beans. His stomach grinded as he tried to keep it down. It was a good meal as always, and he didn't want his mom to think otherwise. It just didn't agree with him.

Due to his father being a manager at a local restaurant, everyone knew how to cook really well. No one was better than Teddy's mom. But that wasn't the problem.

His breaths arrived heavier. Sweat poured down his back. Even balling his hands into fists was too much. Whatever was wrong with him was getting worse. He tried to hide it.

Chatter went on around the table. His father went on with Donny and Casey about the escaped convicts. His mother and Briana were keeping quiet enjoying the meal. This meant they were sure to notice he wasn't joining in with the other guys.

"Are you alright, Teddy?" his mom asked. "You've barely touched anything on your plate."

"I dunno," Teddy said, his focus fading. "I feel off."

"That's because you walked half the town to get back home," his father said. "Take the bus, already. Don't make your mother worry so much."

"Yeah," Donny agreed. "Stop being a handful. You're such a troublemaker, *Theodore*."

The little jerks loved calling him that nerdy name. Teddy rolled his eyes.

Casey laughed. "It's not like there's much to see out there, anyway. Nothing but nature and boring people everywhere. McLeod is so lame. Nothing ever happens."

Donny and Casey were separated by less than a year in age. They were two of a pair. Neither had respect for their older brother or much else. Teddy could think of a hundred different people he'd rather be around. Still, family was family.

"Hush up, everyone," Mrs. MacIsaac said. "No one asked about *his* day. Maybe he had trouble in class. He could have a bully problem. Did anyone think to ask?"

"Who cares?" Donny said. His mother raised an index finger toward him. He sheepishly went back to his food. "Sorry."

"Anyway," Casey jumped in, "do you think one of those escaped convicts has, like, super strength or something, Dad? Wouldn't that be cool?"

The conversation went on without Teddy. He felt grateful for it.

He lamely rolled the lima beans around his plate. Even pretending to eat was tough. He scowled as his stomach twisted.

"You sure you're alright, Teddy?" Briana asked, under the surrounding noise.

He tried to give her a bright smile. "Don't worry."

"What happened? It looks like you've seen Death himself."

Briana paid too much attention to the little things. Despite being the youngest of the four siblings, she acted the oldest most often than not. But she was still a kid. She worried too much about tests; she would have a coronary if she learned Teddy was digging in a junkyard. He couldn't let her know the truth.

"Come on, you can tell me."

"Maybe later."

He pushed his chair back. His knees nearly buckled when he stood up. Thankfully, no one noticed. He couldn't fake it anymore.

Teddy excused himself from the table. He ducked out into the hall and up the stairs before anyone said anything. Drums rolled in his head.

His legs were lead. Each step to his room grew heavier. He shouldered open his door.

The pillow on his bed was much too perfect. He was out in seconds.

Then he was awake.

"What is all this?" he asked into the endless wind.

He stood atop a dune of ash in the middle of endless night. Blackened wind blew under the sunless sky. The land before him was dead.

Only rolling dunes of black slag remained in this scorched world. No scent of maples, pines, or the sights of the tall redwoods remained. McLeod was gone.

He took several steps forward. The pain had vanished, but his weariness had not. He tasted the dust in the back of his throat. A sense of magnetism tugged him onward.

"*Up ahead, Theodore MacIsaac.*"

There was a history here. Long dead voices whispered their forgotten tales in the ashen breeze. Something like magic had once filled these lands. But now, only death remained.

A thread of inevitability ran through him. Was he seeing the past, or the future?.

But, then, he spotted it. A narrow object peeked out at the top of a hill of ash thirty feet away. It glinted like metal. A pipe? No. It was something far cooler than that.

"A sword!" Teddy shouted.

He sprinted through the whistling wind of the dead world. Up ahead was the last light shining through it. A chorus of endless voices ran through his mind. They guided him through the dark. He reached the top of the ashen mound, excitement replacing weariness.

The sword stared back at him, plunged into the darkness of the cinders. The hilt was shining white, unlike the flame-licked blade. Its presence pierced the void. The Red Sword, a blade of stained crimson red, was calling him forward.

"*Theodore MacIsaac, are you ready to heed the call?*"

"If I can be a hero," he said. "Yes."

Chapter 2
Night of Flames

"He's awake," Jonas MacIsaac said.

The grandfather clock in the hall struck a chime. Teddy stretched and sat up on his mattress. Moonlight poured in through the window blinds. Both parents were standing beside the bed.

Before he could say anything, his father threw a hand out on Teddy's forehead. The warmth of his father's calloused hand jarred Teddy.

"What's up, Dad?"

Mr. MacIsaac glanced at his wife, ignoring his son. "He's normal."

"I thought he might be," she said to him. "He's been getting cooler every hour since he went to bed."

"I have?" Teddy asked. "What time is it?"

His father removed his hand and let out a relieved breath. "Late."

His mother's arms were folded. "We came up to check on you after supper, and you were sleeping like a log, so we left you. We just figured you wanted a nap. When we came back later we noticed your temperature was up. It was worrying, at first, but every time we checked on you, it went down further and further. Like the fever just drained out."

"Sorry I worried you."

"You should have told us how you were feeling, Theodore." His father paced around the bed. He stood beside his wife. "If it was something serious, we wouldn't have known."

"Your father's right. What were you thinking sneaking up here without telling anyone? You've been keeping to yourself a lot lately, but this was the dumbest thing you've done yet."

"I know, I know. You guys can ground me if you like."

Bethany MacIsaac's worry-lines faded. She rubbed her reddened eyes. "Are you saying this because you don't feel well, or because you don't want to go to school?"

Teddy bit his lip. He was too obvious.

"If you're not feeling well, you can stay home, there's no question about that," his father said. "But you have been acting odd long before this. You take your time smelling the roses getting to school, and you wander off in the woods on your way back. I don't know what you're doing out there, and I don't like it."

"I just really like the woods, Dad. It's quiet and everything makes sense. School just doesn't."

"The world doesn't always make sense, Theodore. That's part of what makes it so difficult. But you can't keep avoiding it."

"Maybe you got sick from whatever it was that got you stinking like rotten garbage." She caught Teddy's frantic glance to his father. She raised a finger to her son. "And no, your father didn't tell me. I smelled you going up the stairs before he explained anything. I am not going to have you risking your health like this just to avoid sitting in a room with other children you might not like being around. It's school, and it's not fun. But we deal with it."

"That's right, Theodore. From now on you come home directly after school. No more wandering off. No more games."

Teddy sighed. It wasn't that they were wrong; no, he was certain they weren't. Still, an irritation settled under his skin. He was running away. Again.

"You know what? Okay." Teddy raised his right hand in a pledge. "I swear I'll absolutely come home right after school from now on. No more games."

"And you'll tell us if you're not feeling well." Bethany MacIsaac was not asking.

"Yes, Mom, I swear!"

His parents had always been there. When he was sick, hurt, or lost, they'd always been by his side. And yet, he'd hidden so much from them. It was time to stop being a handful.

"Remember, son: a man's promise is iron clad." His father ruffled the hair on Teddy's head. "I'll be back to check on you in an hour. Get back to sleep."

"You heard your father."

His parents lightly glided across the floorboards. The

grandfather clock clicked with every footstep they made back to their room. The door to their room clicked closed. He didn't doubt they'd be back again to check. They always came back.

Teddy threw his legs over the side of his bed. A dream hid itself at the rear of his mind. He was so close to figuring it out. It was important. He lost it when he woke up and saw his father, but it was pushing back out. He rubbed his right hand across his face.

Then, his right palm itched. His left followed. He climbed out of bed over to the window as if being beckoned. Without a pause, he yanked the blinds up. The moon shone through clouds.

It clicked in him. There in the moonlight, he remembered the dream. Simply looking at the coin-shaped outlines on his palms reminded him of everything. They glowed with a white hue, a perfect circle of light.

An urge spoke to him. "*Press them together, and heed the call,*" it said.

This didn't make sense. None of this did. If he'd lost the coin in the junkyard, then he shouldn't have this light inside of him. It was impossible.

He thought back to the junkyard. The light was calling, and he heeded it then. He'd pressed his palms together and said the words back then. The universe broke apart and reassembled in that fraction of a second. The coin had disappeared when he finished.

But, maybe it didn't. The golden glow of the coin was replaced by circles of white lights in his palms. It was a marker. It was inside him. The light was calling, and he needed to heed it again.

"No wonder everyone thinks I'm weird," he murmured. "I get dreams about saving the world with a magic sword while everyone else dreams about getting a girlfriend, making the baseball team, or solving world hunger." He found himself laughing low. "Not that I'm complaining."

Everything was real. He knew it now as he stared at the perfect lights. The dreams, the sickness, the coin, and the Red Sword; they were all real. And all he had to do, was answer the call.

Teddy pressed his hands together, like a prayer. The light shone in between clasped hands. The itch became maddening.

"I beg you," he said, "bestow on me the glory."

Light filled the bedroom. Night became day. The itch vanished in the white veil with the rest of him.

When the brightness faded, he stood alone in the dead land, once more. Ash covered hills lay everywhere. The starless emptiness above remained without a sun, or moon. The black desert had not changed. But the sword was gone.

A roar of some forgotten beast howled in the distance. This was the first hint of life he'd come across here. The faintness of the screech told him it was miles away. He reached to stroke his chin and found a surprise.

On his head was a helmet. It was as strong as metal, though it was light. His hands were also covered in crimson red gauntlets. He felt all over to find he was wearing armor, like a knight. There was a cuirass in front, and faulds to protect his hips. If he had to guess, it reminded him of plated armor from his old stories. The biggest difference was that it was all red. It was all weightless; light as if he were wearing nothing at all. His normal clothes were heavier.

A voice spoke in the wind: "So, you are the Pyre Knight."

Behind him stood a girl. He didn't notice when she got there. She wore a brown robe and dress combination, with white frills along the edges, and a hood over her head. The dress fell longer than her knees, and followed the length of her arms over her fingers. Brown boots shuffled through the ash toward him. A white energy sparked from her like electricity. She was not normal.

She pushed the hood from her head. Deep blue eyes, and a face smaller than his, peered at him. "You're just in time to see the end of the Nameless Kingdom."

Teddy tried not to gape at her. "You're my age?"

"Eighth grade." Dark wind blew her bright blonde ponytail over her shoulder. She straightened it with her small right hand. "I'm Caitlyn West, the Maiden of Faith."

"I'm, uh, Teddy MacIsaac. I'm from McLeod."

"Good to meet you. Do you know why you're here, Teddy?"

"The sword called me." He glanced over his shoulder to find the blade holstered. "I guess it's mine now."

She smiled a beaming grin. "Yes, it is. You are a warrior. You are the Knight of Flames, the Pyre Knight. The Red Sword has the power over fire. It controls the element itself."

"But why do I have it, and why are you here? And where are we?"

"You were chosen by the Coin of Light to find that sword. With it, you're going to help save the world."

He found himself laughing jovially. "Save the world? Awesome! How do I go about doing that?"

"The Order of the Ash did this to the Nameless Kingdom." She stepped past Teddy and scooped up ash. He watched her toss it into the wind. "This place used to have a name, a people, and a history. But that's all gone now. Nothing but ash."

"This place was real," he said, gazing around the darkness. "It existed. Someone actually did all this?"

She turned back to him. No trace of her smile remained. "Yes, they did."

"Okay." He nodded. "Let me know what I have to do to stop this from happening back home."

"I'll come and find you. We are speaking through dreams right now, so my powers can only go so far. We'll talk details then."

"But who is this Order of the Ash? What do they want with our world?"

A roar fell out of the dark. Above them, a snake-like beast flew through the ash. It hacked the air with screeches. It was large, and rather impossible, but Teddy recognized it. It was a dragon. The beast flew high above, built of charred green scales and lots of sharp teeth to go with its claws. Its narrow, orange eyes, glared down through the ash at the two teenagers. Another roar escaped it into the void. However, it didn't approach. The dragon spun a circle in the air and turned back. It was as if it were frightened.

Teddy found his tongue in knots. "Was that actually a dragon!?"

Caitlyn cleared her throat. "I feel like we should go somewhere a bit more private. The next one might be looking for a fight."

"But I want to fight a dragon. Who wouldn't want to fight a dragon?"

She let out a small laugh. "I like that enthusiasm, but we have something to discuss first."

Caitlyn stepped before him, and placed her hands on his shoulders. He tried not to blush, instead staring at her blonde ponytail flopping in the breeze. She was the same height he was which made it hard to avoid her gaze. Her blue eyes stared through him.

Before he could ask what was happening, the world went white. They moved without walking.

He had never seen anything like it. They slid along the ground as if caught in the gust. Then, as soon as the sensation had started, they lifted up into the sky like ascending birds. White light surrounded them, protecting the pair from the endless blowing ash. He couldn't process it. They were flying.

And then they were falling.

When she lifted a hand, the bright sheen lifted from them. It was like gravity woke up and threw him back down like a spiked football. Velocity punched his face through the helmet. His armor rattled with the fall. At the same time, the dark skies had vanished, leaving them in an endless blue eternity. However, it was hard to appreciate the beauty as he fell.

On his descent, he noticed the ground, or rather, the lack of one. The wind whipped against him as he narrowed his view to see what it was far below. It was water reflecting the blue sky he was plummeting through.

He saw himself, a body in red armor, falling toward him in the reflection. He hoped the armor was tougher than it looked.

Then, he became stuck in the air. His body froze in midair. Teddy glanced at the face in the water staring back at him like a mirror reflection. It was an awkward sight. He found himself let down gently on the open ocean. He was actually standing on it.

"What in the world?" Teddy asked. "What was that? How did we get here? Am I standing on water?"

"We were in your dream, so I moved us over to another one." Her face had reddened from before. She was short of breath. "I thought the water-walking was a nice touch. Dreams really are something, aren't they?"

Teddy whistled. "You can teleport? Is that how we got here?"

"Teleport?" she said, breathing hard. "If that's what you want to call it. Boys seem to find the teleportation explanation an easier concept to understand than sliding through dreams. I move within the world, not through it. My power is much stronger in dreams. It takes a lot of energy to do it in real life."

"It's still pretty amazing." He took in the view before turning back to her. "Do you hate good books, or something? Teleportation is a pretty good description for what you did."

She rolled her blue eyes. "Teleportation is disassembling and reassembling somewhere else. Unless you want to have your soul torn apart, I don't recommend it. And no, I don't enjoy fiction very much. Things are bad enough in this world without reading about people who have it worse."

"There's this comic called *The Rangers of the Endless Frontier*. There's this issue where Reuter is captured by the Steel Fist Gang. He is interrogated and tortured for hours."

"That's what I'm talking about. Horrible stuff."

"No, you don't get it. Reuter refuses to sell the Rangers out and he is tortured quite badly. But he never gives up, never gives in. When his friends finally do rescue him, their bond is stronger than before. If you're only looking at the bad stuff, you'll never see the good."

She fell silent. "Is that why you're doing this? It's your dream to be a hero?"

"Well, what about you? Don't you have dreams of your own?"

"I do," she said. "I want to protect this world from evil."

"Other than that. We all have weird dreams on some level."

She blushed. "I want to learn how to cook. Someday. I haven't had the time to learn things like that."

"I can teach you," Teddy said. "My dad is the manager of a restaurant. I can make a lot of things. What do you want to know?"

The girl glanced away from him. "Do you mind if we get on with it?"

"If you say so." He shrugged. "So, what are we doing here?"

"Take a look at the reflection in the water."

It was then that he noticed the reflection was wrong. The water rippled when he laid a gauntlet on it. A man wearing Teddy's red armor stared back at him. The stranger followed his exact movements. On his back was Teddy's Red Sword.

However, it *was* Teddy's reflection. Of that he didn't doubt. The face was of a young man in his twenties, and his pupils were red like flames.

Caitlyn's image had also changed. Her reflection was of a young woman with platinum blonde hair and similarly pale skin; a pretty woman who had an odd coldness about her. Caitlyn's skin was a much healthier shade of white than the mirror image below. She was also much nicer to look at.

"That's us," Teddy said, without thinking.

"Yes, that's what we look like in our world when we wield our Coins of Light. Same armor, same weapons."

"But, who are they?"

"The last people who used these powers."

He thought it over a second. "Then, they're . . ."

"Yes, they're gone."

Other blurred faces faded into view in the ocean. They stretched on for miles. Some were teenagers, some were not. But there were three others that jumped out at him, still blurred. One was a boy sitting in the dark of a warehouse, another standing in a crevice in some cliff, and a third . . . the third reminded him of someone. The third figure was a boy sitting in an empty subway car. Teddy knew him somehow.

The other faces disappeared as quickly as they first

arrived, but he caught a few others. There were girls like Caitlyn, dressed in similar robes as her. There must have been others like him, too. He grinned.

Looking up, he saw Caitlyn crouching before him. She was also taking note of the reflections.

"I mentioned earlier that I was the Maiden of Faith," she said. "My job is to be the rock of the Maidens of the Old World. I'm their leader. We were formed to protect the Nameless Kingdom long ago from outside evils. There is only one evil our predecessors couldn't stop, and that was the Order of the Ash."

"You're a Maiden, but I'm a Knight. What's the difference, other than cosmetics?"

"We were both created to protect. The Maidens purify the innocent and the repentant, and the Knights slay the evil and the wicked. Now that the first Knight of the End has heeded the call, the Order will probably be coming for you."

"But they don't know where I live."

"The Order will sense when a Coin of Light has been accepted, just like we do. They have agents everywhere, probably even in McLeod." She stood up. "When the first Knight of the End appears, it means their greatest enemy has awoken. They will do anything to stop them."

He stood up to meet her. "So, you're saying that I'm a knight that looks like a twenty-year-old who is going to save the world from dragons while dressed in red armor with a sword that is as heavy as a toy?"

"Hard to swallow?" she asked.

"A little bit."

She frowned. Her eyes turned a darker blue which matched the wide ocean around them. "Believing is up to you. There is a lot in this world that we can no longer fight on our own. The shadows no longer hide in the shade; they walk in the sunlight with the rest of us. Things are getting stranger out there. The world is not getting any better. Surely, you've seen examples of what I mean."

He thought of his day, and nodded. If this Order of the Ash was making its move to flatten the world, they certainly had the gate left wide open. Things really were bad.

"So, why me?" he asked.

"I didn't choose you, if that's what you're asking. The Coins of Light choose their wielder based on who the user can be, not who they are now."

"I'm just a kid who likes reading comics and old books. I'm pretty sure they could have found somebody better than me."

"*Better* has nothing to do with it," she said. "You have proven yourself somehow, and in some way. I have no idea how that works."

He threw up his hands. "Okay, I get it. It isn't like I don't want to smash some evil, or anything. But I'm not sure what I'm supposed to do with this power."

She stepped over to him and placed her hands on his shoulders again. He was slightly better at fighting off a blush this time. "We will meet again, Teddy MacIsaac," she said. "But, there are wheels that must be turned first."

They were encased in another field of light, just as before. The white hue overtook his senses. He vanished, as did the world of water. Caitlyn had also disappeared.

He was back in his room. His hands unclasping, he stared out the window and regained his senses. The moon cascaded over McLeod.

Thoughts spun through his mind, just as butterflies tumbled through his stomach. There was only one thing to do.

He pressed his hands together. The words spoke into his ear, and his lips followed. "I beg you, bestow on me the glory."

A blinding light flashed out from his hands, and into the night. He lit up like a lighthouse beacon. When the world cleared, he separated his hands. His test was a success.

Teddy stood several centimeters from the ceiling. His hands wore gauntlets again. The mirror on the inside of his door reflected the truth. It was the face of the twenty-year-old from the dream wearing the red armor. Teddy had become the Pyre Knight.

He moved lightly, as if weightless. His height was easily over six feet now. He was a whole new man.

"It's real," he said, in a new voice. He threw his hands over his mouth. Even his voice had changed. He hoped no one heard that.

The clock revealed no time had passed since his parents had left him to sleep. He could only have stepped out of time somehow. That Caitlyn girl was right about dreams really being something.

He leaned out into the hall. The house remained dead quiet. The other kids slept soundly, and his parents' door remained shut. He let out a breath. He lightly closed the door and returned to the window, stepping lightly. It wouldn't have been fun to explain this to his family.

Then, he fastened his hands together, and spoke the same words as before. The same piercing light shot out into the dark, and the world grew a little. He was puny, little Teddy MacIsaac again.

He fell back into bed, exhaustion overtaking him. A long sleep before his next day at Harding would do him good. He turned over, and sleep arrived fast.

Unfortunately, he woke up again. The clock on his wall told him it was a quarter after four in the morning. And he was no longer tired, sick, or had itching palms. He was fully awake and feeling great.

"So much for it being just a dream," he said to himself.

Chapter 3
Real World Initiation

Teddy didn't like being up so early. Darkness in the morning was not natural. Being unable to sleep left him with few options so he started his day. The grandfather clock clicked away.

He showered, changed, and finished his homework, yet still had time to spare. He flopped down in his father's chair in the living room and thought.

Birds sang outside. The sun slowly peeked through the blinds. A new day awaited, and it terrified him.

If this power was real, then he would have to fight. That Caitlyn girl didn't tell him what to expect; she told him to wait. That didn't sit well. This Order of the Ash could be anywhere, waiting and watching. If they came to his town, his house, he would fight them, and he would do it alone if he must. This time, he could not afford to run.

He wondered about the Coin of Light, and who made it. If something that powerful needed to exist, then what it was counteracting must be terrible indeed. He couldn't imagine what was waiting for him out there.

"Theodore?" his father yawned. "What are you doing up?"

Teddy flinched. He'd been thinking for too long. "Hey, Dad."

The old man shook his head. Mr. MacIsaac was already showered and dressed in his manager's outfit for the day ahead. Teddy had nearly forgotten how early his father woke for work.

"What in the world are you doing up at this hour, Theodore? Aren't you supposed to be sick?"

"I'm well," he said. A blush fell over him. He felt like it was a lie, somehow.

"Are you?"

Teddy nodded. "I'm feeling fine. Don't know why, but I'm really feeling good today."

His father checked Teddy's forehead, and agreed. "Well, the fever hasn't come back, so I'll buy that. Come on, let's get some breakfast before I have to get going."

They sat at the table. His dad dug out two cereal bowls, and filled them with off-brand cereal and milk. Teddy preferred his breakfast simple. The pair discussed yesterday's events as they ate.

"Hey, dad?"

"Yes?"

"How come you didn't hire Rock Carson for the job?" Teddy had found it odd a boy with such a bad reputation would be eager for employment.

"You mean Rochester? Well, there were two reasons. The

first was that I'm not hiring teenagers. They barely show up for work as it is. The second was that he applied for a *full-time* job."

"That's strange."

"Like I said before," his father said with a wink. "You two are a lot alike."

Teddy gulped down his cereal. They finished up their conversation about school and work. His father eventually left for his job, leaving Teddy alone again.

It wasn't much longer when his mother showed up downstairs. She also fussed, and checked his forehead. When she deemed him fine, after asking hundreds of questions, she allowed him to leave early for school. Of course, he wasn't scot free.

"By the way," she said. "I checked your school bag last night."

He gulped air.

"If you ever put dirty boots in your bag again, I will put them on and kick you up and down the street in them until the dirt comes off. Got it?"

A weak smile passed his lips. "Yes, ma'am."

"Remember: home early. Got it?"

She kissed him on the forehead, and left into the kitchen to prepare breakfast. It would probably be a much better breakfast than his, but he couldn't wait to feel jealous. It was time to go.

He put on his hooded fall jacket, and opened the front door. The long walk to school waited. He wanted to leave before—

"Nerd!" Donny said, from behind him. The little jerk stood at the top of the stairs. He wore glasses with his black slacks and dark red sweater. Donny never let irony stifle an insult. He was even shorter than Teddy, though nowhere near as quiet. The jerk was always known as the loudmouth. "Can't wait to get to school, huh?"

"Morning to you too, brat."

In their house, everyone got changed and ready for the day before breakfast. Sometimes, Teddy hated tradition.

Briana followed her brother down the stairs. She blinked twice when she saw Teddy. "What are you doing up? I thought you were sick."

Teddy sighed. "Can't a kid get up early and prepare for school? Why is that so weird?"

"Because no kid is that stupid," she said, tossing her hair back. Her strawberry blonde hair was much longer than Teddy's though she didn't tie it. She wore a simple blue blouse and dress, since she treated every moment of her life as fancy. Unlike Donny, she had a more sensible style.

Casey elbowed by her on the stairs. "He never said he was smart." He wore jeans and a simple white t-shirt like Teddy did. Originality was not Casey's strong suit.

The three of them disappeared into the kitchen. His mother stepped back into the living room, her arms folded. "Remember," she said. "Straight home."

"I got it, Mom." Teddy waved to her. "Don't worry."

He closed the door behind him, and sprinted down the street. Morning found its way out of the darkness. The smell of dew refreshed him. The wind gently passed him over, as did the singing of the birds in the maples he ran past. This would be a good morning run.

Teddy scurried over Mrs. Werner's fence. Her house was as quiet as the rest of them.

The train tracks led him past an old warehouse. The place had been abandoned for years, left alone across from an empty field of dandelions and blowing cotton. He felt eyes on him. A compulsion fell over him to enter the creepy place. An invisible magnet pulled him like in his dream.

It would have to wait. He made a promise to be on time, and he was going to keep it, early or not.

Of course, he was incredibly early by the time he arrived at Harding. The few kids there were half-asleep, and wandering aimlessly through the halls. Some chatted on the steps at the school entrance; others were at the convenience store across the street. It would be a long day ahead for them all.

Teddy sat in his class with his books ready. He ended up waiting until the first bell finally rang. Eventually, his classmates also arrived. Stieg Johns passed him with a sneer.

Morning classes went by as usual. Someone called in a bomb threat, unsuccessfully. Jennifer Yost verbally assaulted Becky Dwyer for stealing her style of shoes. Stieg told some dirty jokes he probably learned from Corey Hoffman. A fight in the classroom across the hall started during third period. The day clicked on like his grandfather clock.

One thing was odd, though. Concentration was easy. He easily copied notes and filed them away. He spent most of the classes processing and actually understanding the material. It was like his brain no longer held him back from thinking. Such little sleep had energized him.

At lunch, he found Stieg in the hallway. He was leaning beside Teddy's locker wearing too-loose clothing, and a smirk. The posing irritated Teddy the most.

"Ran pretty fast yesterday, didn't you, Teddy boy?"

"Get lost, Stieg."

Stieg sidled up to Teddy. "Make me."

"We never had this problem in sixth grade. Why can't you be like that again?"

"Because this is High School, loser," Stieg said, with a touch of anger. "We're not kids anymore."

"This isn't the real world, Stieg. It's just you making High School even worse for the rest of us."

"As if you care about anyone but yourself."

"And what is that supposed to mean?"

"I wouldn't expect a kid still playing games in the woods—or is it a junkyard now?—to understand how normal people think, but I'm not making this place any worse than it already is. Neither is Corey. You just don't get that *this* is the way the world really is. Always has been, always will be. Did seventh grade teach you anything?"

Teddy flinched. Stieg wasn't wrong. He tried to remember the last time he spoke with his old friend. "Did something happen last year, Stieg?"

"Shut up, MacIsaac. Don't act like you care now." He pointed an index finger in Teddy's face. "The field behind the dumpster after school. Come alone. Not like you have any friends left, anyway. It's time to meet the real world, Teddy boy."

"You know, you don't have to be like this. I was just talking to Mrs. Werner yesterday and she—"

Stieg rammed a finger into Teddy's chest. "Shut. Up."

Then the floor rumbled.

A small earthquake erupted. The two teenagers flopped about in the hall. They braced themselves against opposite lockers, and let it pass. As far as earthquakes went, this was nothing. They always passed quickly.

Thirty seconds later, and it petered out.

"That was wild," Teddy said.

"Yeah."

They stared at each other for what felt like hours. Teddy wondered just what happened to Stieg Johns. The kid he knew was gone.

Stieg's eyes widened as if he'd just realized something. He slid from the locker, and out of the hall. Teddy was left alone again.

Later, at lunch, Teddy sat alone once more. His favorite table was the one closest to the exit. It made for an easy escape.

The cafeteria at Harding was near the size of gymnasium. It was filled with creaking benches, cracked tables, and loud teenagers. There was a story that someone choked to death and no one noticed. It was almost assuredly not true, but Teddy could have seen it happening. It was pure chaos inside.

Teddy had made his own lunch after his father left. Salami on rye with a good dab of mustard was Teddy's favorite. He liked cooking simple, and this was as simple as it got. He took a big bite, and washed it down with a cool bottle of milk.

He disposed of his paper bag, and began his escape. "Maybe tomorrow I should make two," he wondered to himself.

While he was thinking, he stepped into a mountain. He shook with the impact, surprised it didn't hurt.

Teddy glanced up to a figure wearing baggy blue jeans, a black and white bowling shirt, and slicked back greased hair. The granite expression of Rock Carson glared down at him. A few kids gasped and pointed at the pair.

"Out of the way, Pintsize," Carson said.

Rock Carson looked like he fell out of a Rockabilly sock hop from some old movie. If he wasn't so tall, or had such broad shoulders, Teddy might have thought he looked ridiculous. Carson's pink skinned face chiseled with jagged edges made Teddy think twice about laughing. The older boy's brown eyes were sharp.

Carson narrowed his green eyes. "You deaf?"

"Sorry," Teddy said, shaking his head. He waved a hand to let the older boy pass. There was no point in causing a fight. Besides, he promised he would be on time to get home. He couldn't afford detention. "Enjoy your lunch!"

The older boy turned, walking backwards, and gestured rudely to Teddy. It was strange that this clown was looking for a job. Carson vanished into the crowd.

Snickers erupted in the cafeteria.

One table contained a group laughing uproariously. Both Stieg Johns and Corey Hoffman were among those guffawing and pointing at him. He waved back to them, smiling.

"Well, that could have gone better," he whispered to himself.

The rest of his day was much the same. Shop class had machinery snafus; math class had more letters encroaching on numbers. It was a bunch of busy work.

But he never got tired. He was as rested at the final bell of the day as he was at the first.

The dream kept coming back to him. The pretty girl who told him such a crazy story had made it seem so real. If the world was about to change, then so should his life. School wouldn't be his world forever: one day he would escape. He shouldn't have to take these classes seriously.

He would have to face whatever was out there. That made him oddly excited. To a fourteen-year-old kid, fighting evil was the next best thing to Christmas. If only his old friends could see him now.

When the final bell rang, he faced his first test of the day. He stepped down the barren hall to meet Rock Carson. The older boy was standing by Teddy's locker.

"We meet again, Pintsize." He wasn't smiling. Rock Carson never smiled.

Teddy sighed. "Can I help you?"

"You have a date in the field. I'm here to escort you. Let's get going."

"I'm not going anywhere with you."

"No hard feelings, Pintsize, but you can't take me. Get your stuff, and let's go. I have a job to do, and I'm going to do it."

"You do know what they plan to do to me, right?"

"None of my concern, I've been paid. But if you want my advice—being a wuss about it isn't gonna solve anything."

Teddy's face reddened. He tried to hold in his anger. "I never did anything to those idiots. I just want to be left alone."

"Welcome to High School," Carson said, still without humor. "You either fight back, or you get beat into the dirt. It's not hard to understand. Now, are you coming, or am I bringing you? Your choice, Pintsize."

"My name is Teddy MacIsaac."

"None of my concern."

"How much is your price? I'll double it." He regretted such a lame tactic, but Teddy had a promise to keep.

"Sorry, I don't work that way. Once I get paid to do something, I do it all the way. If you want to pay me to take revenge on them later, I'm sure we can work out a plan. I'm very flexible that way."

"You've got quite the sick job, man. There's more to life than money."

Rock grunted. "Don't act like you know anything. Now, let's go."

Teddy grabbed his jacket and bag from the locker. He shut the door and locked it up. He threw on his jacket, and followed Carson. There would be no escaping this.

Carson led him through the hallways. They usually emptied out fast after the last bell. Any remaining kids stepped around Carson when they caught sight of him. The creep was intimidating, even for a ninth grader. Teddy thought about turning into the Pyre Knight, and dealing with him that way. But that would bring too much attention to them. Plus, it would be unfair. Rock Carson looked tough, but he couldn't take on a Knight of the End destined to fight evil.

Teddy slapped his forehead. He was losing it. That Knight stuff had nothing to do with this. He would have to deal with it on his own.

Out in the field, a small crowd waited beyond the dumpsters. They were all chattering, and laughing away. Teddy recognized them as the group from Stieg's table at lunch and some other older kids and hangers-on. They were here for a good time.

Hoffman stood in the center of the gaggle. He stuck his thumb out toward Teddy. "Yeah, I can take him. No problem."

There were stories about Corey Hoffman. The main one, was about how he threw a seventeen-year-old on top of a parked car. A lesser one, was how he laughed after getting hit by a van and breaking his arm. Teddy doubted either story were true.

"Bring him here, Carson!" Hoffman called from the field. Corey Hoffman had a round jaw, with a smirk permanently fastened to it. His overweight build was probably the scariest thing about him. Size was all he had, especially compared to Teddy.

Carson pushed Teddy forward into the crowd. The wall of teenagers instantly encircled the smaller boy. It was as if the coliseum gates had closed shut.

Rock Carson held a hand out toward Stieg Johns. "Payment, please."

Stieg glanced from Carson to Hoffman. He was out of the loop.

Hoffman sucked on his own teeth. "Pay him, already. I want to break some bones before an adult shows up."

"Fine." Stieg handed a fistful of small bills to Carson. "Are we done now?"

Carson nodded, and pocketed the money. "Yeah, we're done." He left the field behind for some bleachers thirty feet away.

Hoffman and Teddy faced each other with no way out. Shouts and taunts rocketed around the circle of teenagers. The excitement was palpable.

Their position was strategically chosen by Hoffman and his cronies. None of the windows in the school had a view to this spot in the field. No teacher would see them until it was too late.

Hoffman smiled to the crowd. "So, loser, ready to lose some teeth?"

"I'm still not sure why you're doing this." He glanced at the teenagers surrounding him. No way out.

"Because you're a loser. Does that make you feel any better?"

"I'm all warm inside."

The thug circled around Teddy. Hoffman hopped like mad to the hoots of his crowd, and threw a few fake jabs at the smaller boy. Hoffman had clearly watched too many old sports movies. He was having a ball. The crowd shoved Teddy into the center from behind in their excitement.

"Have a nice nap," Hoffman said. He swung his right hand toward Teddy's face. Teddy didn't notice what the thug was doing until it was too late. He didn't dodge. Hoffman's punch slammed into Teddy's face.

But, something odd happened. There was no crunch. There was no blood. Teddy felt his nose to find it was perfectly fine. No pain.

Whispers fell over the crowd. One questioned why the little one wasn't eating grass. Teddy was starting to dislike these people a good deal.

Hoffman drove forward. An expletive escaped his mouth. He struck Teddy in the cheek with his left hand. He got the same result as before.

"Is your face made of rubber, or something?" Hoffman asked.

Teddy feigned coolness. He was as surprised as any of them, but he needed to keep his edge. This was his chance.

He almost missed Hoffman punching him again. This time, Teddy let it hit him. The swings kept coming. Eight, nine, ten . . . the flurry of strikes didn't stop. They all had the same result as the first.

Eventually, Hoffman began sweating. He panted. The crowd had fallen silent with their boss's building rage. Nobody was laughing.

Hoffman's anger led to a full on primal scream. He charged at Teddy, full tilt.

Teddy sidestepped, sticking his foot out. Hoffman hit

the grass, face first. He slid a bit on his chest before arriving at a full stop.

Once more, Hoffman jumped up. His teeth were clenched, blades of grass littered inside, and his fists tightened to balls of red flesh. He charged Teddy once more.

Teddy knelt to avoid Hoffman's swinging forearm. The larger boy was running too fast to stop. Hoffman ran full-on into Teddy's tucked shoulder.

Hoffman let out a hard breath and a wheeze. He flopped down on Teddy's shoulder, gasping. Teddy lightly pushed forward, hoping to get him off. It worked.

The older boy flew backward through the air. He soared back onto the grass as if a truck hit him. The limp body rolled in the grass an additional two feet before coming to a stop. Hoffman coughed and gagged as he lay still.

Teddy glanced at his hands. That was only a push.

The crowd mulled away from the fight, their hopes of bloodshed thwarted. None dared to look at the pair.

Stieg stuck around to help Hoffman up. He glared at Teddy as he helped the dazed boy up. The pair silently hobbled off toward the school. Stieg glanced back once as confused as everyone else.

Only one of the attendees remained. Rock Carson stared toward Teddy with an open mouth and wide eyes. He slowly stood up from the bleachers as if debating what to do next. Teddy darted off before the older boy could make that decision.

Teddy jumped the fence by the field's edge. He scrambled over it and through the streets towards his forest trail. His legs pumped faster than they ever had before. The wind whipped against him. Before he knew it, he was already at the junkyard.

"What the heck was that?" he asked to himself. His hands shook.

He leaned against the junkyard fence. He still wasn't exhausted. Nobody had followed him.

He massaged his knuckles. If what he did to Hoffman was only a light push, then what about a good punch? He didn't want to imagine it.

A large concrete wall sat a few feet beside him. It was the garage for the garbage trucks. Large graffiti covered the side, reading *Fireball Coming* in oblong letters. The quote was from some urban legend. That was when an idea popped into his head.

"Time to do something stupid," Teddy said.

He threw his fist into the side of the wall.

A large crack broke from the wall, spreading along the cement. Small chunks broke off near the spot of his impact. The building rumbled. That was from a single punch.

Hard breaths fired through his lungs. He could have hit Hoffman with that. Teddy could have put the jerk in the hospital, or worse. Before anyone could see his handiwork, he turned and ran.

The junkyard behind him, he soon passed through the open meadow of dandelions. The train tracks were just up ahead. His conscience bit at him as he continued on.

It didn't add up. He didn't transform, he didn't use the sword. He shouldn't have been that strong. But then, maybe the Pyre Knight was even stronger than that punch.

"The world of ash," he muttered. Teddy skidded to a stop as if someone told him to. If he was going to be up against whatever burned a whole world to ash, then he would need to be even stronger than that punch. It was hard to think about. He was in way over his head.

Teddy looked up from the dirt. The old warehouse from the morning lay down his path to the left. That voice from the morning spoke again. Something was in that dilapidated building.

A chill shot through him. He remembered the Order of the Ash.

Before he could ignore the thought, his feet were already moving. He wouldn't be taken by surprise again. If something was in there, it would regret meeting Teddy MacIsaac.

Chapter 4
The Longest Sundown

Teddy had passed the warehouse everyday on his way to school. It had been abandoned for as long as he'd been alive.

Shattered windows lay between broken bricks and rusted metal. The fence surrounding the building had rusted, and wobbled in the late afternoon breeze. Weeds grew through pavement where the parking lot had once been. The place smelled of rotten wood and ash.

The warm afternoon sun was giving way to the evening. Paranoia or not, he was not going to wait any longer. The day had gone on much too long already.

Rust surrounded the metal doorway, holding it tight. He pushed it lightly. The metal blockade swung open against the inside wall with a crunch. The echo rang out inside the halls.

"Why don't you let everyone know you're here, Teddy?" he whispered to himself. "Maybe they're nice bad guys who just want to have tea with you and chat about the weather. Moron."

Inside, the setting sun flashed through the old, cracked window panes. Piercing orange light brushed across the musty floors, revealing dust like mist by his shoes. The walls were rotting with age.

He followed the narrow grey hall out of the entryway. A low hum like the buzzing of insects echoed throughout the inside. The smell of garbage and ash only strengthened.

Before he went any further, he ducked into an empty room to his left. There the highest concentration of sunlight shone through the shattered windows. This would be his last chance to turn back.

He let his thoughts gather. If he was strong now—just how much tougher would he be with his armor? Anything waiting in this warehouse wouldn't stand a chance against him, and he would also be disguised. He would easily have the upper hand.

Teddy took a deep breath, and clasped his hands together. The sun beamed down on him in streaks of orange rays like rays from the heavens. The words quaked through his mind.

"I beg you," Teddy whispered, "bestow on me the glory."

An explosion of light spun across the room. A warm sensation drew across him like a blanket. Eternity embraced him.

After the brightness cleared, he checked his body. Red gauntlets adorned his hands, and the armor wrapped over him. His height had sprung up, and with it did his longer limbs. The Red Sword was slung against his back. He was the Pyre Knight again.

It was hard to walk slowly through the hall. Controlling his strength was hard enough. It took everything he had to hold back.

The stink grew stronger the closer he approached the back room of the warehouse. The air fell quiet except for the endless buzz swirling on ahead.

The impression grew that he was stepping deeper into the belly of an ancient beast. This place was where darkness went to die, and time stopped just before the kill. Malice oozed from the walls.

He swung open the door to the back room. Impossibilities waited before him. The walls, ceiling, and floor, moved as if made of a breathing inky substance. It slithered about as if alive, buzzing away. The mass pulsed as one organism.

They were flies. Teddy couldn't tell where they stopped and the building began. The walls bulged as if one giant lung.

The buzzing pitched louder when he crossed the hall into the room. The flies parted from the floor with his boot steps.

A figure emerged from the center of the black mass. In the middle of the room, a stranger stepped up through the moving floor as if ascending stairs. The flies parted around the figure.

It was a middle-aged man. He wore a dark blue jumpsuit and greying black hair. He looked normal—aside from his bottom half still being consumed by the dark goop. He stared empty-eyed toward the wall opposite Teddy. A giggle escaped the man's crooked smile.

The insect man turned to face the Knight. A slimy grin was plastered on his face.

"Who are you?" Teddy asked. An urge to cringe rushed over him. The boy still wasn't used to his new voice. "You are trespassing. I'm going to have to ask you to leave."

The figure stared at Teddy with dead grey eyes, and that same slanted smile.

"You are not supposed to be here." A fire rose in Teddy's gut. Words floated to his lips. "I am the Pyre Knight, scum. I live to extinguish the dark. I will not tolerate your presence in this world!"

The man's jaw cracked when it opened. "Yes! The Master will be excited to learn I have found you! I will be rewarded with ninety-nine new years of service." His voice was like shattered glass.

"I think I should take you to the hospital, monster. Maybe the mental ward."

"The light beacon led me here. You sent it last night. Do not pretend you didn't want to be found, Knight. You exist to destroy my Master! We know it."

The Order knew about Teddy, just like the girl said they would. The Knight slowly moved his hand to his sword.

"My brothers and sisters have been searching for your kind all over the countryside." The freak lazily gestured around the room. "We have been searching. Town after town, and city after city. The Coins of Light must be destroyed. We've been restrained by the Master so long. It will be so nice to finally be able to kill."

Teddy cocked an eyebrow. The Order knew more about the Pyre Knight than he thought.

"Last chance to give up," Teddy said, in his best heroic voice.

"Make me, Pyre Knight."

Teddy slowly moved to the center of the room. The flies dispersed with every step he made. His right hand rested on the hilt of his sword.

"Unfortunately for you," the gross man said, "the Knights of the End have long been a thorn in the side to Master Jero. I cannot imagine the ninety-nine glorious years in service he will give me for killing you."

"Ninety-nine? I have no idea what you're babbling about."

"This is the offer my Master gives you," the man said, outstretching both arms. His skin covered itself in the black flies. "Courtesy of Master Jero the Boundless, I will kill you, Pyre Knight."

The strange man's body stretched in directions it was never made to. His hands grew matted black hair and stretched crookedly into claws. At the same moment, his arms, legs, and torso, twisted and grew bulk. His voice hardened to a roar, and his face twisted to match the rest of him. There before Teddy MacIsaac was a nine foot tall bug man.

"I guess talking is off the table," Teddy quipped.

The creature dashed forward. It checked into Teddy with the force of a three hundred pound hockey player—or a rocket-powered Zamboni. The force sent Teddy backwards into the hallway.

The wall broke out from behind him. Teddy skidded across the dust covered floor. It smarted. He felt like Corey Hoffman landing in the grass.

Teddy stood back up. "That's a no, then."

The monster didn't reply. Teddy wasn't sure it could. The thing didn't even move like a human anymore. It robotically stepped forward, its claws ripping open the rest of the wall Teddy had flown through. The monster howled at its prey.

The boy sighed. "I'm starting to regret being diplomatic."

It bolted towards him. Teddy rolled sideways. The freak crashed down into the hallway floor where the boy had just been. Its claw scrapped the dusty cement. Its momentum carried it through the rotting wall into the next room. The warehouse rumbled.

The insects from the fly-covered room hummed louder. They poured into the hall around the Pyre Knight, and toward the bug beast. The flies swirled around the larger creature, and slipped into its black fur and skin. The monster puffed up and expanded even more. The buzzing now only sounded through the beast's body.

There was no humanity in the beast's eyes. This was not a fight Teddy could afford to walk away from. Striking first is the only option when it comes to predators. He could not let it escape.

But he'd never fought before, not really. Teddy knew how to throw a punch, thanks to his father, even if he never threw one in a fight. This was different. It wasn't just a silly schoolyard brawl. This monster was an abomination out of a fever dream. It shouldn't exist.

The monster leaped down before him. Two larger tree trunk arms smashed down against the Knight's shoulders

The force slammed him downward into the cement, cracking it. The room spun.

It leaped onto his back, and bit into his armor.

"Get off!" Teddy shouted.

But he was lucky. The monster's gnashing teeth only scraped and scratched at the armor. Instead of broken bones and torn skin, Teddy didn't receive so much as a bruise. It couldn't get at him.

Teddy reached behind him, and gripped onto its thick neck. It flinched. He pulled it off with one hand. It struggled against him as he ripped it off his body.

Finally, Teddy stood up. He still held it tight. With a twist of his arm, the creature soared forward.

The monster landed on the floor with its full weight, ripping into concrete. It skidded over the length of the rotted out room.

The monster flipped over as it spun along the floor. Its feet kicked against the opposite wall before striking. The wall broke up on impact. It howled once more. The creature shot forward, its claws swinging, toward Teddy's neck. Its speed was still tremendous.

The Knight brought back his right fist, and planted it into the beast's gut. The monster froze.

A gust of dirty air filled the silence.

The creature fell forwards, and tumbled over.

Teddy brought his hands together as the enemy dropped. He swung them upwards like a rising sledgehammer under the creature's chin. The beast lifted from the floor. It struck the ceiling, and plummeted back down. Chunks of metal broke loose above.

As it fell back down toward him, Teddy waited. He rammed his fist into its face. The creature soared backwards across the room. It broke through two sets of walls, and slammed against the end of the original room of flies. The building shook. Cement and metal broke off the walls and ceiling.

The warehouse was now more or less one giant room, with broken concrete walls and rubble all over. The creep wasn't quite as fast as he first thought. Teddy could do this after all.

The monster groaned, and stood up once more.

"Now what do I do?" Teddy looked around. There was nothing but the two of them. The warehouse was crumbling. If that was all his punch could do, he was in trouble. This fight would never end.

"*Use the sword,*" the voice from the junkyard said. "*It is right behind you.*"

The beast stomped over rubble toward him. It grinned madly. Sunset rays from shattered glass glinted off its teeth.

The Knight reached behind his back. The sword hilt released heat into his hand once more. An impression of burning red flames danced in his mind's eye. Teddy let out a sigh. He jerked his hand forward, and pulled loose the blade. A deep crimson light shone off the charred sword before him. It was shining as if licked by the flames of Hell; it hungered for demon blood. The Red Sword begged to be let loose.

The monster charged forward. Its heavy steps thundered in the barren warehouse. It paid no attention to Teddy's outstretched sword.

"Wait!" he shouted.

The beast pounced upon the Pyre Knight; and the Red Sword ran through its chest. It whined out a cry.

For a moment, the world stopped.

It bellowed as it fell backwards, and the sword slid loose from the wound's opening. The monster fell to one knee. No blood spilled from the gash.

Instinct fell over Teddy. He lunged forward, and ran the beast through again. A bright red flash burst from the blade, and into the hollow wound opening. Sparks lit inside the blade.

A tornado of flames danced from the Red Sword. The white light shone through the crimson blade.

Red fire burst like a geyser. It gushed through the monster. Flames splashed over the warehouse walls. The ceiling sparked under the inferno. The blaze poured out all over the place.

Where the monster had been stabbed, something odd was happening. Two bodies separated from each other, as if the fire had melted them apart. The first was a middle-aged man in a jumpsuit. The second was a screeching black beast that was little less than a shell. They split from each other.

The middle-aged man hit the floor with a dead weight. He was unconscious.

The bug monster was all that remained in the heat. The shell was incinerated on the spot by the red flames. It howled out in vain. Within seconds there was nothing left but ashes in the scorched cement floor. The black ash itself was consumed by the blaze.

Teddy brought back his sword, and the fire ceased pouring out of it. But the warehouse still burned. It spread all over. The ceiling began to twist and curl under the heat. It was time to go.

"What in the world did I just do?" Teddy asked. The sword decided not to respond. "Fine, be that way. I'll just get us out of here then."

He sheathed his sword, and sprinted over to the unconscious man. The jerk was still breathing. Teddy lifted him up and put him over his shoulder.

The fire had already consumed the entire building. The heat beat against his armor. It didn't bother Teddy, but he wasn't so sure about the unconscious man. They needed an exit.

"You know, you're pretty light," he said to the unconscious man. "I feel like Orson Buchan in issue nine of *The Rangers of the Endless Frontier*. Now all I need is about a hundred cyborgs to beat to death with my magic sword while I rescue the Baron's daughter from the pirate ship. Sure, it's a bit different from that, but it's still pretty cool!" He laughed as the flames licked against him. "So cool!"

The red flames were melting the ceiling, and ate into the concrete. This fire played by different rules.

The Pyre Knight slammed his knee through the exit. The strike smashed it from its hinges. A second kick sent off into the empty grass field thirty feet away.

The dark orange sun cascaded over the pair as he stepped outside.

Behind him, the warehouse was fully consumed with red

flames, but none spread to the surrounding grass. It was as if they were held to their location by some invisible force. Only the building was coated in fire.

Sirens began squealing in the distance. It wouldn't take long for the rest of McLeod to notice his handiwork.

He found shade from the flames behind a nearby dumpster, and laid his enemy down. The jumpsuit man was still out of it. It didn't look like he would be getting up anytime soon.

Teddy only had a small window of time. Nobody had arrived to check the fire out yet, and the trucks would take a bit longer to get there. The very last thing he wanted, was to be caught or identified. If anyone knew what happened then more of these creeps would show up. The sirens were getting closer. He needed to get going.

He placed his hands together, and said the words once more. The armor vanished in a flash of light. He was a kid wearing normal clothes and a backpack again.

Leaving the man behind the dumpster, Teddy left for the train tracks. He'd extinguished the monster—his job was done here. The police could handle the rest.

Shouts and machinery yelled out far behind him. He was far ahead of them now. He had made it to the fence bordering the train tracks and Mrs. Werner's house.

Thankfully, Mrs. Werner wasn't on her porch. The last thing he wanted was to involve her in this. Teddy ran through her yard, and out into the streets.

The neighborhood was dead quiet other than the sound of fire engines. Even the birds had fallen silent. Smoke billowed from where the warehouse had stood miles off. He tried to forget about it.

The truck was nowhere to be seen when he finally reached home. It was strange that the old man wasn't there. Teddy scratched his head, and went inside.

An odd quiet waited him inside. His family wasn't there. It was as if everyone in the world vanished.

"There you are," Mrs. MacIsaac said.

Teddy jumped. He choked down his nerves, and turned to meet her. "Hi."

She was leaning against the entrance way to the study. Her arms were folded and her mouth pressed into a straight line. She was clearly upset about something.

"Where have you been?" she asked. "Watching the fire with everyone else?"

"Sort of," he said, playing cool. "You didn't go?"

"Your brothers got excited and went on their bikes to check it out. Your father closed up for a bit to watch it, too. Briana's upstairs doing homework."

"Sounds like Dad and the Bozo Bros." He scratched underneath his shirt collar. "So, uh, what's up?"

Her mouth hardened. "You were in a fight."

The hair on his neck stood up. She knew. There was no way to explain this and not sound crazy. He tried to work out what he would say before she exploded.

"The school called while you were playing in the forest. When your father gets home, we're going to have a long talk. And you're not going to be going out again for a *long* time."

He'd totally forgotten about his fight with Hoffman. It felt like ages ago.

"But, Mom!"

"Don't start whining. It's embarrassing for a boy your age. Sit down, and don't move from that couch until your father gets back. I've had it with your acting out, Teddy, and I'm not going to put up with it anymore. It's time for you to grow up."

He sighed, and fell into the living room couch. Sirens rang out in the distance as he made himself comfortable. This day would never end.

Chapter 5
The Longest Night

To no surprise, Teddy found himself grounded.

Of course, his brothers couldn't miss this opportunity to mock him. They went on about how lucky Teddy was to drop Corey Hoffman in a single hit. This was easy pickings for them. They never missed a chance to mock Teddy, even over such a lame fight.

But no one in his family knew the truth. They couldn't know about the warehouse.

Teddy was the Pyre Knight. He was unbelievably strong and fast. He incinerated a monster into less than ash. He might actually be invincible.

And that scared him just a bit.

He lost control of the fire, and let it burn down a warehouse. Not to mention, despite being so much stronger than his enemy, he took much too long to defeat it. It was sloppy work. Were he in a public place, someone might have died. He'd have to do better next time. Because he well knew there would be a next time.

He sat alone in his room, staring out his bedroom window. The events of the day replayed in his mind.

On the radio, the newscaster went on about two things. They marveled at the fire being red instead of orange, and how it went out after burning the warehouse down. Almost like magic, the fire disappeared.

The man found by the fire was named Keith Anderson, originally from New Sun City. There was nothing wrong with him except being covered in smoke. No one could figure out why he was there at all.

The fire department found no evidence of arson, so Anderson was let go after questioning. The only information released to the public was that a man in red armor started the fire. The local media went wild.

Pundits on the radio seized this as an opportunity to jump to wild conclusions. They pinned the man in red armor as being responsible for the missing populace of Moonmere, as well as being the culprit of vigilantism in New Sun City. The news predicted terrorism, a cult of homegrown locals, corporate fat cats waging war with competitors, and all sorts of idiocy that never came near the truth of it.

Although it wasn't as if Teddy knew the whole truth, and he was actually there.

But he didn't regret anything that happened. If he had to do it again, he would still incinerate the monster to dust, and he would still accept his punishment for being late and fighting at school. At least he could breathe easier knowing that freak would no longer hurt anyone else. At the end of the day, it was still a victory.

The knowledge of the monster's defeat was enough for him to sleep easy. His eyelids drooped. A yawn escaped him, and he slowly slid into slumber.

And then he woke up an hour later, his batteries completely charged.

Teddy sat up, and blinked. It was past midnight. Everyone in the house was still asleep, and here he was, ready to get started on the day ahead.

"Now, what do I do?"

But, he was also grounded. Not only could he not sleep; but he couldn't leave the house, either. It wasn't the best combination of circumstances.

The grandfather clock rang out in the hall.

He rolled out of bed, and quietly stepped out of his room. If he couldn't go out, he could always stay in. The rest of the house was still his.

Down in the basement sat his father's study. A strong pine scent grabbed him. Everything was cleaned and organized as usual. There were weights in the back room, books on shelves in the front, and a computer smack dab between them. He would need them all tonight.

Teddy got on his father's workout bench. He gathered the weights his father would lift, and tried them out for himself. He lay down on the bench and took a breath before giving it a try.

He tried the bench-press, pushing the weight up from his position on his back. From what he remembered, the average man could lift around 165 pounds. That was around normal for a man his father's age, so Teddy decided to start there. He counted to three, let out a deep breath, and lifted the weights.

It was basically cardboard.

He added more and more weights, but found they were just as light. His father had up to 400 total pounds of weights lying around, and Teddy used them all. He lay on the bench and tried again.

It left him astonished. He got the same result as before. It was a bit weird, if not awesome.

"Okay," he said, putting the weights back. "Looks like pulling back on punches in the future might be a good idea."

He left the weights behind for the study. His strength tested, now he needed information.

The bookshelf was organized immaculately. Teddy browsed for books on knights and anything about a group like the Order of the Ash. He flipped through wat he could find. There was nothing other than a few history books, and old novels, about knights, but not the Knights of the End. He'd hit a wall.

Teddy turned on the computer, and began his search anew. He was never grounded from using the computer, since he rarely used it anyway. For once, he was glad to be raised such a luddite. He made a mental note to thank his parents for that someday.

Unfortunately, the internet had little of value. It had more stories like his father's books: histories of knights from ancient ages, novels and short stories, and differing definitions on what a knight was supposed to be. The information was useless.

There were some archived stories of a vigilante in New

Sun City that the news spoke of, but no solid descriptions that weren't rumors. While looking through dead end reports, he found some rumors of women wearing robes appearing at night. Teddy instantly thought of Caitlyn West. New Sun City was one strange place.

There wasn't much else to find. The only other knight report was of a man in green armor spotted in the countryside not long after the disappearance of Moonmere's populace. That was the last of the rumors. Teddy had hit another wall.

"So, nothing on Maidens, or Knights, huh?" He leaned back in the computer chair and stared at the basement ceiling. He had to search for something more specific. "But what about the prison break from last March?"

The prison break had far more information available. The three escapees were named Felix Barfield, Lorenzo Sims, and Stephen Gaines. They were a trio of bank robbers busted on their first attempt a month before their escape. Teddy sat forward in his chair. The story of their capture was confusing.

The three were in possession of empty firearms when they were arrested. They were sabotaged by Stephen Gaines, who called the cops ahead of time. It was never explained why he did this. Barfield, from his comments, didn't even realize what was happening, as he was caught sitting in the getaway car. He maintained his innocence up until he disappeared in the prison break. Neither Sims nor Gaines ever commented at all on their attempted robbery. All three had been missing since their escape in March.

"I got grounded for getting in a fight and staying out too late," Teddy whispered to himself. "Can't imagine what these guys will get when they get caught."

He decided to do a search for the Moonmere disappearances. There was no information he could use.

Moonmere was a small mountain town that no one paid much attention to. That was until one day a few weeks back, when the entire population of a few thousand simply disappeared. There were all sorts of crackpot theories as to what happened, but no answers. It was as if the whole town got up and walked away to parts unknown.

Teddy still knew nothing. If this Order of the Ash was behind it, he still didn't know what they were planning.

But there was one discovery he made in all his research that gave him heart. He was not alone in this. The world had many secrets hidden in plain sight: secrets that were waiting to be solved. If they were all related, then he was a piece of something much bigger than he first thought. He was a Knight of the End, after all.

Teddy stretched his arms and legs, and sighed. Criminals and ghosts were not much of a lead to go on. He needed something more solid to look into. A name would be enough.

The boy tapped a finger against his forehead. "Wait a second. I've got a name: Caitlyn West."

But even she was a dead end. There was not a single school picture or article to be found anywhere. She had no online presence, at all. She was very discreet.

While searching, he came across a legend of a man made

of stone—the man who was supposedly Darryl's killer. Teddy found some message board posts over a year old about a fat man who could walk through solid stone in New Sun City. They had to be about the same man. But if Darryl really was killed by this Stone Man, then Teddy would be the one to find and stop him. Teddy made a mental note to talk to Mrs. Werner as soon as possible.

He turned off the computer. That was all the information he could think of searching for.

Teddy fixed up the study, and left the basement. He still had too much time to waste. Unlike the computer, he was banned from the television, so that made his choice of what to do easier. He grabbed his backpack by the door, and unpacked it.

He did some homework in the living room to calm his mind. The irony didn't escape him. But, it wasn't enough. He finished his work by a half-past three in the morning.

Being grounded was particularly tough in the middle of the night. All he could do was take a hot shower, change, and eat breakfast. He thought about his day ahead and found himself bored rather quickly. Eventually, his father shuffled down the stairs.

The old man yawned, and stared sideways at Teddy.

His son waved, meekly. "Hi, Dad."

Mr. MacIsaac quietly stepped past Teddy into the kitchen, and set up the coffee maker. The old man returned up the stairs without a word. The shower started. Teddy waited for him by the bottom of the stairs.

When Jonas MacIsaac emerged again, he was fully

dressed for the day ahead. He returned down the stairs, passed Teddy once more, and sat in the kitchen. Teddy sat across from him at the breakfast table.

"So," Teddy said. "What was the deal with that fire yesterday?"

"You heard your brothers gushing about it at dinner. It was quite a sight. What do you think caused it?"

"I dunno." He shrugged. "Gas leak?"

The old man laughed. "I doubt it. But I've never seen anything like that before. Red fire is certainly not natural. The firemen couldn't even put it out, and when the warehouse burned to ground, the flames just went out on their own. None of the pictures or videos people took of it came out clear, either. No wonder everyone's going on about it. It's almost like magic."

"I'm sure." Teddy cleared his throat. "Do they have any leads on who did it?"

"I'm surprised you didn't see anything. We were worried since you were so late, but you still didn't see anything even though you pass by the place on your way home every day. You're lucky your mother didn't roast you over a spit when you got back."

"Actually, I have a more pressing problem."

"I severely doubt it, but let's hear it."

"I need to leave early this morning. It's important."

His father's brow rose. "You *want* to go to school early?"

"Not even if I was threatened at knifepoint. No, I need to talk to Mrs. Werner before school starts."

The old man took a sip of coffee. "I'm sure it can wait

until after school, when you come back home and finish your homework. Then you can give her a call."

"Dad," he said, trying to keep his tone level. "Please. It is important."

Mr. MacIsaac sighed. "If it's so important, why don't you tell me what it's about?"

That was a minefield Teddy wasn't ready to cross. It wasn't that he couldn't trust his father, but he also couldn't just tell the old man about his dreams. It was too crazy. His parents already thought Teddy was childish and irresponsible, and if they thought he was dragging Mrs. Werner into his delusions, then they would never trust him again. He couldn't tell them. Not yet.

But he also wasn't going to lie.

"I will tell you everything later, Dad. Trust me. It's a long story. Kind of complicated."

His father stifled a yawn and shook his head. "It's getting harder and harder to trust you, Theodore. You haven't been acting normal since you started at Harding last year. In seventh grade, the teachers complained that you never paid attention; in eighth grade, you're getting in fights on top of it. You need to start being honest with me. Did you really have to hit that boy?"

"Dad, I already told you. He charged at me, and I pushed him back. Ask anyone who was there. I didn't start anything. I finished it."

"You nearly cracked one of his ribs." Jonas MacIsaac's voice hardened. "Don't lie to me. Never lie. A fight is one thing, but this is more serious than a simple school yard fight, isn't it?"

"What can I say; I'm stronger than I look. I didn't mean to hurt him that bad. I just wanted to stop him. That's all it was. There isn't anything wrong with that. Is there?"

His father locked his gaze with the boy's. Teddy refused to glance away. It felt like an hour before the old man spoke again. "Tell me why you want to speak with Mrs. Werner."

"It's private."

"I'm your father. Try again. You don't have privacy until you move out."

"This isn't about my privacy. This is about her, and Darryl."

The old man paused and glanced at the kitchen table. He finished off his coffee, but did not reply.

"Please, Dad. It's really important."

His father stared at his son with a wrinkled nose for a few moments.

"Alright," Mr. MacIsaac said. "You can go. Just realize that you're not grounded for fighting, even though that was what your mother was most upset about. There is something going on with you. If you don't tell someone soon, something bad is going to happen. You are grounded for breaking your promise, being late, and for lying. These are not traits worthy of real men. You always wanted to be a hero, right? Well, this is your chance. Straighten up, and do the right thing."

"I understand, Dad. Really. I will tell you later. But, right now, I really have to go."

"Then go. But if she's not up, you leave. Don't pester her. The poor woman has been through enough. After you see her, you go straight to school. No wandering off."

"I got it, Dad. I won't." Teddy shot out of his chair and to the front door.

"And be polite!"

"I will. Thanks, Dad!"

"Don't you want any breakfast?"

Teddy stopped at the door. "I, uh, already ate before you got up."

His father stared cockeyed at him once more. "What time did you get up?"

"I'm an early riser these days." Teddy winked. "Really, I'm a whole new man."

"I'll remember that when mowing season returns. Lawn maintenance awaits no lazy teenager. Now, get going."

Teddy tied his sneakers, put on his coat and backpack, and left for Mrs. Werner's place. It was nice to get out again.

The morning air cut into him. It wasn't any colder than usual, and yet he felt it through his jacket and down to his bones. A frost clung inside him. He didn't shake, or shiver. It was as if there was a sheet of warmth just over his soul keeping the chill out. He ignored it, and continued down the street.

Teddy knocked on Mrs. Werner's door. She usually slept until nine or so, but sometimes she would be up early. It depended on if she felt well or not. He hoped this was one of her early days.

Her living room curtain opened momentarily, breaking the heavy shadow on the porch. A figure stood in the window, and vanished as quickly as it arrived. It looked like this was an early day.

"Mrs. Werner," Teddy called out. "It's me, Teddy MacIsaac. I need to talk. Can I come in?"

There was a pause. Then, a series of clicks rang out behind the door. It swung open with Mrs. Werner standing behind it. She had heavy bags under her eyes.

"What are you doing here so early?" Her tone was rough. "Don't tell me you've been out all night."

"Me?" Teddy scratched the back of his head. "I'm only fourteen, ma'am. I'm here because I wanted to talk with you before school starts. Can I come in?"

She eyed him up and down, suspiciously. She was clearly debating calling his mother. After a second or two, she finally waved him in. The door shut and locked behind him.

The inside was coated with old flowery wallpaper. There were antiques littered throughout the walls and shelves. It was a bit of a time warp in Mrs. Werner's house. Teddy hadn't been in a house like this since the last time he visited his grandmother's home. That was ages ago.

He followed his host, and the smell of coffee, through the halls. The place felt so empty.

In her kitchen, Mrs. Werner turned off the radio and sat at the table. Teddy sat across from her.

She said nothing, waiting for him to speak his piece. Birds chirped outside the window. The quiet was nearly suffocating.

"Ma'am," he said. "I need to ask you about Darryl's attacker. What was his exact description? I hope this isn't too rude of me, but I need to know."

She didn't miss a beat. "He said his attacker was a man

made of stone that didn't look like he was made of stone. He looked like a fat man, until his skin hardened to stone like a grey shadow fell over him." She stirred her coffee cup, not looking at Teddy. "He wore a dark blue jacket and a baseball cap over his head. He was about six foot tall even and overweight, probably near four hundred pounds. One tiny earing in his right ear, and the face of a bull. That's everything Darryl said about the criminal."

Teddy took a deep breath. That was the same description as the rumor. He couldn't tell Mrs. Werner anything about being the Pyre Knight, but he could get her son's killer. He could stop the murderer. It was his duty.

"They never found this guy with a description like that?" he asked.

"I think they have an idea who he is," she said, with a bitter smile. "But they were looking for a man who can turn to stone, and attacked people in bad neighborhoods. There was no murder weapon found, and no one could possibly believe in a stone man attacking people. It's too unbelievable. He stopped not long after Darryl died, and the police just figured that was it. They didn't dig any deeper. The case is closed."

"You don't believe he just stopped, though."

She stared long at the table before glancing back at him. "Mr. MacIsaac, there is a lot of evil in the world. We've seen a bit of it. Relatives backstabbing each other for money and property, coworkers knocking friends over for promotions, and those are just the little things. We believe that's all the evil we can deal with, so that's all the evil there can be. But there is a lot we don't see, dear. And the worst enemy is one you don't see coming. I believe my son was the victim of one of them."

Teddy thought back to Keith Anderson, the man in the jumpsuit. He had transformed into a monster that lived deep inside of him, and lost control. But while Anderson was nutty, this Stone Man was a whole other level of insane. This was random malice. Darryl was not the victim of a grudge—he died for no reason.

"And this happened in New Sun City, ma'am?"

"Yes, in King's Park near the subway station. What is all this about, Mr. MacIsaac? Is there something about Darryl you wanted to know?"

"It's just this project I'm working on. Listen, ma'am, Darryl was a good guy. I didn't know him long, being that he left town when I was a kid, but I know he was grateful to have a mom like you. He kept me in line when he babysat me."

"I know."

"He was also the one who gave me my first adventure book. He made them sound so magical. That's why I can't just throw them aside. Visiting a world of possibilities, a world of adventure, is what shows me this world can be saved—that there is something worth protecting. Darryl believed that."

"I know," she said, her eyes watering.

"I'll get out of your hair." He got up and approached the back door. "Thanks for your time, Mrs. Werner."

He swung the door open. The sun was shining bright

across her backyard. Morning was finally showing itself. Behind him, he heard Mrs. Werner call out.

"Yes, ma'am?"

"What I said about throwing those books away? Forget it."

He grinned. "Sure."

"Have a good day, Theodore."

"Something tells me today will be a good one. You have a good day, too."

He hopped the fence, and bolted down the tracks. His speed easily carried him. He was going to be on time—he still had a promise to keep.

The Stone Man was the only lead he had about the Order of the Ash. The murderer had to be connected to them with powers like that. But Teddy didn't know how he could take advantage of this knowledge. There was little he could do from McLeod.

He soon reached the warehouse. It was nothing but a pile of ash now. A crowd filled the area separated by police tape, as police officers and firemen inspected the debris. It was hard to imagine he was responsible for all of it.

The crowd chattered on. Teddy couldn't hear them from the tracks, but they were probably going on about the same rumors his father mentioned. Everyone looked ill at ease.

In the crowd of dozens, were a few people that didn't look like they belonged in McLeod. Three figures dressed in trench coats, three piece suits, small chains around their necks, and sunglasses, wandered the crowd. They all had the same pale face, and greasy black hair. It was hard to spot details from his distance, but they all looked like the same man. Whoever they were, they were searching for something.

Or someone.

Teddy pulled up the hood on his jacket and kept moving down the tracks. Thankfully, no one was looking his way.

He left the crowd behind for school with one thought remaining on his mind. The Order of the Ash was definitely here.

Chapter 6
The Longest Morning

Harding was somehow worse than usual. The other kids avoided Teddy, giving him sideways glances as he passed them. The teachers sidestepped him in the hallways. He knew it was because of Hoffman, but only the warehouse fire tugged at him. He had more important things to worry about than what others thought of him.

The PA system blared. "Will Theodore MacIsaac please report to the main office? Theodore MacIsaac to the main office."

"Oh, great," he said, opening his locker. He tossed his bag and coat inside. "I'm guessing they want my blood now."

He swung open the door to the main office. The odor of turpentine instantly crushed his nostrils. The walls were painted a nasty and murky light grey like a sewer. He'd never seen a more sterile place.

He handed the secretary his ID card: the one with the picture of him sneezing. She gave him a pink slip and sat him down next to the Assistant Principal's office. They called *him* there, and yet he had to wait for them.

"Such a well-oiled machine," he whispered under his breath.

After five minutes of wasted time, the door to the Assistant Principal's office was thrown open. A man wearing an old faded grey suit, and badly-trimmed, thinning, brown and grey hair, poked his head out of the doorframe. His plump cheeks grimaced at Teddy.

"Next," the Assistant Principal said.

Teddy stood and stretched, and followed him in.

He took the slip from Teddy, and motioned vaguely to the chairs before his desk. "Sit."

Rock Carson sat in one of two chairs facing the Assistant Principal's desk, his hands behind his head. He leaned back when he noticed Teddy.

"Hey, Killer," the thug said.

Teddy froze. He'd almost forgotten that Carson was there in the field when the fight broke out. The thug probably sold Teddy out to get himself a bigger deal. Teddy sat beside Carson, paying the older boy no mind.

The Assistant Principal sat in the chair behind the desk. "Quiet, Mr. Carson."

"Yeah, yeah," the older boy replied.

Rock Carson always looked like some Rockabilly reject. He wore a bowling shirt colored dark blue and green, black baggy jeans, and had his hair slicked back. Dark circles under his eyes clashed against his white, lightly freckled skin. He still didn't smile.

The Assistant Principal looked over the slip, and nodded to himself. "Now that the gang's all here, this should be easy."

"With all due respect," Teddy said. "What is this all about, sir?"

"He's looking to nail someone for the fight yesterday." To Teddy's surprise, Rock answered first. The older boy didn't bother to look at anyone while he spoke. "We're the only ones without alibis, and Hoffman's friends sold us out. So we're getting thrown under the bus."

"You didn't sell me out?" Teddy asked.

Carson tilted his head at the younger boy. "Why would I do that?"

"Kindly shut it, Mr. Carson." He snapped his attention from Carson to Teddy. "Mr. MacIsaac, you know our rules about fighting."

"I was only defending myself."

Rock sighed, his tone flighty. "It doesn't matter."

"Silence, Mr. Carson." He once more turned to the younger boy. "Fighting is never permissible on school grounds, even in self-defense. You should have found a responsible adult to settle your grievances. Did you not sign a student contract telling us you promised to obey the rules, Mr. MacIsaac?"

Teddy tried not to laugh. "I skimmed it."

"Everyone does," Rock interrupted. "It also says I promise not to commit suicide, or bring a gun to school. If I wanted to do either of those things, do you think I'd care if I signed a sheet paper? But that's just the stupidity of

Harding. I can't wait to get out of this town."

"Last warning, Mr. Carson."

Rock threw up his hands in surrender, and leaned back in his chair.

"He's not wrong, sir," Teddy said. "I did what I had to do. I don't regret it."

"Be that as it may," the Assistant Principal continued, "self-defense is no excuse for violence. You should have found a teacher or a peer mediator."

An urge to slug the man rose. Teddy tried to calm himself before responding. He sat forward, his fingers threaded together. "There weren't any around."

"Again, Mr. MacIsaac—"

"The halls were empty, and the big guy here found me after class. He brought me directly from my locker to the field. There was no choice but to either fight Hoffman, or him."

The Assistant Principal snapped his fingers at Carson. "Is this true?"

Carson shrugged. "I was paid to stomp him into the ground if he ran away. When we got to the field, they built a ring around him. There was no situation where he couldn't fight back without getting hurt. Hoffman's gang is a pretty stupid bunch, but it was a smart plan on their end. Rules can be gamed."

"Kids always find a way to break the rules, sir." Teddy needed to appeal to the Assistant Principal's sense of fairness. "I was just doing what I could at the moment."

"I see," the Assistant Principal said. He folded his hands

under his chin as if weighing his options.

"I'm glad you see it my way," Teddy said.

The man in the suit leaned back in his chair, and began scribbling something on a sheet of paper. His disinterested expression didn't as much as twitch. He had clearly done this many times before.

After a few extra seconds of scribbling he finally looked up again.

"Detention for a week," he said, "for both of you."

Carson let out a groan and fell back in his chair.

Teddy stood up. "For what? I didn't have any choice!"

"There is always a choice, Mr. MacIsaac. Just because you did not see a way out does not mean there wasn't one available. Maybe if you spend a week in detention without any distractions, the two of you will begin to think things through instead of mindlessly plowing into dangerous situations."

Carson yawned. "Sure, if it didn't work the first hundred times, it'll work the next time."

"This isn't right," Teddy said. His fists tightened. "This isn't fair."

"Life isn't fair, children."

"In this case, you're just making an excuse for your own decision," Teddy said, through gritted teeth. "This is a useless punishment, and you know it."

"Excuse me, Mr. MacIsaac; I believe I was being generous with your sentence."

Rock laughed. "You don't know the first thing about generosity. You and this whole rotten town. You're just thinking about yourself and your job."

"Generous?" Teddy asked. "I didn't do anything wrong."

The Assistant Principal stood up, the veins in his forehead pounding. "Then that just proves you're both still children. Now, shut your mouths."

"Better a kid than an adult like you," Rock said, his teeth bared in a grin.

"Alright, a month's detention instead," the suit said. "Stick around if you want more. Now get out of here and get back to class. Get yourselves an early start for once. Have a good day, gentlemen."

The two students left the office for the empty halls. Teddy felt the anger melt from him the further he got from the Assistant Principal. Reality eventually caught up with the boy. It looked like another bad day at Harding was ahead of him.

"Don't worry about it," Carson said. Teddy flinched at the voice.

"I'm not."

The older boy passed him in the hall. Rock Carson gave him a wry smile, and ran up the stairs with surprising speed. Teddy now knew why the rockabilly reject never smiled. An expression like that could break mirrors. At least he was gone now.

At his locker once again, Teddy pulled out his books for Math. He thought about algebraic equations as he made his way to his next class. The Assistant Principal's words still twisted in his mind. A month's detention was a real raw deal.

He remembered he had his phone with him, and slipped

it out of his pocket. He had to call home.

Teddy hated phones. Nobody ever talked the same on the phone as they did in real life. He even wore a watch so he wouldn't need one of them to check the time. It was better this way. He didn't need a phone for anything. Nonetheless, he would have to use it now.

He called home. Nobody answered, so he left a message. He wasn't anticipating his mom's reaction.

After his call, he sat in the empty math class. He threw his books up on his desk, and kicked his feet up next to them. No one would be there until class started. Boredom kicked in.

He thought back to those suits at the warehouse. They were looking for the Pyre Knight. They had to be. Sooner or later, they would figure out the Knight of Flame's identity as a shrimpy fourteen-year-old. He needed a plan before someone in town got hurt. Teddy had to beat them to the punch.

He thought of the pretty girl. Caitlyn West, the girl from his dream, was nowhere to be found online or in real life. But he still needed help. There had to be someone he could talk to.

"Wait a minute," he said, his voice echoing in the empty room. He remembered the image of the teenagers in his dream—the ones in the water's reflection. There was one on a subway who looked sort of familiar. He might have known him. "No way."

He brandished his phone, and dialed an old friend. Matthias Matthew Sova, his best friend from elementary school, was now in New Sun City. That was the center of all this weirdness. Matt was attending some private school. Something about that figure in the reflection reminded Teddy of his old friend. He decided to give it a shot.

Unfortunately, no one picked up. Again.

He decided to leave a message. "Matt, it's me, Teddy. I have to talk to you as soon as possible. It's pretty important, so call back when you hear this. I know we didn't part on the best of terms, so you know I wouldn't do this otherwise. Please, call back when you get this."

Eventually, the bell to change classes rang, instructing the prisoners to move from cell to cell. Teddy's math teacher, Mrs. Cindy Sands, arrived first to set up for her class. She didn't pay Teddy any mind.

She was in her thirties, had the face of a hawk and sandy brown hair cut short, and was married with a kid. Despite that, Mrs. Sands didn't really seem to like children very much. Teddy had a hard time learning algebra from her, and he figured he wasn't alone in that.

The rest of the class slowly filled with students. It appeared he was still being ignored, since even Stieg silently passed him to his seat.

"All right, everyone," Mrs. Sands began, "sit down and get your books out. Did everyone complete the worksheet assignments from last night?"

She looked strangely tired. Most of the class was spent with her stifling yawns between lessons. They weren't quite that boring.

No one made any jokes during the whole class; no one

really spoke out, either. It was almost like a normal pleasant day. He was beginning to forget what those were like.

Another announcement on the PA blared near the end of the class. He was half-expecting his expulsion from Harding this time.

"We will now have a special assembly on recent events," it said. "Please leave your classrooms in single-file, guided by your current period teacher, toward the second floor gymnasium. Thank you."

The second floor gymnasium was absolutely huge. They had never called an assembly there before. The auditorium was sufficient for holding a few classes of kids. This must have been a big announcement.

"Mrs. Sands," Ashley Michaels asked. "What is this about?"

Stieg shrugged. "Probably about the psycho that burned down the warehouse yesterday."

"The word is *pyro*," Curtis Simon said, from the front row.

"Same difference."

"Enough," Mrs. Sands said. "We had an early staff meeting today, and I'm not in the mood. Get in line."

The long line of students met in the hall, winding from every classroom all the way up to the second floor. It was unusual to call all the students at once, instead of one grade at a time. He tried to hold back his excitement, and his dread. It was not going to be about anything he didn't already know.

Teddy surveyed the scene as the classes piled into the

gymnasium. The kids all had different theories for the assembly, but no one had a clear idea.

"I hear they're shipping some us off for military testing," a ninth grader said.

"No way, it's got to do with the water supply. Someone poisoned it."

"It's probably about that kid who keeps calling in bomb threats. Rumor is, they've already got a psychiatrist lined up for the poor sicko."

Another kid laughed. "They're probably holding casting calls for that *World's Stupidest Kids* show. We have a lot of good candidates for that."

"Speak for yourself," some eighth grade girl snapped.

Mrs. Sands hushed her students when it was her class's turn to file in. The gym was filled with students of every grade. Every teacher and hall monitor attended, as did the security guards. The place was almost like a weeded out concert hall.

There were people everywhere. The front office was left unattended since the faculty was all milling about near the front of the stage. If anyone was calling in a fake bomb threat, they were not getting through today. It looked like everyone in the school was there.

Across the crowd, Teddy spotted Rock Carson amongst the ninth graders. The older boy casually waved to him, and turned back to the stage. He didn't look too happy to be there.

"Perfect place for a set up," Teddy muttered.

Mrs. Sands grimaced at him. "Mr. MacIsaac, will you

kindly shut your mouth? The presentation is about to begin. It's safe to say that this is important, or we wouldn't be here."

Something about his teacher looked a bit off. She had been sweating since they left the class, and her pupils were dilated. Her aggressive attitude wasn't anything new, but her impatience was. This was more than fatigue. He decided not to push her any further. He'd had bad days before, too.

Eventually, the crowd died down. Several staff members crossed the stage, fumbling with the microphones. Some kids laughed. It was business as usual.

He almost breathed a sigh of relief. His nerves buckled when he caught a glimpse at a set of four people standing at the back of the stage. One of them looked exactly like the three Teddy saw at the warehouse that morning. He had the same pale face and greasy hair. But that wasn't what froze his blood.

The fourth figure was a fat man in a suit. He was around six foot tall even and overweight, probably over four hundred pounds. He had one tiny earing in his right ear, and the face of a bulldog. It was the man Darryl Werner described in every way, except without stone skin. He smiled blandly to the crowd.

The feedback from the Principal's mic caught everyone off guard, except for Teddy. His knuckles tightened. The Order of the Ash was right there in front of him.

Chapter 7
The Proclamation

The Principal had no charisma at all. It was agonizing. He spoke as if reading from cue cards or a script despite having nothing of the sort. His voice could pull a sugar junkie down from a high.

It started as a speech on zero tolerance policies before turning to the subject of bullying. A comment on what a fine school Harding was drew scoffs from many in the crowd, but that was the biggest response he got.

Five minutes in and he was still endlessly prattling. He babbled on and on.

And on and on.

"I wonder how many years of this job it takes before your soul dies," some kid said. A teacher shushed him.

Teddy's eyes began to glaze over. An elbow tapped his ribs.

"Hey, loser," Stieg Johns whispered. He kept staring at the stage. "You know that Corey is transferring schools because of you, right? His parents pulled him out last night. He's going to Riverview now."

Teddy's bored stare remained on the Principal. "This is me caring."

"About the same as always, eh, MacIsaac? Selfish kid."

"What's your problem?" Teddy snapped in his quietest voice. "I am not selfish. He deserved what he got, and you know it. I'm not sorry for what I did."

"Yeah, well, watch your back. I don't know what you did to beat Corey, but it won't work again. The rest of us will get you. Count on it."

"Get a life, Stieg. I mean an actual life. Take up gardening, or sailing, or raising puppies. Just do something far away from fighting. You're not cut out for it, just like your pal Hoffman isn't."

"You stupid—"

"Boys," Mrs. Sands interrupted. "Feel free to talk trash outside of my supervision. As long as you're here, kindly shut up."

The four figures at the back of the stage moved behind the Principal. They scanned the crowd. The three men dressed in suits, and the woman dressed in a black skirt with matching top. They were eager to get at the microphone, giving passing smiles to the faculty and the crowd. All four of them looked like they hadn't slept in ages.

The Principal went on: "With me here is a member of a fire department from out in New Sun City. They are here to remind you all of the importance of fire safety. It was their employee who was caught in the warehouse. He was doing an inspection when it started, probably from some vandal. Let this be a lesson to you all to be aware of your surroundings. Now, please welcome Mr. Morris."

The gangly man in the black suit strode over to the microphone. Teddy recognized him as the one that looked like three other suits scoping out the crowd at the warehouse. The other two triplets were nowhere to be seen. The suit had messy black hair that was not combed right, yellow circles under his brown eyes, and a smirking grin. He had the air of a professional speaker, which clashed with the unwashed way he looked. He straightened his tie and beamed a smile down at the crowd.

"Good afternoon, everyone," he said, drawling out every word. The lone woman in the quartet leaned forward and whispered into his ear. He feigned surprise at whatever she said. Teddy couldn't help but think he'd seen her before. "I'm sorry, I mean, good morning."

"Way to go, genius!" some kid shouted.

The crowd laughed.

The voice was hushed fairly quickly, as were the giggles that arose from the comment. The man at the microphone remained smiling with white teeth bared. He didn't look very happy.

"I'm sure by now you have all heard of the pyromaniac who attacked our employee. We have reason to believe the fire was caused by an outside party, not of this town. But, just in case our hunch is wrong, I wish to say something to all you young happy people. Now, while it is fairly obvious to everyone here that playing with fire is wrong—"

"We learned that in first grade!"

A seventh grader laughed. "Speak for yourself."

Another hush arrived from the teachers. More giggles erupted.

The suit waited patiently for quiet to return.

"Anyway," he continued, "what I am trying to say is that if anyone here knows who the arsonist is, to make sure to inform those at your local fire station. This is a very serious matter."

There were no other interruptions. Something about the man's dead smile seemed to put everyone on edge. His happy expression did not match his tone.

"If the arsonist is out there among you all, I only have one thing to say," he said, his smile hardening. "Do the proper thing and come forward. It is the right thing to do. We will go a lot easier on you. If you admit what you did, maybe we'll even get to become good buddies and best friends."

He paused, but no one took advantage of the situation to make a joke. Many of the kids glanced away from him.

"That is all." The gangly man spun around, and marched to the back of the stage. He mumbled something about hating kids as he wandered away.

The Principal took the stage again, oblivious to the mood. He went on about the dance from last week. The crowd's attention petered out again. School activities were rather trivial compared to the possibility of an arsonist at large.

It took another five minutes for the Principal to wrap things up. The crowd applauded when he finally finished.

The crowd finally filed out.

Stieg shouldered Teddy on his way out. "Watch your back, loser."

"You don't want to become good buddies, Stieg? I thought that speech was rather inspiring."

He made an obscene gesture at Teddy. Unfortunately for Stieg, Mrs. Sands caught him and demanded he apologize. Stieg rolled his eyes. Teddy would have stopped to hear the rest, but he had a class to get to.

The rest of the day went as expected.

Shop class was set up so oddly. It was essentially one giant room split in two. The class had one side that was a standard classroom for lectures, and a second side with the machinery separated by a wall with a double door between them. Thankfully, they spent more time in the classroom side, so Teddy didn't have to see any girls like Katie Robertson fainting. He had a low tolerance for seeing girls looking sickly.

He checked his phone at lunch and found no messages. Matt Sova never called him back.

"The one thing I use this stupid thing for, and it's useless at that, too." He checked his watch. If Matt didn't call by now, he wasn't going to call at all. He probably thought Teddy was playing a game.

After the final bell, Teddy entered shop class for detention. The class was almost barren. Mrs. Sands was supposed to oversee detention, though she had yet to arrive. Teddy closed the door behind him.

There was only one other boy in there with him. It was Rock Carson.

Carson sat at his desk with a comic in hand, reading intently. He didn't bother to look up. "You have to put your phone on the teacher's desk."

"I do?"

"Otherwise you'll get another day, or week, of detention. Depends on the teacher we get and how bad of a mood they're in."

Teddy slammed his phone on the teacher's desk. He didn't care if he had to give it up. Phones were useless.

"Where's your phone?" Teddy asked. He sat in the desk beside Carson.

"Don't have one, don't want one, don't need one."

Teddy eyed the comic. "*The Rangers of the Endless Frontier*. Wow, that's a classic."

"As if you know the classics."

"Let's see," Teddy paused, pretending to reach into the depths of his memory. "Fifty-two issues, drawn by Jim Thomas and written by Marty Garfield. Had just over a four year run. It ended, like, back when my grandfather was a kid. It's about a gang in a frontier land with no borders who band together to bring law back. Very action packed. They fight strange beasts from the darkest depths and robot sentinels from the city. I liked the Fake Sheriff story the most. They don't make them like that anymore."

Rock's mouth fell open for half a second. He quickly went back to his comic.

"You like this stuff?" Teddy asked.

"Yeah," Rock said. "I do. It was a time when good guys were good. Bad guys were bad. Choices mattered.

Consequences. Now, you can't open a comic without someone being raised from the dead for the sixty-third time. No drama. The Rangers are different."

"Honor, valor, friendship, life above all, truth, persistence," Teddy said, a smile breaking through. "Not much you see these days. Now it's all about bad people doing bad stuff to each other. Personally, I don't think people are all so bad." He remembered yesterday's fights. "Well, most of the time."

Carson placed the comic on his stomach. He scratched his hair and stifled a yawn. "I don't like people very much. All they want is what they think they deserve. Best to just walk away from them all and be your own man."

"I've heard the rumors." Teddy slid into the seat beside the older boy. "Is that why they call you Rock? Because you have the people skills of a pebble?"

"My full name is Rochester Carson. My dad thinks it's manly. I've beaten people up for not calling me Rock. So that's why they call me Rock."

"Sounds a bit over the top."

"Strike first and hard before your enemy does. You should have learned that yesterday against Hoffman. How hard did you hit him, anyway? For a kid your size, he shouldn't have flown back so far."

"I just knocked him off balance. It was a fluke."

"So modest."

"Hey, I don't regret beating bad guys." Teddy leaned back in his chair. "The Rangers wouldn't."

Rock chuckled. "You got that right."

Teddy glanced toward the door. Mrs. Sands still hadn't appeared.

"Teacher's late," Rock said.

"How long do they usually take to get here?"

"Usually before me. I don't know how they do it. Sometimes I think teachers can walk through walls, or teleport."

A vision of Caitlyn popped into Teddy's head. He smiled. "Teleport, huh?"

"Not literally. And why are you grinning?"

Teddy wanted to tell him it wasn't so far-fetched, but decided against it. He was starting to doubt Caitlyn West was even a real person.

As if on cue, the door opened. Mrs. Sands stumbled into the doorway, and slammed the door behind her. She limped, sweating profusely, toward the teacher's desk. Around her neck, she wore a sort of small chain that looked somehow familiar to Teddy. She looked far worse than she did in the gym.

Teddy stood up. "Are you alright, ma'am? You don't look so hot."

"Sit down," she said, flatly. "Detention begins now."

He obliged, falling back into his chair.

Rock threw his backpack on his desk, shuffling for something inside. He removed a math book and binder and slammed it on his desk. After getting what he wanted, he whipped the bag back under his seat. Rock Carson simply couldn't be subtle.

The older boy's hands flew up. "Excuse me."

"Quiet," she said.

"But I don't understand my homework."

"Not my job."

Rock scratched the back of his head. "But, uh, isn't that your *only* job?"

Just then, the power in the building went off like a light switch. Rock flinched. Teddy felt the butterflies in his gut again.

Mrs. Sands stood up. She removed the lone phone sitting on her desk, and threw it on the floor. Without a pause, she stepped down on it and smashed it to rubble. Teddy wasn't as offended as he should have been.

"Are you going to buy him a new phone, Mrs. Sands?"

"Shut up," she said, limping forward. She threw both of her hands down upon the desks before the boys. The wood cracked, and both students jumped in their seats. "Stupid noisy kids should just be silent."

Teddy gathered his courage. "There is something wrong, isn't there, Mrs. Sands?"

Her body began to distort under the black shade of the darkened classroom. Skin twisted. Her mouth fell back into the jaw, and a black fuzz of hair sprouted through her skin. The face of an insect sprang from where hers once was. Bones cracked and bent.

Teddy jumped backwards out of his seat, and Rock fell out of his chair.

She was no longer Mrs. Sands. Their teacher had transformed into an insect monster, just as Anderson did in the warehouse. The smell of ash flowed from her.

"What is going on?" Rock shouted, his voice warbling.

"Not something good," Teddy replied.

Her body twisted into a parody of a human standing erect. It twisted and popped in the darkness that grew around her. The insect monster stared down at the two teenagers.

"So tell me, boys," she said, her voice no longer human. "Which one of you is the Pyre Knight?"

Teddy stepped backwards. He fell back against the door to the other half of shop class. His palms itched.

Chapter 8
The Order's Invasion

The claw struck Teddy in the waist. It sent off the floor and through the shop class door behind him. Splinters broke against his back.

He slid on the chunks of wood on the floor into the machinery room. His brain rattled as he flipped over. Searing pain shot through his back, though he was physically fine. He thanked his lack of injuries on being the Pyre Knight.

Someone yelled, and Teddy glanced up. The thing formerly known as Mrs. Sands had fastened its claws around Rock Carson's throat. The older boy kicked and thrashed, but couldn't break its grip.

"One of you must be the Pyre Knight. Teenagers are the most common wielders of the Coins of Light and those creatures center in schools during the day. I will take you upstairs to the others, and we will dissect you both."

Rock began to gag.

Teddy growled. He'd forgotten there were other

detentions going on. "There are other kids in detention?"

"We have them until we rid ourselves of them. One of them has what we are looking for, so they will remain alive until we receive what we seek."

"Let Carson go. You're not going to find what you're looking for by hurting him."

"Will I have to tell you to shut up again, boy?"

"It doesn't matter who you are," Teddy said. "I'm going to stop you."

Teddy ran forward. His incredible speed carried him across the floor. He struck the monster in the chest, shoulder first. The impact knocked it back. It tumbled backwards through the air, screeching the whole way. It let Carson go as it flew back.

The monster crashed through the teacher's desk. Broken wood erupted around its massive body.

Rock fell to the ground, coughing. Teddy helped him up by the arm.

The beast flipped around in the rubble. Its horrific wailing could have brought blood to Teddy's ears. Desk splinters scattered over the floor as the monster rose.

Rock wheezed. "What is that thing?"

"Not Mrs. Sands." Teddy glanced through the broken door behind him. The monster blocked the normal exit, leaving only one option left. The machinery room had an emergency exit. He bolted through the broken door. "Let's get past the woodcutters. We're going out through the back exit."

"You don't have to tell me twice."

The pair dashed across the workshop. They weaved around the large wooden worktables and the powered down machinery. The monster screeched behind them.

Desks broke apart in the classroom they had escaped from. The monster still hadn't followed. The teenagers didn't look back.

Teddy kicked the door open at the back of the room. It flung out into a barren white hallway toward their escape. There was a short hall that led to the emergency exit at the end. It was so short; it had no room for a security camera. From there, it was only a small dash to the outside world.

"Watch out!" Rock yelled.

A heavy weight, like a concrete block, struck Teddy in the spine. He tumbled forward across the floor, the world flipping around him. His body spun to a stop inches from the emergency exit. The light from the cracks of the door blinded him.

Behind him, the monster held Rock by the back of the neck. It glared at Teddy before pinning Rock with his chin to the wall. He thrashed about uselessly.

In the creature's free right claw sat the small chain that was around its neck. Attached to the chain was a small crystal vial filled with a tiny amount of black liquid. The liquid stunk of garbage. The monster squeezed and shattered the crystal, and the liquid poured out. The liquid was absorbed into the beast's skin.

"Now to end this," the monster said. The liquid gathered into its right claw.

The black liquid became a tiny ball of pure darkness. The

darkness drifted only an inch up from its claw, spinning like a tiny planet of its own. The fake Mrs. Sands gazed at it in awe with its beady, bug-like eyes. It jabbed the darkness into Rock's back, cackling away.

Rock let out a scream.

Teddy sprang forward from the floor.

With a wave of its left claw, it batted Teddy backwards. He skidded backwards with his feet still planted on the ground. The drywall broke behind his body. A cough escaped him with the impact. He slid down to the floor on one knee.

"You stay there, Pyre Knight," the monster said, with the same flat tone of Mrs. Sands. "This won't take very long. I just have to get rid of the witness, and then we can go upstairs. The Captains are dying to meet you."

Teddy barely heard its words. He was more concerned with Carson. If he couldn't help the older boy this way, he had to think bigger than his own strength. One option remained.

"I beg you," Teddy said.

The monster laughed. "Begging won't help."

He brought his hands together. "I beg you, bestow on me the glory."

A flash of light flooded the hallway. Teddy's body became near weightless. His limbs grew with his height, and he was someone else again. The world became somewhat smaller.

He flew forward, faster than his last charge. He delivered a solid punch to the insect beast, square in the jaw.

Flesh crunched. The monster soared backward down the hall with the hit. It spun in the air, falling back into the machinery room. It crashed into a workshop table.

Rock slid listlessly to the floor. He muttered unintelligible sarcasm as he regained his senses.

The beast stood back up. It slurred its words. "I thought it was you. Thank you for confirming it. But it does not matter who you are. You are in the way."

Teddy drew his sword. Flames danced off the blade. "I don't have any idea what you want," he said, with his new voice, "but you will never get it. I will send you back to the ash!"

"Pyre Knight," the beast said, its voice dropping any semblance of humanity. "You are wanted by my Master. You are fortunate; he is allowing you the chance of joining him without further bloodshed. No one will have to die like this one before you will."

"Pintsize," a voice squeaked out below him. "What happened to you?"

"Stay still, Rock. This isn't going to take long."

His sword shone a red light. Licked flames from the steaming blade brushed the white walls of the hall. It left no scorch marks, almost as if he had willed them not to touch anything but his target. If Teddy could control the flames to this extent, maybe he could avoid what happened to the warehouse this time. It was a gamble, relying on the red fire, but he trusted in the Coin of Light. This power was a gift, and he would use it right.

"The first Knight of the End has made his choice, it

seems." The beast slowly slunk back through the hall towards them. "It is a shame it had to be a foolish child like you."

"I'm not one of you, am I? So I can't be that stupid."

He held his sword forward. Flames danced from the tip. The blaze swirled through the air, and pierced into the enemy. Its high-pitched squeals were consumed by the red fire.

Mrs. Sands' body struck the ground between the two warriors. She was out like a light. The remains of the beast sparked into ash where it stood. Within seconds, it faded into nothingness before even touching the floor.

The hallway was clear. The beast had been exterminated. Teddy sheathed his sword.

Rock stared at the slumbering Mrs. Sands, and then the Pyre Knight. He squinted as if trying to figure out what happened to Teddy MacIsaac.

"Rock," he said, "you need to take Mrs. Sands outside."

Rock's lip quivered. "Uh, sure, man. You got it!"

The shaken teenager wobbled to his feet. He pulled Mrs. Sands next to him, putting her arm around him. An ounce of fear passed over his glance toward Teddy.

"But, what about you?"

"I've got an appointment upstairs," Teddy said.

"You gonna be alright?"

"The other kids in detention are in trouble. I've got to go. Just stay outside until this is over." He glanced at where the ashes from the monster should have been. "This probably won't take long."

Rock carried Mrs. Sands to through the exit. He glanced back a few times, but said nothing.

Teddy bolted down the hall back into the school. The power was still out, but it wouldn't stop him.

The others were in danger—McLeod was in danger. Teddy might have been the one to summon these creeps here, but he would also be the one to throw them back out.

He didn't know how, but the Order of the Ash knew the Pyre Knight was a teenager. There was only one possibility he could think of. The man in the suit hated kids. He must have figured that either the Pyre Knight was a student, or the Pyre Knight would come to the rescue of kids. Either way, some teenagers get killed. Teddy really wanted to ram his fist down the jerk's throat now. These Order guys were sick.

At the stairs to the second floor, he spotted something strange. Three teachers stood at the top of the steps, staring down at him. Their eyes were beady and full of emptiness. They had black fur on their arms. He wondered what exactly happened at the teacher's conference that morning. An infection had spread.

Before they could approach, he sprinted up the stairs. He removed his sword, and threw his flames forward. The monsters were struck dead on with the blast. His sword ran them through, leaving their bodies to hit the floor. They were deep in slumber, turning back to normal.

He kept moving.

Around the corner, he found three students. Two ninth graders and a tenth, stared back at him. They were huddled in a corner, shivering. Teddy warned them to get out, and they complied without an argument. He watched them run down the stairs. He needed to hurry to the gym.

The halls were as empty as they were silent. Up ahead, a high-pitched squeal emitted from behind the doors to the second floor gymnasium. He charged onward.

Teddy kicked open the door with as much strength as he could imagine. The door broke off its hinges. It soared across the open floor, and crashed into the opposite wall of the gymnasium. The door broke into pieces on impact.

He tried to hold in his shock. His strength still surprised him.

"Well, if it isn't the guest of honor," a familiar voice said.

The gymnasium was still set up like it was that morning. About a dozen students were concentrated in a circle before the stage. They were guarded by teachers that looked as infected as Mrs. Sands. The Principal and Assistant Principal stood by, beady eyes flashing. In Teddy's opinion, the latter looked about the same as usual. The teachers didn't budge an inch. Only the kids weren't infected.

"Stay put," Teddy told the teenagers.

He recognized most of them as Hoffman's former cronies. One of them was Stieg.

The kids whispered among themselves, as Teddy approached the stage.

On the stage stood the four figures from that morning, no longer hiding behind suits or a human appearance. They had given up covering up what they really were.

The speaker from earlier stood before them. His hair

moved as if made of worms, and his eyes were orange like headlights. His grey skin with black fur reminded Teddy of a reptile or insect that couldn't have existed. Like the other three, and the monsters Teddy had already fought, he was wearing a small chain around his neck. He still looked like he hadn't taken a bath in a year.

"We were waiting for you, Pyre Knight," the speaker said. "Now the fun can begin."

"You have a strange sense of humor, villain."

The woman grinned. "He doesn't look like much. Even if he looks like Tola, he doesn't have near his power or ferocity." Her hair was pale white, her eyes black, and her face was cracked as if about to shatter into a million pieces. She looked like a ghost, no longer resembling the pretty woman from that morning.

She flew a foot off the ground, still staring down at him. Purple energy crackled around her. This woman was somehow different of the others.

The third of the group was a veritable monster. It was a half-man, half-tiger hybrid, complete with stripes and a tail. The beast said nothing with arms folded, watching Teddy with beady black eyes. It was built like a bodybuilder, towering at near eight feet tall.

Then there was the last one. At the end of the line was a fat man. He wore a blue coat and had a single earing. He was around six foot tall even and had skin made of stone. It was the Stone Man that killed Darryl Werner.

Standing before the Pyre Knight was the Order of the Ash.

Chapter 9
Brawl at Harding High

"Glad to meet you," the insect man said. His voice echoed through the enormous gymnasium. He leaned over the front of the stage. "I appreciate you coming here to meet us."

Stieg and the students passed their attention between the Pyre Knight and the four members of the Order. They were completely still

"Who are you four supposed to be?" Teddy tried his best hero voice.

"We four," the woman cut in, "are members of the Order of the Ash. I am the Phantom Maiden." She pointed behind her. "They are the Stone Eater, and the Manslayer."

The Stone Eater leaned against the back wall at the back of the stage. He glanced at the ceiling, not bothering to look at the Knight. Come what may, Teddy would get him.

On the other hand, the Manslayer kept its narrow gaze on the Red Sword. Its tongue passed over the tiger muzzle where a human face had once been. It was very excited to see the Pyre Knight.

"As you can tell by looking at me," the orange-eyed bug man said, "I am the Parasite."

Teddy laughed. "That is quite the apt name."

"Were you in the crowd earlier, Knight? I'm quite the speech-maker, wouldn't you say?"

Teddy bit his lip to stop his response. These monsters had to believe he was not a student. "You are responsible for the man in the warehouse, then?"

"I am exactly what my name suggests," the Parasite said. "Master Jero has blessed me with the power to infect and multiply, and he has promised immortality. If he has a request, I will attend to it. That includes searching his enemies out, and annihilating them."

"I have already destroyed some of your infections, Parasite. This is your last chance to leave, before I destroy you next."

"Big talker, Sir Knight." The woman played with the strands of her white hair. "But you are outmatched, and outnumbered."

"I will defeat you all, nonetheless," Teddy replied, in his best hero voice. His odds were not good, but it didn't make a difference. "Fight me however your warped honor dictates, but know I will fell you all here. As the Knight of Flames, a protector of the innocent, and one of the Knights of the End, it is my duty."

The Parasite nodded. "Very well said. Four on one is a bit unfair, true. Still, some of us have other jobs to accomplish. We did not only come to this town to play with you. One of us will be enough for you."

"I wish to battle the Stone Eater." Teddy held back his vitriol, but some of it still slipped out. If nothing else, he would avenge Darryl and his mother.

The Stone Eater yawned. "You're not ready for me, pyro. I'm only in this town on General Snow's orders. I have no interest in what you, or these clowns, do."

"That was a tad harsh," the Parasite said, still grinning.

"If any of you want him, he's yours." The Stone Eater leaned deeper into the wall behind him as if it were thin air. He fell backwards into it. A bulge ran along the wall like a moving air bubble until it also disappeared.

The students gasped. Stieg looked as if his brains were going to melt.

"Well, I've still got a job here," the Parasite said. "So, I'm afraid to say I must also make my exit."

"You're not going anywhere!" Teddy shouted. He couldn't lose two of them.

The Parasite sprouted giant wings out of his back. They fluttered like the wings of a fly. He lifted off the ground, his wings carrying him high. His greasy grin continued beaming down at Teddy.

"It's a shame, but we will not meet again."

"Stop!" Teddy called out.

The enemy dove toward the emergency exit behind the stage. He crashed through the doors, and out into the afternoon sun. There was no way to catch him with the remaining two hanging behind.

Teddy took hold of his sword, and concentrated. A voice, like the one in the warehouse, was trying to tell him something, but there was too much interference. He focused on it, and faced his remaining two enemies.

"*These flames are yours,*" the voice said. "*They will burn what you will them to destroy. Control is key. Do not let wrath throw you from your goal.*"

"What are you doing, Sir Knight?" the Phantom Maiden asked, a hint of fear in her voice.

Teddy faced the crowd of students surrounded by the infected teachers. He remembered control. These flames were part of him. He would use them to their fullest.

With everything he had; he threw the red flames forward. The flames sailed through the crowd.

Several students screamed and fell over themselves to escape. But it was pointless. The flame passed right through them. They were not Teddy's target.

The twisting blaze struck the teachers. Just like before, the flames separated the teachers from the parasite monsters. It burned the monster into ash, and the teachers fell to the ground, unharmed. The ash, as before, became nothingness.

The students glanced at their unharmed selves, and then the unconscious teachers. The flames had already gone out. Stieg wiped his forehead of his fear.

"Get your teachers out of here!" Teddy told the kids. "You will not want to be around for the rest."

They nodded in unison. The students went for the open doorway that Teddy broke through earlier. They brought the teachers, pulling and dragging them the whole way out. Teddy watched them go.

"And now," the Knight said to his enemies, "it is your turn for incineration."

The Phantom Maiden flew upwards away from Teddy. She drifted just below the high ceiling. "I don't think that will be happening."

Teddy started forward, leaping onto the stage. He went right for the Manslayer.

The Manslayer extended both arms, bracing for the attack. A smile fell over its face. The monster wanted this.

"What do you say we take this outside?" Teddy said, under his breath.

Teddy charged shoulder first into center mass of the Manslayer. He lifted the tiger-man off the floor. His momentum carried the two of them across the stage, and into the back wall of the gymnasium. The school rumbled with the impact.

The strike burst a hole to the outside world. Teddy carried the Manslayer out into the afternoon sky. He had forgotten they were two stories up.

They flew straight on, until gravity pulled them downward.

Teddy pulled his body close to in a ball. The cement road below drew closer. He braced for impact.

He struck into the pavement. Concrete exploded around his armored body.

"That was odd," he said, gathering his bearings. His armor was light, and yet the weight broke through stone under him. He hadn't quite figured out these powers yet.

He stood, and the broken pavement fell from him.

Everything was fine. His armor was still solid and in one piece.

Above, the Manslayer continued soaring in an arc across the street. It landed directly on top of a parked car, and metal exploded under its body. Its weight dented the vehicle. The car alarm went off.

Passing vehicles swerved to avoid the chaos. Bystanders on the sidewalks scattered and shouted.

It took a moment for Teddy to remember they were still in front of the school. There were bystanders everywhere.

"That was quite a hit, Sir Knight! Tola would be so proud!" The Phantom Maiden cackled as she passed above him. She moved as if made of the wind, her black robes blowing against her. "That armor is impressive, is it not? I wonder what we can do to break it."

"Don't you think there's enough breaking going on out here?" Teddy shouted into the sky.

"Everything will be ash eventually, just as it did the last time."

He wondered about the strange woman. "You knew the last Knight of Flames?"

"Of course I did. He had the very same face you're wearing now. He was so very full of hope for the future. What a sense of justice and law he had. And now he's just a memory of a dead age."

Teddy thought back to the world in his dream. He remembered finding the Red Sword plunged in a black dune. It was the only thing left of that old world. She knew what had killed the last Knight.

"I am not him," Teddy said.

"There is no doubt about that, Sir Knight. He was a good deal smarter than you are."

"Who are you?"

"See?" She cackled. "Not very bright."

He saw it out of the corner of his eye—a crumpled ball of metal soared toward his head. He ducked back. The projectile grazed his helmet, scraping it. The metal ball smashed into pieces on the brick wall of the school behind him.

The Manslayer stood on the street, staring over at Teddy. It held the remains of the destroyed car over its head. The steel twisted under its grip. It tossed another chunk of metal toward Teddy.

"This is one messed up dodgeball game," Teddy muttered to himself.

He waited for the projectile to get close enough. It was a veritable fastball. He made his move, and dodged. The chunk smashed against the road beside him.

Teddy weaved forward. Balls of solid metal crashed into the road around him. The Red Sword deflected what didn't miss. He figured he'd return the favor.

He plunged his sword into the pavement below, and wedged it in. When it was deep enough, he pulled back. A chunk of road lifted with his blade. He threw it toward the Manslayer.

The Manslayer punched the chunk of road out of the air. Concrete sprayed out. It punched the next three blocks of pavement Teddy sent at it. They threw concrete back and forth as they closed in on each other.

The warriors paused when they reached the center of the road.

A smile fell upon the tiger-man. It knelt down, and leaped up into the air. The pavement broke under it as it bounded. Its powerful legs carried itself higher than the three story school.

"You have to be kidding me," Teddy said.

The Manslayer twisted in the air. It shot downward as if kicking off the sky itself. The wind whipped against its orange and striped fur.

Teddy knelt down, aimed carefully, and jumped. Road broke under him. The height of his leap surprised him. It carried as much power as the Manslayer.

The two met in midair. The Manslayer brought down its claws. The Pyre Knight swung his sword. They struck each other dead on. A crash of metal echoed throughout the afternoon sky.

Teddy had batted the Manslayer with his sword. Its chest gave a crack. The monster flew downwards with the slash. It crashed down through the roof into the convenience store across the street. The building shook and the windows shattered.

Teddy landed on his feet, the road breaking under his boots. Stars shone before him.

He ran a hand over his helmet and felt a wide fissure. Pieces had dislodged from his helmet and fell into the road. The Manslayer's strike had hit its mark. Another hit like that and he would lose more than his helmet.

"Hey!" Teddy called out into the busted up store across the street. "Everyone alright in there?"

No answer emerged from the broken building. A short, balding man with a nametag ran out of the building. The lamp post in front of the store fell over into the broken glass of the front window.

Sirens sounded streets away.

The woman swooped down from the air, between the store and Teddy. "Don't get ahead of yourself, warrior. There are two of us here."

His helmet breaking, he didn't want to risk another fight. He grit his teeth. "Stand aside. I don't know what you want, but you're both done here."

"What do we want?" A light sparkled in her dark eyes. "Kingdom. We want kingdom. As you can plainly tell from the helpless fools running away from you, this world needs a dependable leader to unite it—to protect them from the fear that consumes them. Jero the Boundless can bring them together. Unless you want this world to end up a desert of ash, you will let us through, Sir Knight."

Sirens lit up the street. Police cars whipped around street corners, and blocked each side of the road leading from the school. They took cover behind their cars.

"If you cared about this world," Teddy said, "you wouldn't be doing this."

"I treat worthless humans exactly the way they should be. It is not much different than the politicians your stupid people elect over and over. If you haven't reached paradise by vote yet, when will you? If anything, we are taking meaningless decisions out of your hands."

The woman placed a hand forward. A purple field of energy surrounded her, and crackled like lightning. Her energy reminded Teddy of someone, but he didn't have the chance to remember. A bright flash burst from her hand and disappeared. She smiled.

The purple lightning struck Teddy in the helmet. The world dimmed, and his head screamed. He fell to one knee. His insides swam.

"Oh?" she said, with feign surprise. She lifted the back of her hand to her lips. "I'm truly sorry, Sir Knight. Did I break you, already?"

He grimaced, unable to speak. His eyes watered. Illness shot through him. One wrong move and he would lose consciousness.

A voice amplified by a megaphone shouted down the street: "This is the police. Put your hands up and throw down your weapons."

"Isn't this entertaining, Sir Knight? The ants believe they can defeat a wolf!"

He struggled to answer. His throbbing head stopped him.

"This is your last warning," the officer shouted. "Put down your weapons, or we will open fire!"

Teddy's wooziness prevented him from complying. Purple bolts of lightning fired through his brain. He could only watch the Phantom Maiden raise her hands toward them.

Purple energy swam around her. She laughed. "Such meaningless prattle."

The police fired upon them. Their bullets ricocheted off of the broken pavement and Teddy's armor. The woman only cackled again.

The bullets had frozen in midair before her, caught in a purple haze. Electricity flashed. The barrier of purple energy surrounding her had not budged. The fired bullets fell uselessly to the road.

Bullets clanged off Teddy's armor as he stood up. Everything in his mind burned. He wouldn't be able to stop her next attack on them.

"Keep watching, Sir Knight," she said, a hideous grin showing teeth flashed down at him. "This is how it will always end for those who defy the Order of the Ash."

A bolt jumped out of her right hand. It struck into the cement, and exploded. The road before the cops overturned. It fell backwards on the police cars, crushing them into the street. The officers dove out of the way, taking cover behind rubble.

Screams shouted everywhere.

She sighed, turning back to the injured Knight. "You see," she said, "this is the best they can do. This is *all* they can do. Do you see my point now? It is a waste of time to protect them. They will just die."

"The only waste of time here, is hearing you ramble," a woman said.

Teddy glanced up.

The Lightning Maiden soared through the air toward them. Just as in Teddy's dream, she wore the same robe-like brown dress with white edges. The face behind the robed hood was not that of Caitlyn West, but of the face from the water reflection. Like Teddy, she had transformed into another body.

"Are you alright?" the Lightning Maiden asked him. "Sorry I'm late."

The new arrival drifted down between the Pyre Knight and the Phantom Maiden. Teddy thought he saw something off about her.

Then it hit him. The Phantom Maiden and the Lightning Maiden shared the same face. It was as if they were the same person. This woman was not just another villain.

"What is going on here?" Teddy asked. His head creaked and rattled.

"I'll tell you later", the Lightning Maiden said. Her hands flashed white. She held them up to the Phantom Maiden. "For now, we have to stop the two of them."

Before he could answer, a blur struck into him. The road had broken open just before him, and a body charged through it. The figure was the Manslayer. The tiger-man had charged him. His armor cracked in the hit.

It ran forward. The Manslayer carried him backwards. They burst back into the school. It was as if the monster was returning the favor from earlier. Brick wall after brick wall broke behind Teddy's back. Thunderous crumbling of stone rang out.

Then, the Manslayer stopped.

Teddy continued soaring backwards. He flew back through the Administrator's office and through a large brown desk. He rolled to a stop. Finally, he regained his senses.

He stared up at the Manslayer. The beast looked down upon him, breathing heavy. A wide, charred red gash gaped across its striped chest. A grimace of rage fell over its whiskered face.

Teddy glanced over the office. There were no civilians. He could go all out.

"I am the Pyre Knight," Teddy said, catching his breath. "I live to defeat evil. This is nothing."

The Manslayer roared, and lunged. Teddy dodged the first swipe for his head, but not the second. With a full-on slash, the beast struck.

The Pyre Knight's helmet shattered into pieces. Teddy fell to the floor. The sickness inside of him rejoiced.

Red filled his vision.

Sweat gathered on his forehead. He'd forgotten his own injuries. Any remaining illusion that the Pyre Knight was invincible fell apart with his helmet. The next attack would decide it all.

He rolled back up, and smiled at his enemy. If he was going to go out, he was going to take the Manslayer down with him.

Chapter 10
Gathering Storm

The Manslayer swung deep for his head. The Pyre Knight weaved out of the way.

It was at that moment he realized he'd left his sword lying on the floor. He had no opportunity to go for it without losing his head. "I'm going to pound your face into paste, furball."

The Manslayer growled. Its chest still steamed from the earlier attack. The monster brought its claws up toward its opponent.

If it wanted a fist fight, then Teddy MacIsaac would give him one. The Knight tightened his fists.

The red gauntlets gleamed as he punched his fists together. He imagined a concrete wall would be nothing compared to this monster.

They brought fists against each other. The Knight traded hard punches with the tiger-man, rattling bones with every strike. They exchanged punch after punch, fur and armor chunks flying with the hits.

The Manslayer landed a punch in Teddy's gut. The armor creaked as he was lifted off his feet. In the same motion, the enemy grabbed Teddy's shoulder. It slammed him down, face first. The floor cracked.

A foot crashed down for his head. He rolled away. The stomp broke a hole in the laminate floor.

Surges of purple pain fired through Teddy's head. He rolled to his knees, his head still throbbing. The lightning still lashed out against him. He needed to end this soon.

Teddy flipped back up. A claw screeched against his chest, scraping the armor. He gripped the Manslayer's wrist before it fell back. He spun the beast around, and flipped it onto his back. It thrashed, trying to escape his hold.

With as much strength as Teddy could muster, he threw the Manslayer forward. His arms whipped like a lash. The monster rocketed across the room. It slammed through a wall at the end of the open office space. It didn't stop. The Manslayer smashed through several more walls. The building shook. It crashed through half the length of the school before finally stopping. Six rooms and a hallway began to crumble between the warriors.

The Manslayer did not move.

"That was fun," Teddy panted out. "Other than my head being ready to explode."

Crushing pain gripped his mind. Purple flashes ripped through his veins.

Everything blackened. His face struck the dented floor with a dead weight. All he could do was watch his sword lying on the floor. He watched it break apart and disappear before him. The world vanished with it.

His mind fell into dreams, dreams fell into nightmare, and nightmare fell into abyss.

Then, he was far above the world, looking down on it. He floated in an endless darkness. The earth below had been scorched clean to ash, the animals and peoples nothing but dust and bones. The world was dead. A black swirl of cloud covered everything.

One figure stood at the world's center. Teddy recognized the spot as the same as where Teddy had found the Red Sword. This lone figure was the last man left in the world. It was a man wearing red armor.

The man plunged his sword into the dune before him. His armor was cracking, disintegrating with the rest of the world.

He was the last Pyre Knight, and he was dying.

The man howled a scream that struck Teddy to the core. Hatred filled the Pyre Knight's being. As the man died, his armor shattered into the dust. His body crumbled into the wind and vanished. Only the dead world remained behind.

A voice spoke from the sword on the mound. "*There isn't anything left here.*"

"That was you, wasn't it?" Teddy asked. "You were the last Pyre Knight. You burned this world to ash. Not the Order."

"*I did. I let my wrath consume me, and I covered the world in flames. They are all gone now. As am I.*"

"You mean I can do all this?" He gestured around the ashen world. "I can destroy the world?"

"*You can save it, or destroy it.*"

"I don't know what's worse. That I can do this, or that you already did."

"*There is nothing to be done about this now.*" The blade's voice held a somber tone. "*You have seen what the Order of the Ash is willing to do to your home.*"

"I have."

"*The question is simple. Will you allow this to happen again?*"

With those words, the dream circled around the boy's head like a drain. The dead land fell away to nothing. It sunk back into the darkness to wherever such a place was to be swept into. He fell into the void.

His eyes shot open.

The world slid before him in a glorious white hue. He moved with it as if being pulled along. It reminded him of the dream where he first found the Red Sword.

In the haze, he thought he saw the girl. She stood before him, facing outward. Her arms were outstretched. Blonde hair tumbled across her blue eyes, her small frame silhouetted against the piercing white. The blinding heat kept his headache at bay.

They were moving through the world, sliding as if guided by an invisible force. The white hue pulled them through broken bricks and stone, and eventually through trees. He couldn't tell what was happening.

"Don't worry, Teddy," the girl said. "You'll be home, soon enough."

His eyelids fell heavy, and he was out again. He was only

asleep for a second, when the song of a robin woke him up.

He blinked and saw the clear orange sky above. The setting sun hung overhead. It broke through treetops and the maple scent of the forest. He was no longer in the dead world. Everything was back as it should be.

Teddy clutched his head, the pain still fresh. His helmet was gone, as was the rest of his armor. The transformation had left him.

"Guess I'm not dead," he whispered to himself. His palms glowed faintly under the shades of oak branches.

"Not yet, Pintsize," a familiar voice replied.

Teddy sat up. A treeline lay ahead of him. He recognized the forest path he'd traveled many times on his way home. Across from him, beyond the trees, lay the ashes to the warehouse fire. The lot was surrounded by police tape. The officers and bystanders had long since left behind.

He remembered the fight, and sat up. He needed to get moving.

"Whoa, calm down." Rock Carson was leaning against a maple, breathing hard. His skin was oddly pale. "We're pretty far from Harding. Nobody's gonna find us here. Relax."

"You got Mrs. Sands out of there, right?"

"I always do what I say I'm gonna do. I left her with some cops. Compared to her and you, I got out of this mess pretty well. Although, I *did* lose my bag and comic in that whole mess." He coughed into his hand. "That was one of my favorite issues, too."

"Did anyone see me transform?"

"Only me."

"What happened after I went dark?"

Rock smiled, weakly. "You were dragged out of the school, like you are now with no armor. The guy who pulled you out was one of those suits in the assembly. It was the quiet-looking guy with the combed back blonde hair and sunglasses. He didn't stick out next to the fatty, the gross dude, and the hot chick."

That could only have been the Manslayer. "He helped me? That doesn't seem right."

"He told me to get you to safety, and just left. Walked away. Nobody saw him, or you, since they were too busy paying attention to the two broads fighting across the street."

"He spoke?"

"Yeah. Said next time he wouldn't hold back." Rock choked out another cough. "Weird guy. Oh, and no one died in that whole mess. Can you believe it? You are like some kind of hero or something. But how are you holding up?"

Teddy was fine, considering. His body ached, he was drained, and he could hardly stand. Not to mention, his armor was damaged, the last Pyre Knight destroyed the world, and his enemy let him live. This would not go down as one of his favorite days.

"Forget me," Teddy said. "Are you alright, Carson? You're coughing quite a bit there. She hit you with that darkness sphere pretty good before I got her off of you. Maybe you should have stayed behind."

"The dust from that rubble is just bad for my allergies.

You torching her probably stopped whatever it was she was trying to do to me. I'm fine."

Teddy asked for a play by play as to what happened with the women, but Rock only shrugged.

"The two chicks fought for a while," Rock said," throwing electricity or colored lightning or something. Then the ugly one with the white hair ran away. That happened a bit after that guy pulled you out of the building and left. After she left, the pretty one flew off in the opposite direction. It's crazy at the school right now. We slipped out just before getting pulled into it."

Teddy slid back against the oak behind him. "I still don't know how we got here."

A new voice spoke: "That would be because of me."

A girl sidled between two pine trees. It was Caitlyn West, no longer transformed. She looked the same as when he first saw her in the dream. Without her robes, her dress was much plainer with a denim skirt, a blue hoodie, and red sneakers. Her hair was still tied in a pony-tail, and her blue eyes were still sharp. She had the eyes of a girl on a mission. Her height was the only thing that tipped him off that she was actually a teenager, and not an adult. She was about as tall as he was.

She passed Rock and kneeled by Teddy. She checked his head.

"I told you I was coming," she said.

He smiled. "Just like a girl to be late."

Rock laughed in between his coughs, and Caitlyn smirked.

"Very funny," she said. "Now, you wanted to know how we got here?"

He nodded.

"Do you remember the place with the endless water and skies? I brought you there. I can do that outside of dreams, too. It's my thing." She let out a relieved breath. Teddy had no injuries. "It just takes a lot more out of me to do it in the real world. We're gonna have to walk back the rest of the way."

Teddy stuck out his right hand. "Good to meet you for real, Caitlyn."

She shook it. "You already did."

"I don't have any idea what is going on here," Rock said. "Have you two met before, or not?"

"Sorry, I can't get up to greet you properly," Teddy said, ignoring Rock. "I might have overdone it a bit in that last fight. I'm still working out the kinks in this whole Knight thing."

Rock wheezed. "Man, does everyone in this town have a power other than me? This is dumb. You're both short, too. How old are you, kid?"

"Kid?" The line of Caitlyn's mouth hardened. "I'm in eighth grade, tough guy. I'm gonna be fourteen in April. Not that it's any of your business. Do you have any tact at all? Who do you think you are calling me a kid?"

"Alright, alright," he replied, rolling his eyes, "just ease up, Princess."

"How many of the Order are here in town," Teddy interrupted, "are there more I haven't seen?"

"Just the four of them," she said. "Although, the Parasite can infect others and make them into his puppets. If we're going to stop any of them first, it should be him."

"Right." Teddy was more interested in getting the Stone Eater, but he wouldn't mind wiping the grin off that cocky freak. "What are we doing out here, anyway? Couldn't you have just brought us back to my house?"

"I can only slide to places I've been before. I passed over this wreckage earlier to get to you."

"Oh, right!" Teddy said, a laugh bursting from him. "You can fly, right? Isn't that amazing?"

Rock's pale face brightened. "That's right! She did!"

"I can when transformed, yes." She paused, glancing at each boy with a puzzled expression. She blushed. "But, it's not that amazing."

"It's just like Duchess Tallulah from the Rangers," Teddy said to Rock. The older boy nodded back to him.

Her smile fell. "Let's just get back to your place, Teddy. We were on the way there when that whole mess at the school started. The others should have gotten there by now."

"So, wait," Rock said, raising a hand. "You can teleport, and fly?"

"I don't teleport. I slip between spaces and come out in a new place. Nothing breaks down and reforms, I just move. Now please stop with your dumb comic book talk."

Rock feigned hurt. "That's harsh, Princess."

"It's alright, Rock, she just doesn't like stories."

Rock stared at him sideways. "How do you know that? You've never seen her before, have you? This makes no sense. I still don't know what the deal is between you two."

"Enough, boys." Caitlyn raised her hands. "That can all

wait for later. I have a question first."

"Shoot," Teddy said.

"Do you get a lot of earthquakes here?"

He nodded. "Not sure how it matters, though."

"I checked the warehouse ruins while you were out of it. There was a tunnel deep under the remains. It looks like it goes on for miles in multiple directions. They spread all over town, and probably all over the countryside. It wouldn't surprise me if they were already watching this town. When you transformed, someone was hiding out in McLeod. No wonder they got here so fast."

"I'm not very lucky, I guess," Teddy said.

"Luck has a bit to do with it," she said. "But you and me, we're a lot alike. We get pulled like a magnet to evil when we get too close. The Order knows that. That's why they draw us to places out in the middle of nowhere. Easy pickings. They would have found you eventually, even if you didn't hit them first."

"Then I'm glad I burned the monster and building to ashes when I did."

"You should be." She pulled a shattered vial from her pocket. "This is what I came to the warehouse for."

Teddy whistled. "All four of those guys at the school were wearing those around their necks. So was Mrs. Sands. I guess the guy I beat here did, too."

Rock glanced back and forth between them. He squinted at Caitlyn's hand. "What are you talking about? I don't see anything."

"You wouldn't." She stuffed it back in her pocket.

"People without powers can't see them. That's how no one found it at the site. It's broken now, anyway. Won't do anybody any good."

"But what is it?" Teddy asked.

"It's an artifact from the Nameless Kingdom," she said. "Darkness pools in the vial. In a pinch they can shatter it for some extra power, or they can use it as a weapon. But it's very risky. No one knows what the energy will do to the user. Thankfully, there aren't many of these left. You did a good job breaking it."

Teddy blushed. "Just doing my job."

"This is your dream, isn't it? I remember you being excited the last time we talked."

"It is my dream," Teddy replied. "But what about you? Still looking to learn how to cook?"

She stared at him, befuddled. "We have other problems right now."

"Can we go already?" Rock's breaths tightened. "I feel nervous out in the open."

Rock's coughing had continued to bother Teddy. "You aren't looking any better, Rock. Are you sure you're fine?"

"Teddy's right," Caitlyn said. "You don't look so good."

"I'm fine! Really, I don't need any help. Let's go before someone spots us around here."

Caitlyn and Rock hoisted Teddy back up. He regained his balance. His body still ached, though his head no longer hurt. The lightning had finally worn off.

They traveled down the train tracks. The tracks were barren.

Rock continued informing Teddy of what the younger boy missed while he was out. It made Teddy think of his dream. That ashen world could easily become this one. It was a lot of power of a teenager to wield.

"This dead end town is more exciting than usual," Rock said, chuckling.

Caitlyn shook her head. "We're just lucky no one died. The Order doesn't usually attack in the open."

"Oh, man!" Teddy's hands flew to his head. He'd completely forgotten. "I lost my phone, so I never told my folks I'm okay. They don't even know where I am. They're going to kill me."

"Don't worry," Caitlyn said, waving him off. "They know you're fine."

"How do you know that?" he replied. "In fact, how do you know anything going on in McLeod? How does anyone? I searched online, and nobody seems to know anything about the Order of the Ash."

Caitlyn frowned. "There are people who know. If there's anything you should have learned through all this, it's to have a little faith. You're not alone here." She walked ahead of them.

Teddy cocked an eyebrow. He didn't understand her at all. Beside him, Rock shrugged.

"What happened to that black sphere that hit you, Rock?"

"Let it go," he said, acid dripping from his words. "Nothing happened. You should worry more about yourself. Can you even beat these guys? They took you out without even trying."

That was true. Teddy's armor was cracked open and the helmet was totaled. His sword had faded away. There wasn't any way to know if they could be fixed. He could only hope they would be fine.

"I'll ask her about my powers when we get back," Teddy said. "We've got other problems right now. For instance, you need to tell me what's up with you."

Rock shook his head, and left Teddy behind.

Teddy sighed. "Suit yourself."

Above the group, dark clouds covered over the remains of the falling sun. Sirens flooded the coming night over the neighborhood beyond the forest. The blackbirds had fallen silent with the setting day.

Eventually, they exited the forest. They had slipped away down the train tracks without anyone noticing. There was only a little further to go.

Sirens grew farther away with each passing moment.

As tired as he was, Teddy didn't relish getting home. It would be impossible to explain this whole mess to his parents. There was also Caitlyn and Rock to consider. There was no way his folks would understand. Teddy wondered how many weeks punishment he would get for leveling a school.

Chapter 11
The White Light

The three teenagers crossed the tracks toward Mrs. Werner's house, and Teddy was glad for it. The sun had dropped low, and night was around the corner.

The sirens had died down off in the distance, but Teddy still didn't want to be outside. Being caught out in the open at a time like this would arouse much suspicion. The Order was still out there, too.

They arrived at the fence Teddy had scurried over so many times. Thankfully, they had still not been spotted by anyone.

Caitlyn stopped short. She sighed, leaning against the fence.

Teddy scanned the train tracks. "I'm pretty sure it's clear. Something wrong, Caitlyn?"

"Yeah, I, uh," she said, fumbling for the words. "I need a boost over the fence."

A pause followed. She didn't look them in the eyes. Teddy and Rock stared at each other.

Then they burst out laughing.

Caitlyn sighed.

"Are you kidding?" Rock's laugh grew hoarse. "You flew across town, fired lightning from your hands, and teleported—"

"—*Slid*," Caitlyn interrupted, still looking away.

"Right, *slid*." Rock rolled his eyes. "You slid the three of us out of harm's way, and now you need the two of us to help you over a stupid fence. Are you for real?"

"It's just a fence, Caitlyn. I climb over it every day. Is it the dirt?"

Her face brightened beet red. "I was transformed when I did all that stuff. When I'm not transformed I have . . . problems with stress on my body. My bones aren't very strong."

"You aren't just playing with us?" Rock asked.

"No, I'm not. Nobody knows just what it is, but my body is very weak when I'm not the Maiden of Faith. It's been like that forever. Now, can you lovely boys stop being boys and help me?"

"Well," Teddy said, "since you asked so nicely."

Teddy knelt, jumped, and scurried up the fence. He landed on the other side as he always did.

He turned to Rock and gestured at the older boy. Teddy used the same thumbs up signal the Rangers used in most of the old issues.

Rock nodded back to him with a dopey grin.

Caitlyn's attention darted back and forth between them. "Oh, please don't let this be something stupid."

"Ease up, Princess," Rock said, standing behind her. "Just remember to tuck and roll."

"Tuck and roll what?"

She didn't get to find out. Rock leaned down, and pushed her up the fence in a single bound. She scrambled to find her balance at the top.

She turned to chew Rock out, and her hand slipped. Her foot slid with it, and she fell backwards into Mrs. Werner's yard.

His body reacting much too fast, Teddy knelt forward. He cushioned her fall with outstretched arms. She was lighter than he expected. Blue marbles shone into his eyes as he checked her over.

"Are you alright?" Teddy asked.

"Yeah, I am," she said, slowly. "Thank you."

Rock landed beside them with a grunt. He let out a dry chuckle.

After a beat, Teddy let her down. She straightened her skirt, and glanced away.

There was no one on the porch. Mrs. Werner must have left to see the chaos at the school with everyone else. Teddy was oddly glad for it. He didn't relish having to tell her about the Stone Eater. Especially since he let the monster get away.

"Pintsize," Rock said, behind him. His voice staggered through coughs. "Sorry, I lied."

Teddy turned to face him. "It was that orb, wasn't it? Why didn't you tell me what was wrong?"

"What orb?" Caitlyn asked. "What's going on?"

Rock tripped to his knees, clutching his heart with left

arm outstretched. He gasped as he hit the grass, face planting into the dirt. They didn't even make it to the gate.

"Something's inside," Rock forced out. "It's clawing."

"We've got to get him inside," Teddy said to Caitlyn. "He was hit with pure darkness from one of those vials. I thought I stopped it when I blew the Mrs. Sands monster away."

"He didn't say anything sooner?"

"He wouldn't tell me if it got him or not. He has a head of cement. I kept asking him if something was wrong."

Rock gasped. He tried standing, but failed. "I don't need your help. Let's just keep going."

"Let's get him inside." Teddy glanced to the deck chair on the porch. She kept a spare key there. "I don't think Mrs. Werner will mind."

He unlocked the back door, and shouted for Mrs. Werner. There was no answer.

Teddy leaped back over the porch railing. He hoisted Rock up by the shoulder.

"Clear a way," Teddy said to Caitlyn. The exhaustion was fighting against him. "I'm going to put him in the living room."

She ran ahead into the house. The girl moved fast for someone with weak bones. The scrapping of moving furniture sounded from inside the door.

For some reason, Rock kept speaking.

"What was that, Rock?"

"I never even found her," Rock spewed. "I never found her."

Teddy tried to keep him talking. "What are you going on about? Who didn't you find?"

"She didn't leave. But she's gone. I was going to find her. Show everybody what happened."

"Over here!" Caitlyn called.

Teddy carried Rock through the kitchen and out into the living room. He put the older boy down on the couch, his back nearly giving out. Teddy felt like collapsing, himself.

"This isn't good," Teddy said. "I saw him hit with that orb back at the school, but I thought it was destroyed. He looked okay at the time. I didn't even think about it."

Caitlyn nodded. "Even with all his coughing, I believed him when he said it was nothing. He's really used to keeping things secret."

Teddy remembered Rock's mumblings moments earlier. "A real enigma."

"This is bad, Teddy. At this rate, he isn't going to make the next hour, never mind the night."

"Okay, but you must have dealt with this before, right? How do we take that thing out of him?"

"I've never dealt with this before," Caitlyn said. "The vial is the most potent pooling of the Dark there is. Members of the Order use it on themselves to enhance their own dark powers. That's why they're so valuable. Why did they even use it on Rock?"

Teddy took a deep breath. "Because he'd seen too much. They wanted him to suffer."

"I don't know anyone who can heal non-physical wounds like this, and I can't slide him anywhere since I'm tapped out. Do you have any ideas?"

Rock thrashed mindlessly on the couch. Teddy thought about how to help the older boy, but nothing came to mind. The red armor was broken, and the sword was gone. He had no weapons to use. All Teddy could do was plead for a solution.

"*There is a way to save him,*" a voice whispered into his ear.

Teddy grimaced. "I've been waiting for you."

Caitlyn blinked and gazed around the room. "Waiting for whom?"

"*Kneel beside him.*"

Teddy obeyed and kneeled beside Rock. At this point there was nothing to lose. Teddy gazed into his own palms. The heat of the Coin of Light burned through his thoughts. A very strange idea occurred to him.

Rock threw his arm sideways, and knocked a lamp from the end table. He was still babbling. Teddy thought this over once more.

If he didn't do this just right, Rock would die—and maybe so would he. If he gave too much, he might save Rock, but lose his life. There had to be a right balance—a right way to do this.

"*Trust the light to guide you. Listen.*"

"What are you doing?" Caitlyn asked.

"Probably something very stupid," he said. "If I don't make it back, tell Stieg Johns he was right about me. I let this happen. If I thought of someone besides myself, we wouldn't be here."

"Just tell me what you're doing."

"Oh, and tell my brother Donny that the jerk still owes me five bucks. Debts continue after death."

He raised his hands above the delusional boy. The voice whispered to him, and he knew what to do. If Teddy was going to do this, he would have to put it all on the line. No holding back.

Caitlyn spoke behind him once more. "I would really like to know what you're doing."

Teddy pressed his hands down on Rock's shirt, over his heart. The world had fallen silent outside his task. The words came to Teddy just as easily as they had back in the junkyard. He knew what to do. It was all so clear.

"I beg you, bestow on me the glory." A light shone from between his clasped hands down onto the older boy's shirt. Heat escaped Teddy's palms. "You're going to make me a promise, Rock."

"Yeah?" he panted out. His eyes were held shut due to the pain. "What's that?"

The energy rushed out of Teddy like an airlock. A haze of happiness, sadness, and death, swirled through him. Exhaustion was coming on. Eventually, the energy would leave the boy, and he would die.

But then a strange thing happened.

The younger boy went numb: all feeling closed off. Emotions locked out. Only the clear light of his coin floated around him like steam, or smoke.

The numbness broke within a second. His thoughts lit, his bones tightened, and his heart emptied of all feeling. Joy overcame all senses, and tears formed in his eyes. The world made sense.

The Coin of Light pierced through. Incense passed through his nostrils. He could grab hold of the light.

One wrong move from Teddy, and it would all be over.

The light held him tight. His insides all pulled back together, as if puzzle pieces locking in to a bigger picture. He held on with all his strength. Silence flooded the room and enveloped the pain.

Teddy pulled back, and the world kicked in again. The light between his hands muted, as if on cue. The room regained color, and shape.

"The promise is simple," Teddy rasped.

In between his hands laid the Coin of Light. Its perfect shining essence was a heavy weight. Teddy showed it to the older boy.

"I've got a coin here. If I give you this coin, you have to promise me that you will do exactly what you saw me do today. You will fight. You will do the right thing. You will live beyond yourself. Understand?"

Rock's attention stayed locked on the coin, his eyes as wide as a child's. "You want me to get my butt kicked?"

"This isn't the time for joking around, Rock." The light of the coin began to fade. The words perched on Teddy's tongue. He had to finish this fast. "I want to save your life, and I will, but this is about more than us. I know you have honor, and I need you to use it. You have to promise me."

"Promise you?"

"A man's promise is ironclad," Teddy said. "I need you to make it."

Rock fell silent. Short breaths rocketed through him. The ball was in his court now, and he didn't seem to know what to do with it.

The older boy closed his eyes and muttered. For a second, Teddy thought Rock was going to snap, but a strange calm came over the sick boy instead. Rock's eyes were now shining, red as if he choked something down his throat. His stare was still fixated on the coin.

After a pause that felt like a century, Rock nodded.

"You're putting me on the spot." He wheezed; sweat pouring down his neck and onto the couch. "I don't know what you think that coin will do, but this is an easy choice. You've got me. Whatever I have to do, I'll do it. That's a man's promise."

The young knight took hold of Rock's clammy hands. They were as cold as the night. Teddy forced the older boy's hands open and shoved the coin in between them. He gripped Rock's hands together with his own, and placed the sick boy's hands down on his heaving chest. Rock's breathing slowed as the coin touched him.

Teddy leaned forward, and shoved Rock's hands down on top of his chest. A bright light illuminated out of the coin, and blinded Teddy. Rock let out a yell. The sound of escaping steam rang out from the coin.

The light expanded, and then vanished. The coin had left with it.

When his eyes cleared, Teddy found his fingers running across his face. They were not his normal hands—they were armored.

He felt all over. The red armor covered Teddy again. However, it remained cracked and broken from his earlier battle, with his helmet still missing. His sword was on his back as if it had never left.

"Teddy," Caitlyn whispered. She pointed at Rock. "What did you do?"

He stared down at the couch.

"Well, now," Teddy said. "Did not expect that."

Rock lay, sleeping; only he wasn't just Rock anymore. He wore whitish grey armor. The armor had the same broad shoulders, breastplate, and helmet that the Pyre Knight's armor had. It was like Teddy's armor, only with a different color. However, the older boy's body didn't change—he was still Rock Carson under the armor. He was now a Knight.

Teddy tried to form words for what had occurred, but came up empty. Even Caitlyn had fallen silent behind him. It was simply unbelievable.

Rock turned over in his sleep, and fell from the couch. He clanged against the wooden floor face first.

Teddy flinched. "Whoops."

"Now that's a mood killer," Caitlyn said. "Still . . ."

"My word," a voice from behind Caitlyn said. "What is all this?"

Both Teddy and Caitlyn whipped around. Mrs. Werner stood back in the hallway. She glanced at all three of them, wiping sleep from her eyes.

"Theodore," she said. She had seen Teddy transform. "What . . . what *is* all this?"

"Ma'am," Caitlyn interrupted, "I'm sorry to ask like this,

but I need to know if I can use your phone. It's extremely important."

Mrs. Werner nodded blandly, still focusing on the Pyre Knight, and the boy on the couch behind him. Her shocked expression turned to puzzlement.

There was a clank behind the Pyre Knight.

Rock had fallen off the couch. The older boy was back to normal, sleeping on the floor. As if on cue, the lump of a teenager began to snore.

"You have got to be kidding me," Teddy muttered.

Mrs. Werner stood before him. "Theodore. Explain."

Teddy tried his best to explain what was going on. He did his best to leave out details about the Order and his dreams. She didn't need to be thrown in the deep end like that. Mrs. Werner nodded at his explanation.

She listened to his every word. Thankfully, she didn't call him insane even once.

It went better than expected.

Caitlyn hung up the phone, and checked on Rock. Teddy lifted the slumbering teenager back onto the couch as she made sure the older boy really was just sleeping. She apologized to Mrs. Werner for barging into the old woman's home.

"I see what you're talking about, Theodore. But I'm not quite sure I believe it. Why would these monsters attack a school of children, and why would they be looking for you? This armor aside, you're still just a boy. You have nothing to do with any of this."

That wasn't quite true. But she couldn't know about the

Stone Eater. Not yet. Not until Teddy handled that monster personally.

He placed his hands together, and the armor disappeared in a flash of light. Back to his normal height, she let out a relieved breath.

"I'm sorry, ma'am, but I'll have to explain that later. I'm sure my folks are worried, so I've got to get back home."

She glanced at Rock who was busy snoring. "That boy can stay here until he wakes up. It does look like he has been through the ringer. But I do expect an explanation for all this."

"I swear, ma'am," Teddy said. He held up one arm. "I promise. I will explain everything later."

Mrs. Werner nodded. "Tell Beth your friend is here when you get home. She isn't going to believe any of this."

"Probably not, ma'am."

He bid her goodbye, and bolted out her front door. Caitlyn followed quick on his heels.

The two of them huffed, low on energy. It wasn't a long to run, but every step was like a lead weight. Being drained was no fun. At least the streets were deserted, so he didn't have to worry about the neighbors.

They rounded the corner to Teddy's house. His mind tumbled at a million miles a second. So much had happened. Rock was some sort of knight now, Darryl's murderer was in town, Harding had a knight-sized hole in it, the Order was in McLeod, and the girl from his dream was right there beside him. Things were going south. All this, and the sun still hadn't set.

He grunted to her. "You could have warned me she was standing there."

"She was standing behind me," Caitlyn said, breathing hard. "I was distracted. I was more focused on whatever it was you were doing. What *were* you doing?"

"I dunno."

"It just came to you to give a piece of your coin to someone else?"

"A voice gave me a hint."

"That sounds likely," she said. There was no sarcasm in her voice. "I was talking to my cousin. He said he made it to your house. He calmed your folks down, too. They're fine. Better than we are, anyway."

"Right, we're okay, I guess. Other than my armor being totaled."

"What are you talking about? Your armor isn't totaled."

"How's that?" He slowed down to let her keep up. "It looked pretty well done to me."

"It usually takes at least one sleep, eight hours, for our powers to repair themselves. It takes longer depending on how damaged or injured we get. They self-repair. Your helmet and battered breastplate is not as bad as it can get, so you should be fine. Just try not to get hit so much next time."

"Next time, huh?"

He thought of Stieg's words during their last argument. Teddy might not have caused the mess at the school, but he still had a responsibility. Next time, he would have to see it through.

They reached his front lawn, after taking far too much time. He was ready to accept whatever punishment came his way. As long as he was finally home, he didn't care what happened to him.

The two teenagers entered the house, and a tornado of voices burst from the living room.

Before Teddy could get two feet in the door, he found himself in the grip of a bear hug from both his parents. Caitlyn pretended she didn't see it.

"Hey, guys," he said, breaking free. "This is Caitlyn West. She was at the . . . uh . . . the school."

"We know." His father nodded to the girl. "Nice to meet you, but your cousin already told us you two were on the way here."

"Hello, Caitlyn," his mother said. Her voice was not as frosty as Teddy expected. "You both need to go into the living room. Now."

There was a full house in the living room. Teddy's siblings all sat on the leather couch with another young boy next to them. He had blonde hair like Caitlyn, and was chatting excitedly to Teddy's brothers. Teddy had never seen him before. The boy jumped up when he saw Caitlyn enter the room.

"Sis! Good to see you!" The boy plowed directly into Caitlyn.

A young man in a blue suit stood by the window, looking out. He looked to be college age judging by his carefully combed hair. Teddy could easily tell he was the cousin Caitlyn was talking about. The young man had a mature air about him.

"The goofy kid is Colin West, my brother," Caitlyn said. "The older one is Kevin Scott West, my cousin."

Teddy shook their hands and introduced himself.

"I've been waiting to meet you for a while, Theodore," Kevin said. "Caitlyn has told me so much about you already."

Teddy leaned over to her, "You told him about the dream?"

She shrugged. "I told him what I knew."

"Thanks for bringing her back," Colin said, interrupting them. He shuffled his sister off to the couch. There he introduced her to Teddy's brothers and sister.

Teddy's parents entered the room behind him. They were whispering something they didn't want him to hear. They stepped over to where the kids were.

"Cute kid, Caitlyn's brother," Teddy said.

"He'll be more than that one day," Kevin Scott West whispered. "But enough about that. We need to catch up. I'll have to start with how we got here."

Mr. West described it as best he could. The three visitors first arrived in McLeod hours earlier. They had traveled all night to get there from New Sun City. The city had been having problems of its own, which meant none of the others could afford to leave. Caitlyn was the only hand they could spare. The Order was a nuisance in more places than just McLeod.

"Why didn't you call first?" Teddy asked. "We're in the phone book."

"Nobody answered," Kevin said. "That and we couldn't

be sure they weren't tapping phones around here. When drove into town we got to hearing about some sort of a problem at the school with a sickly-looking woman dressed in black. Caitlyn took off so fast she forgot to even bring her phone with her."

Teddy shrugged. "Girls."

"I heard that," Caitlyn said from across the room.

"She didn't even wait to tell us she was leaving," Kevin said. "Scatterbrain."

"Alright, alright, I get it." Caitlyn threw up both hands. "Next time I'll tell you where I'm going before I run off. I think we have more important things to discuss."

"She's right," Teddy's father said. "We still don't know anything about what's going on. Who exactly are you three, and what does Theodore have to do with what happened at the school?"

Kevin nodded. "Alright, Mr. MacIsaac. If everyone will just sit down, I'll explain what I can."

Mr. West waited for everyone to find a seat before he began. Only Teddy declined to sit. His nerves forbade him.

"This is what I wanted to talk to you about," Kevin said. He turned up the volume on the television. "This is why I'm—*we're*—here."

The local public channel held an emergency broadcast. It had been repeating since Teddy entered the room. On the screen was amateur footage of the attack on the school. The footage bled a lot, blurring oddly whenever the Pyre Knight, Lightning Maiden, or any of the members of the Order, were on screen. It faded worse with each replay. No one on the broadcast knew what to make of any of it.

"That footage," Keven said, interrupting the newscasters, "will be useless soon enough. Our technology wasn't built to capture this sort of otherworldly power. Soon enough it will be dismissed as a prank."

The screen showed a period of time Teddy was not around for. Caitlyn was battling the Phantom Maiden out in the street. A white light flashed from Caitlyn's hands which disrupted the sirens on the police cars, and the camera footage. She fired a bolt of white lightning at the pale woman, barely grazing her. The two fired back and forth at each other. Eventually, both Maidens took off into the sky, and the footage looped.

That was obviously the moment when the Phantom Maiden ran away, and Caitlyn left to find Teddy. He decided it best not to mention it in front of everybody. It was confusing enough as it was.

Casey broke the silence that fell over everyone. "So, who exactly are they?"

No one answered. Caitlyn and Mr. West both glanced at Teddy.

He didn't like to lie, it was unbecoming of a proper hero, but telling the truth would be difficult. It was far too unbelievable. But then again, he would have to tell them one day.

"I know who they are," Teddy said. His family glanced at him. He swallowed his nerves.

Kevin nodded. "You might as well tell them. Sooner or later, someone will find out, and things will get complicated.

Secrets tend to do that. As you can tell by that awful footage, the world is going to find out eventually."

Teddy's mother glanced between them. "What is he talking about, Teddy?"

"Theodore." Jonas MacIsaac looked his son in the eye. "The truth."

Teddy crinkled his nose and closed his eyes. There wasn't much choice.

"I'll start," Mr. West said. "You see, these attackers are members of a group called the Order of the Ash. They are not from this world, but from a place that no longer exists. They are led by a man named Jero the Boundless, who exists to, well, do this." He pointed to the television screen. It showed the moment the Manslayer charged Teddy into the school. "They were defeated long ago by three heroes: the Ocean Knight, the Zephyr Knight, and the Pyre Knight. They are called the *Knights of the End*. That red fellow you saw in the footage? That's the Pyre Knight."

Caitlyn sat forward. "Jero escaped to this world ten years ago, and has been rebuilding the Order ever since. They're going to do to this world what they did to the last."

It was an insane prospect to entertain. Teddy knew it would be a hard a sell. His parents had no patience for outlandish fantasy. He readied himself for an explanation.

"Alright," his father said, rubbing his temples. "So, what does this all mean? Why are these people here?"

Mrs. MacIsaac nearly jumped from the couch. "You mean you believe this crazy fairy tale, Jonas?"

"As much as I can understand," he said, slowly choosing

his words. "You've seen the footage, Beth; you've heard about those escaped convicts months back, the strange blurred photographs from all over the country, and the rumors of vigilantes in New Sun City. Then there were the Moonmere disappearances. There is too much that doesn't add up. If this story is concocted, then I don't want to know the truth."

"What does Teddy have to do with this?" Briana asked, getting to the point.

"The arrival of the Knights of the End means the final battle is about to begin," Mr. West continued. "We win; we get to go on the same as we always have. We lose; we sink to the bottom of the food chain. The Knights of the End were the ones who beat Jero the first time, but they are all gone now. The ones who are chosen to wear the armor against the Order are those who have proven themselves worthy of it. Only they can slay the Darkness with their elements, and send it back into the abyss.

"That's nice," Casey interrupted. "But like Bri asked: what does this have to do with *Teddy?*"

Donny grimaced. "Do you need our brother as a human sacrifice or something?"

Mrs. MacIsaac eyeballed the boy. He glanced at the floor.

"Well, that's up to Teddy to tell you." Mr. West gestured to the new Pyre Knight.

Teddy stood in the archway to the living room, away from the rest. He couldn't think of what to say. The entire room had eyes on him.

He decided to go for it. Teddy clapped his hands

together, and stated the credo well-embedded in his mind. Everyone in the room shielded their eyes from the white flash.

"It has a lot to do with me," Teddy said in his new voice. "Because I'm the Pyre Knight."

Every voice in the room exploded.

Chapter 12
Under the Surface

For the first time since he received the Coin of Light, Teddy had realized how much he preferred to be alone. He sat on the front porch, letting the cold evening wind wash over him. It was a welcome change from the chaos inside the house.

As a kid he'd spent many hours in his backyard, and in the woods, slaying monsters from the furthest reaches of space and the most desolate pits of Hell. He was a hero out among the maples and flowing grass fields. Now his dream is reality, and his parents didn't take to the news well. He couldn't blame them; he still had trouble believing it.

But there was no time to worry about that. He had to find the Order before they struck again. They were still hiding in McLeod.

He yawned, looking out into the empty street. Most of the neighbors were still checking out the mess at the school. Teddy couldn't remember the last time the neighborhood was this quiet.

"Your folks were fairly reasonable," Rock said. The older boy sat on the railing beside him, arms folded. "That could have gone worse."

"What could have?" Teddy asked

"Well, everything."

Rock first arrived at Teddy's house after a good hour's nap. He made it there post-haste after Mrs. Werner gave directions and scolded him. He was mighty confused when he stepped inside to the avalanche of voices. Teddy took him aside, and the two decided to wait on the porch for things to cool down. That was hours ago.

"How much worse could it have gone?" Teddy asked. He leaned back in on the deck chair. "Those guys in the comics are able to keep their identities secret for most of their lives. I blew my cover in less than two days. On top of it, the Manslayer beat me to a pulp, and let me live for some reason I just don't get."

"At least, you don't have to make up ridiculous lies about going to the bathroom for two hours at a time whenever trouble shows up. That's something."

Teddy stifled a laugh.

Rock cracked his right knuckle and grimaced. He ignored his left. "People worrying about you, is a good thing. You are lucky."

"I don't feel very lucky." Teddy felt the back of his neck. It still ached. "Have you ever been thrown through a school, Rock? It hurts. A lot."

"Actually, I'm hoping to punch some of these Order of the Ash psychos through some walls, myself. That'll teach 'em some manners. It's been a dream of mine since—"

"—issue twenty-nine of the Rangers," Teddy interrupted, "when Edgar Marshall rocket-punched the Steel Bandit out of the third floor of the hotel."

"Wow, you sure know your oldies."

"That was a good issue. It is nice meeting someone who actually read it. I mean, someone born after the Paleozoic era."

Rock laughed. He leaned over the Porch railing, and spat into the grass below. "That guy who pulled you out of the building—the guy you said was the Manslayer? That guy reminded me of the Steel Bandit. You know? More interested in crushing his enemies than achieving his boss's goals. But I could be wrong."

"He didn't care about who I was underneath the helmet. Maybe I can get through to him."

"Don't get your hopes up. I was more freaked out by the ugly chick. She had the same face as your girlfriend did when she was transformed. There's something going on there. Did the Princess tell you about what's up with that?"

"No, we haven't had a chance to speak since we got back." He paused, and glanced at Rock. "Shouldn't you call your parents? You know, let them know where you are?"

Rock fell silent. The night air swirled across the porch. The older boy's wrinkled bowling shirt blew in the wind. He looked up at the endless sky for a long time.

"Something wrong, Rock?"

"My dad's in the hospital. Has been for a long time. He probably doesn't have much time left. My mom's been gone for a while now. I don't really have a family to worry about me."

Embarrassment washed over Teddy. He tried to make sure Rock didn't see him punch the side of his own head. "Sorry, I didn't know. No one really knows anything about you. I can't imagine what it's like for a parent to just leave like that."

"She didn't leave, Boss. She disappeared after visiting my aunt out in New Sun City. No one's ever been able to figure out what happened. That's why I've been trying to get out there. Unfortunately, getting a job is not that easy around here. Your dad also apparently doesn't hire teenagers."

New Sun City again. It looked like Teddy would have to look into the place himself. If he lived through *this* mess, that is.

"I'm living with my uncle and his wife," Rock continued. "They don't really want me there, so they don't care where I am, as long as I'm not embarrassing them. You hear your folks hollering at everyone and everything in there? That's because they care. That's how it should be."

"Yeah, when they come out here to tear out my guts, I'll take comfort in that."

"Here to help."

Teddy paused. Doubt had been eating at him for some time. "One dumb teenager against monsters that can rip up roads, grow giant bug wings, throw purple lighting, and can turn into stone. Will I be able to beat these guys?"

"No," Rock said, flatly. "Not alone. We're pretty hosed, if all we have is you, Boss."

The Pyre Knight burned down a warehouse, demolished a school and convenience store, and almost got innocent people killed. So far, Teddy's record was pretty lousy.

"You definitely got that right," Teddy said.

"I was about due to get something right." Rock craned his neck back. "I think you're being called."

Teddy listened. Rock was right. A frost spread down the younger boy's spine.

"Well," Teddy said. "Guess I better get this over with."

He left Rock behind for the house.

The kids all but avoided him when he stepped past them, huddling around the television. Caitlyn and the other visitors were sitting on the leather couch. The mood was eerie. The house had rarely ever been this quiet as long as Teddy had been alive.

He climbed the stairs to his room. His father stared out the window and his mother sat on the bed. Teddy closed the door, and waited for the hammer to drop.

His father spoked first, calm and collected. "This is going to take a long time for us to understand, Theodore. A long time."

"But first," his mother said, "there is one thing we wanted to tell you."

He slowly approached his parents. His embarrassing ordeal at Harding still etched in his mind. For the first time since getting it, he was beginning to think that receiving the Coin of Light was a mistake. Nothing but calamity had followed—calamity that someone more worthy could have dealt with. He steeled himself.

"Mom, I—"

Before he could say anything, they pulled him in. It was another hug. This one was even tighter than the first one. If he wasn't the Pyre Knight, it would have broken him in half. Tears welled, but it was mostly because of how sore and tired he was. He was now glad he had shut the door behind him.

"What are you guys doing?" he asked.

Jonas MacIsaac took hold of his son's shoulders. "You not only saved that man in the warehouse, but your teacher, that boy downstairs, your school, and the whole town, from these monsters. You did that, Theodore. You were in over your head, and you still tried to save everyone. You have no idea how proud we are of you."

"It wasn't much, Dad." It was actually embarrassing to think about. "I didn't have much of a choice."

"You always have a choice, Theodore. Your mother and I raised you to make the right ones and, even though we don't understand everything going on, that you made the right choices when it truly counted means everything."

"You're not mad?"

"It's just like your father says, Teddy. You might be strong now, and maybe you can do a lot of bad things, but we have faith that you will keep making the right decisions. You showed it today."

"I did?"

Mr. MacIsaac ruffled his son's hair. "You need to stop asking dumb questions."

"I don't know if I'm in trouble here, or not," he said. "Didn't I mess up bad today?"

"You look like you've been in a war." His mom kissed him on the forehead. "Get changed and get some sleep."

He blinked. "That's it? No grounding?"

"We'll talk more in the morning," his father said. "Mr. West and his cousins will take the guest room, and your new friend will take a sleeping bag in your room. We'll sort through all this in the morning."

"I hope we can," Teddy replied.

Whatever Mr. West discussed with his parents, they didn't bother sharing it with Teddy. He didn't even bother to ask about dinner, it was doubtful that anyone was all too hungry, anyway. It was simply too late, and he was too tired, to worry about it now.

But, sleep was a fickle mistress.

Teddy slept exactly one hour, once again, and awoke at midnight. Just as before, that single hour of slumber was enough to fully charge him. A bit of pain still lingered, but the exhaustion was gone. Now he sat awake with nothing to do, except think unpleasant thoughts.

He turned over in bed.

Rock stirred on the floor. He'd fallen asleep in seconds after putting down the sleeping bag. The sight of him there made Teddy uneasy. Rock had almost died twice because of Teddy.

He really wasn't much of a hero.

Teddy left his bedroom to fight off the negative thoughts. He stumbled down the hall in his undershirt and boxers, stepping lightly. The rest of the house slept soundly.

At the stairs, he met a figure sitting on the top step. It was Casey, staring at the front door a floor below.

Casey hadn't said one word to Teddy all night. He quietly sat beside the kid.

"Hey," Teddy whispered. "What's up?"

Casey kept his stare locked at the front door, as if expecting a monster to burst inside. He didn't even acknowledge Teddy's existence.

"You should be sleeping, Casey."

"Everyone else is awake; it's just no one will leave their rooms. Except for that Colin kid. He's watching TV downstairs. It's been a rough day."

The muted light of the television spilled out into the bottom of the stairs.

Teddy put a hand on his brother's shoulder. "But you should still be in bed. At least, try to get some sleep."

Casey never said much outside of joking around with Donny. He was the silent type, very sarcastic. Teddy had never seen him lose his cool since the boy kept himself bottled up. He didn't expect that to change just because Teddy was the Pyre Knight.

"The footage of you in that Knight get-up is gone, you know."

"It's what?"

"Faded to nothing but static. The newswoman couldn't explain it at all. People online are already calling it a prank. No one is going to believe any of this. Bunch of jerks."

"Easy, man. It isn't like this is easy to understand. According to Kevin, our technology wasn't made to deal with this kind of stuff. Once they see it for themselves, they'll understand."

His brother laughed and shook his head. An awkward silence settled in.

"Harding's closed indefinitely," Casey said. "They said it on the public access channel, when you were talking with mom and dad. I don't know if our school will still be open, or if Donny, Bri, and me, are out of luck. Maybe school will be canceled forever. Who knows? We can't just go to school with monsters out there, can we?"

"You know," Teddy said, trying to pick the right words. "I'm glad no one was seriously hurt, but Harding was a terrible school. On my list of concerns, going back there tomorrow was at the bottom next to apologizing to Corey Hoffman."

"And what are you going to do when Harding opens again?"

Teddy shrugged. "I'm never going back there, Case."

"So, what?" Casey let out a short laugh. "You're going to be a professional crime fighter now, is that it? This isn't one of your kid games. You're a short, long-haired, fourteen-year-old comic book freak, Teddy. It was a mistake to give you those powers. Mom and Dad, or Donny and Bri, might not say it, but you're totally out of your league here. You can't do this. You're just a kid."

"You say that like it's an insult."

"But it's true."

"Maybe," Teddy agreed. "But I'm going to do what I have to do. That's what a man does, right?"

Casey stared at him, bewildered. It was as if they were speaking different languages.

"Well, whatever," Casey said, shaking his head. "Do what you want. Not my problem."

"Is that all that's on your mind?"

"Uh, no, actually." Casey blushed. He glanced over his shoulder to make sure no one was watching. "Between the two of us, that Caitlyn chick is mad hot. Think she has a boyfriend?"

Teddy smirked at his younger brother. "Isn't she a little old for you? You shouldn't be talking about your elders that way."

"Yeah, right. She's the same age as you, and you sure as spit ain't my elder."

Teddy shrugged. "I'm pretty sure she isn't into smart aleck kids who still sleep in space robot pajamas."

"Aww, what do you know?"

"You're right; I'm completely out of my depth." Teddy stood up and clapped his brother on the back. He made sure to hold back on his strength. "Go to bed, Casey. Don't worry about things you can't control. You're right; it's not your problem. I'll do what I have to do, and you do what you gotta do. Right now, that means getting some sleep."

Casey slowly shuffled back to his room. Teddy watched him go, thinking about the kid's assertions. They weren't wrong. Teddy really didn't know what he was doing. Still, it stung that his own brother wasn't more supportive about this whole mess. But, that was Casey, after all.

Teddy descended the stairs for the living room. The flashing light of the television nearly blinded him.

Caitlyn's brother, Colin West, was alone in the living

room. He sat on the carpet staring up at the screen. The boy wore jeans and a green sweater. His blonde hair was styled like someone put a bowl over his head. His plump cheeks made Teddy think the boy was much younger than he was.

"You should go to bed, kid," Teddy said with a smile. "I'm getting a bit of a déjà vu here."

The public access channel was repeating its earlier broadcast. There wasn't any new information, which made it weird that the kid was still watching it.

"I'm not a kid, and I could say the same to you." Colin kept his gaze forward. His cool blue eyes stared through the television as if watching into a world beyond it. "I already slept. One hour a night is enough for me."

Teddy's mouth almost fell open. "Are you a Knight?"

"I'm not a Knight of the End," the boy said. "I'm here because Kevin thought it would do me good to meet you before the others did. He seems to think I'll be something special, but I just don't see it."

"Well, who knows?" Teddy fell into the couch behind Colin. It would be a long night keeping this kid out of trouble. "With a sister like Caitlyn, I'm sure you've got a talent, or two."

"She can't cook, you know."

Teddy held back a laugh. "It appears to be a sore spot with her. Girls. Who knows, right?"

"Speaking of Caitlyn, I was wondering about something. She said that you saw other Knights in that dream where you first met. Did you recognize any of them?"

"I think I knew one," Teddy said, thinking of Matt Sova.

"But it's hard to tell. I tried to call him earlier today, and again on the porch, but there was no answer. I think I was just mistaken."

"I doubt it. Don't know how this works, but I've seen some strange things in New Sun City. Usually if you have a hunch about something, you should look into it."

"And I'll be sure to get back to him if he ever answers my calls. For now, I just wish I knew what I was supposed to do next *here*."

"Me too. Well, keep watching this. Maybe we'll catch something we missed."

They watched the news for half an hour, when the mood changed. The ground began to shake. It quickly grew to a heavy tremor. One of McLeod's infamous earthquakes had hit.

Picture frames bounced off the wall. Teddy nearly fell from the couch.

It started out rough, but tapered away in seconds. It was as if a giant were running underground, slamming into stone, and sprinting far west of them through the woods. However, it was still nowhere near as bad as the one that almost took down the mall. That was the still the worst one.

Eventually, the world settled. Teddy regained his bearings.

Colin turned to him, his eyes wide. "How long have you had these earthquakes for?"

"A couple of months. Why?"

"You might actually get your chance to prove yourself sooner than you think. The Order travels underground. If you've been having these earthquakes for a while, then they've been here just as long."

"I don't follow. Are you saying that quake was leading somewhere? It's happening for a reason?"

The boy paused for a second, and then nodded.

"Yes," Colin said. "The Order has a base somewhere in McLeod."

Chapter 13
Revelations

"I only slept like an hour last night, and I feel great!" Rock took a large bite of toast, spraying crumbs all over the table. He glanced around the expanded breakfast table. "Anyone else?"

The MacIsaacs, Caitlyn and Colin West, and their cousin, were all present. They were all dead quiet. The mood at five in the morning was much too oppressive. The earthquake from the previous night certainly did not help.

"I only sleep one hour," Teddy said. He took a gulp of orange juice. "Ever since I got the coin I only need an hour of sleep to recharge."

His father glanced up from his plate. "So that's why you've been up so early. You've been up all night."

"Unsupervised," Mrs. MacIsaac said. Both Casey and Mr. West nervously shifted in their seats.

"So," Rock said, ignoring the atmosphere," how come you never hired me at the restaurant, Mr. MacIsaac?"

"We're not hiring, mainly. The other reason is that the

last teenager I hired posted online about a great party he was at . . . after calling in sick on us."

"Ouch."

Jonas MacIsaac shrugged. "We haven't had the best of luck."

"What was the deal with the earthquake last night?" Donny asked. He didn't appear to notice he had brought the sour mood back. "We usually don't get them that late at night."

"It felt like it was traveling west," Colin said.

"Like it sprouted legs and ran?" Donny wiped his chin of crumbs. "Are you kidding me?"

Colin grinned sheepishly. "Is there anything out west in McLeod?"

"Just trees," Donny said between bites. "Trees, trees, and more trees. Lots of grass, too. There's forest everywhere. You should ask Teddy about what's out there. He's always out there. Dude's got no life."

Teddy shared a glance with Colin, and went back to eating silently. It wasn't like there was anything out of the ordinary out there. Teddy had been all over McLeod's forests. He'd been down the trails, in the meadows, and over the steep hills. He'd never once seen anything suspicious. He made sure to reassure Colin of that fact.

"When you're finished eating," Mr. West said, "I'd like to talk to you outside, Teddy. You too, Rochester."

"It's Rock," the older boy said, chewing on more toast.

Donny giggled. "Is that because your head is thick?"

"No, it's because the last kid who called me Rochester

ended up kissing pavement." He grinned at Donny, crumbs filled his lips.

Donny fell silent.

"Lovely," Briana said. "Have you ever thought the reason you don't have any friends is because you have the manners of a pig?"

"I always thought it was because I once stood up at the lunch table and said I would roundhouse kick anyone who sat next to me. If they believe you can do it, you can scare kids to do anything."

Briana closed her eyes and pushed her plate forward. For someone who prided politeness above all, Rock Carson was too much to stomach. "And this is the company you keep, Teddy?"

"Believe it or not," Teddy said, wiping his mouth. "He's pretty decent compared to what you'd normally find in High School."

"Thanks, Boss!"

"That wasn't much of a compliment," Caitlyn interrupted. "You almost threw me over that fence yesterday when all I asked for was a simple boost. It's like you're incapable of doing anything without going all out. Didn't you hear me say my bones are weak?"

"Ease up, Princess. You're in one piece aren't you? Anyway, in High School, the strongest rules all. It was made for people like me." He nodded to Teddy and Caitlyn. "You guys are eighth graders; you should know this by now."

Briana groaned and rolled her eyes. "It they're like you, then I'm never going there."

"If you don't watch your tone, young lady," Mrs. MacIsaac said, "you'll never make it to the next grade, never mind High School."

The table fell silent. Briana pulled her plate back and continued eating without complaint.

Everyone went on with their breakfast.

Teddy's father was whispering something under his breath. The old man was leaning over his plate. Teddy leaned forward to ask his father what he was saying when Jonas MacIsaac burst out laughing. The old man leaned back in his chair.

The other kids stared at him in disbelief. His wife and Mr. West continued eating like nothing was wrong, apparently expecting it to die down.

Teddy felt the bug in him, and a tickle in his throat. Unfortunately, he couldn't hold it in, and burst out laughing. He laughed good and hard. Everyone stared at him like he was insane.

"What's so funny?" his mom asked. Her tone remained sharp.

"Nothing, Mom," he said, the laughs dying off. He felt one hundred pounds lighter. "Nothing at all."

Breakfast ended and the table cleared. The group went their separate ways.

Mr. West stepped out onto the back porch followed by Teddy, Rock, and Colin.

Caitlyn had already left by the time they went outside. A white light engulfed her when she put her hands together, and she was gone. She'd gotten a call saying she was needed, and used her powers to slide back to New Sun City. She mentioned she probably wouldn't be back until the evening. Sliding took too much energy from her to keep popping back and forth.

Teddy didn't get to talk to her much. She still wouldn't talk to him about comics, or books, and she grew oddly hostile when Rock teased her about it. It was like she was intentionally being difficult. But it wasn't like Teddy knew much of anything about teenage girls.

The sky grew no lighter when they got outside. Overcast clouds had taken over. He didn't like the idea of bringing an umbrella with him to fight the Order.

Autumn leaves littered the backyard. The maples bared their barren limbs, killing the last remnant of color inside the fence. Birds still perched upon the branches, singing the only sound in the neighborhood.

Mr. West sat down at the picnic bench at the back of the yard. He brushed his seat, and the others, clean of leaves. Colin sat beside him, and the two teenagers in front.

"So," Rock said. "What's up?"

Rock wore yesterday's clothes, not having much choice. At least Teddy was able to put on some sweatpants and a thick flannel shirt over his blue t-shirt. Rock slid on his tattered jacket.

"I'm going to preface this by saying we don't know much of anything about the Knights of the End."

"You brought us outside to tell us this?" Teddy asked.

Mr. West cleared his throat. "The Maidens of the Old World, of which Caitlyn is a member, is a different matter."

Teddy blushed, and Rock laughed.

"Long ago in the Nameless Kingdom," Mr. West said, "there were those that could harness the very life force of the universe. A group calling themselves the Order of the Ash wanted it to rule over everything. They wanted to be God. Magicians learned incantations and spells to bend this life force to their will, and invented the Dark Energy, corrupted life force. They used this power to enhance themselves to a veritable godhood and they used it to create monsters. It was sick. The Order, led by a particularly adept Dark Energy user named Jero, attacked the kingdom, and nearly leveled it."

"After seeing what they did at the school," Rock said, "I believe it."

Teddy nodded.

"Some of those in the Order began to break with Jero, whether because of moral differences, or because he was getting too powerful, but, either way, they were all wiped out. Only one escaped, and completely disappeared." Mr. West took a deep breath. "Years later, he resurfaced. On his person, he carried a chest containing ten perfectly made coins. These coins harnessed a different kind of energy."

Teddy leaned forward. "What kind?"

"He called them the Coins of Light. They were blessings bestowed on those worthy to destroy the corruption of the world. They were made of the life force the Order had corrupted for its own use. They were a direct line to the Light itself. The polar opposite of those bathed in the Dark.

"The coins were not all used, some even vanished, but

five maidens arose using the power of the light and became guardians of the people. They purified the poison the Order spread, and protected the defenseless. The Maiden of Faith was the leader of these Maidens of the Old World, wielder of white purifying lightning she called the Blind Lightning. They protected the old order from the new."

"Caitlyn's predecessor." Teddy remembered his own predecessor, and the world of ash. He cringed. It didn't fill him with warm thoughts.

"That's right. But there were three other warriors who also emerged. They were slayers of evil, and the strongest knights that ever emerged from the Nameless Kingdom. Three elemental Knights powered by the Coins of Light appeared. They were the Knights of the End—the ones that would end all corruption once and for all."

"We don't know much about the Knights," Colin interrupted, "because you're the first one who awoke in this world. All we know is that there are three of them."

"And how do you even know *that*?" Rock asked. "Let's be fair here, there's no way either of you should know this sorta stuff."

Mr. West and Colin glanced at each other.

"I can sometimes get messages from the Nameless Kingdom," Mr. West said. "That's my ability. It's like a message in a bottle delivered directly into my mind. That's how rare they are."

"Ten years ago," Colin continued, "the Order of the Ash first arrived here in this world. They've had time to grow. And now they're ready to wipe us out."

"Seems simple enough." Rock scratched his left knuckle.

Teddy shook his head. "Did you know they would attack McLeod after I got my coin?"

"I have to admit," Colin said, not meeting teddy's stare, "I lied to you last night. I do have one single ability. I can sometimes see events before they happen, usually the birth of evil in this world. I saw the Parasite infecting one of your teachers in a vision, though I didn't know who it was at the time. I can only see fuzzy pieces, but this time I caught one thing on the desks. I saw the name of the school among the paperwork."

"That is how you find the Order when the attack, I take it." Teddy pointed a thumb to Rock. "Did you see what happened to Rockhead here when he was attacked?"

"I can only foresee events in my sleep, and not everything. That wasn't part of what I saw."

"Anyway, enough about all of that," Teddy said, before Rock could crack a joke. "I'm more interested in what you guys want with me."

Rock nodded. "Yeah, good point."

"We're here to help you save this town from being leveled." Mr. West brushed leaves from the table top. He grimaced. "Now that they know you're here, they're going to try to take your home."

"I'm the reason they're destroying the town?"

"No," Colin interrupted, "they would have destroyed it sooner or later. It's what they do."

"But I don't think they expected *two* of you." Mr. West glanced at Rock. The well-dressed man lost his grimace.

"I've never heard of a Knight gifting abilities to another. Not even in the legends. We're in uncharted territory here."

Rock cracked a wide grin. "So we've got the edge now, don't we? Boss here can just make a Knight army, or whatever, and we'll flatten the lot of them. No problem."

"I can't, Rock," Teddy said. "I felt it when I *knighted* you, or whatever you want to call it. A lot of power choked out, and almost drained me whole. If I did it again, it would probably kill me."

The older boy growled. "Then you shouldn't have done it at all."

"I, for one, would feel much better if Teddy never attempted that again," Mr. West said. "We can't afford to lose one man in this fight. We're lucky enough to have an extra Knight around."

"So, here's what I've been eager to know," Teddy said. "Why did you three specifically come here? It wasn't just to help me save McLeod."

Mr. West paused. Cold wind blew through the barren trees, and some squirrel hollered in the distance. Autumn went on regardless of Teddy's situation.

"To be frank," Mr. West said, "we came here to recruit you. The Order is stepping up their game, and we're quickly biting off more than we can chew. It's no coincidence that Caitlyn was the only Maiden who could make the trip with us. The others are dealing with further problems. We need more hands."

New Sun City was where Darryl died, and it was the source of many rumors. There was much about it Teddy needed to see for himself. But it still wasn't McLeod. It wasn't home.

"I'm not leaving McLeod," Teddy said. "This town won't survive without someone to protect it. If I go to New Sun City with you, who will stop the Order from attacking the people here?"

"I know what you're saying, Teddy, but they're not *just* here." Mr. West straightened his tie. "They've been popping up all over the country. The only constant is that they always come back to New Sun. That seems to be where they're based. If we can stop them there, we can stop them everywhere."

"I'm not saying I don't want to help."

Mr. West raised both hands. "Just think about it. That's all I'm asking. Think about what's happening here right now and multiply the populace and the monsters. It isn't hard to imagine why I'm here begging you for help."

It was a good point, but Teddy would have to consider it later. He didn't have time to think about it now. New Sun City probably did need help, but McLeod still needed it more.

"If I can fix McLeod, I'll think about it. For now, I have to focus on what's in front of me."

"Whatever Boss decides, I'll go with. Simple as." Rock stood up from the table. "Are we done now? It's not getting any warmer out here."

Mr. West's reply was cut off by Teddy's mother. She was calling to them from inside the house.

The trio piled into the house. Mrs. MacIsaac stopped Teddy at the door.

"What did you talk about?" she asked.

"A lot," he said. "I'm going to need to think it all over."

"Well, before all that, you're going to need to call Mrs. Werner." She handed him the phone. "She called while you were talking outside."

"She's up?" Teddy asked. That was rare. "Okay, I'll give her a call."

Teddy slid up the steps to his room, and closed the door behind him. He dialed Mrs. Werner's number.

The overcast soured Teddy's mood. It reminded him of the Order. He couldn't help but imagine a blanket of ash strangling the world just like the monsters wanted. A chill ran through him.

"Yes, Theodore," Mrs. Werner said. "I saw the news on the public access channel. The situation looks exactly like you explained it yesterday. I'm sorry for doubting you. How are you all feeling this morning?"

"A little shaken," he admitted. "Thankfully no one was killed."

"What was happening at your school? It looked like a man in red armor was protecting it. He wore armor just like what you wore yesterday. Theodore . . . you can tell me what's going on."

"They are a group of monsters who aim to destroy us all. I was given a gift to help stop them. It didn't go so well yesterday, but next time will be a different story." One of these invaders had killed Mrs. Werner's son, and his old friend, Darryl. Teddy's mouth went dry when he thought of it. This was no game of pretend.

"The radio had an interview with one of the boys that was in the school during the attack. It was your old friend Mr. Johns. He mentioned four strange people had lead the monsters. One, he said, was a man made of stone."

She knew.

"It doesn't matter who it is," Teddy said. He held his composure. "The Pyre Knight will put a stop to them. I thank you for helping my friend yesterday, but you don't need to worry about this. We've got it."

"What are you talking about? You're just children. You can't be planning on finding these monsters. Not after what happened to the school." Mrs. Werner's voice dried up. "Not after what happened to Darryl."

She wasn't wrong. If he continued on this path, he would eventually meet the man who killed Darryl Werner. He would have to stop before the murderer struck again. He swallowed the lump in his throat.

"Darryl took care of me, ma'am. This is the least I can do."

Mrs. Werner didn't reply.

"I'm going to do what I have to, ma'am. But you could give me a bit of assistance. Did Darryl say anything about the man of stone before he died?"

"Just that," she said, choking back a sob. "Just that the walls moved oddly in the alleys before he was attacked. I didn't know what Darryl meant, nobody did. We just thought he was delusional."

"This will help me find the stone man and bring him to justice, ma'am." He made sure to annunciate every word. "I

give you my promise that we will stop him. We will save McLeod."

She paused. "I guess I can't stop you." Her voice remained hoarse.

"I will bring him to justice," Teddy repeated, trying to keep calm. "For Darryl, and for you."

"Please keep safe, Theodore. Darryl would not want you throwing your life away."

"I know, Mrs. Werner. I won't."

He said his goodbyes and hung up. Teddy looked out the window.

The Stone Eater may have been at the top of his list, but there were three more to go after that murderer. If the others were as dangerous as the Manslayer, stopping them would be nearly impossible.

The kids were calling him from downstairs, but he already spotted it outside his window off in the distance. It looked like the ground was melting into the sky in tiny streams of black dust. But they weren't dark clouds, or dirt, but a swarm of bugs. The insects filled the air above McLeod. They were pouring out from clumps of earth all over the neighborhood and out of the woods.

The Parasite was on the move.

Chapter 14
Infestation

There were bugs everywhere. News reports blared on the radio, and the public access channel struggled to show their bleeding footage. Horrid abominations of green hornet-like insects, the size of fat cats, were swarming the skies. Teddy watched them outside the window as they mingled high above rooftops.

The newscasters gave status updates. People that were stung slid into a fever and then a coma. This would happen within an hour of being attacked. No one could discern the source of the insects, except to say that they appeared to be coming out of holes in the ground. Teddy instantly thought of the underground tunnel that Caitlyn mentioned.

Mr. West sat in the guest chair in the living room. He leaned forward, staring out the window. "They're calling you out, Teddy."

Rock leaned against the archway to the hallway, arms folded. "No way is anyone going out there with all those bugs flying around."

"They know that Knights have a sixth sense about these things," Mr. West said. "They know he'll have to leave to stop them. It's like getting a cat to pounce on a juicy robin. The Parasite is putting out the bait."

"What do we do, Kevin?" Colin asked. He'd been sitting on the couch beside Teddy's brothers. "Do we call Caitlyn back?"

"She can't leave the others right now. They need her just as bad. We'll have to handle it without her until things settle down in New Sun City. I'll give her a call when we figure out what to do here."

"The Manslayer has seen my face," Teddy said. "Why didn't they just come here?"

Mr. West shrugged. "I don't know. Not everyone in the Order works in a straight line. The Manslayer is a bit of a mystery compared to the other three. We have no idea what motivates that one."

Rock smiled to himself. "Honor."

There was a chance Rock was right. After all, if the monster didn't kill them in their last brawl when it had the chance, then it only stands to reason that it didn't give them Teddy's identity. It didn't want its allies to know who the Pyre Knight was. There was no other possibility.

The insects spun higher and higher into the sky, blocking every bit of blue. The morning greyed further. Specks of dark clouds peeked through.

"Well, okay," Teddy said. He'd made his decision. There wasn't much else to do.

Teddy ducked out of the archway toward the front door.

He grabbed his green jacket. A flood of footsteps gushed behind him.

"I'm going to slay some monsters," he said over his shoulder. "Don't wait up."

Rock stepped beside him. "Sounds like fun. I'm in."

"Wait," Mr. MacIsaac nearly growled. "We need to talk about this first, Theodore. Don't rush out there like a fool. Who knows if you won't be affected by those insects? This is incredibly dangerous."

"Doesn't matter, Dad. The longer I wait, the more chance there is that someone else will get hurt."

"At least let me take you in the truck—"

"I can't risk it. If they attack us, you'll be a sitting duck. I think you know that, too. There's only one person who has a chance out there, and it's me."

"And Rock!" Rock said. "Rock, too! Hello? Did you forget about me?"

Teddy smirked. "I heard you the first time."

Mrs. MacIsaac stepped forward, and hugged her son tight. The pressure was intense. "Please, let's just talk about this, Teddy. You don't even know where they are."

"I don't know where I'm going yet, but I'll know soon enough." He let her hold him a bit longer. "The Coin of Light will guide me. I'll find them, and I'll stop them."

"Your armor should be fixed," Mr. West added. "It's been a whole night since you used them last."

Teddy nodded. "The bugs seem to be mostly congregating around the center of town. Near the old mall. I'll torch 'em all."

"Please, Teddy," his mother said. "You can't go."

He pulled free of his mother and kissed her once on the cheek. "Don't worry, Mom. I'll be back by dinner."

Teddy slipped on his running shoes, and zipped up his green jacket. He threw open the front door, and the stink of ash blasted into him. A chill flew through his bones. The Dark was waiting for him out there.

He took off down the walkway, and waved back to everyone.

Down the street he ran, his shoes kicking up dust and pebbles. He checked the skies to make sure the bugs hadn't noticed him. Another pair of sneakers knocking up against pavement distracted him. He was being followed.

"So, where to, Boss?"

"I didn't ask for any help, Rock."

"A ranger never lets his friend go in to battle alone, does he?"

"We're Knights, not rangers."

"And?"

Onward they ran. Thankfully, none of the insects made a move toward them. It was like they were waiting for a signal of some kind.

The teenagers had already run several blocks in a matter of minutes. Rock had no problem keeping up with Teddy's speed.

"You're fast," Teddy noted.

"I could say the same to you. It's so weird. It's like gravity is on my side. It's so easy to move."

"That was how I beat Corey Hoffman without even trying."

The older boy snorted. "I could have folded him like laundry before this. I wonder what I can do now."

Teddy didn't answer. If Rock's powers were as crazy Teddy's were, they would certainly find out soon.

Whenever Teddy ran, he gathered a vague shape of a destination in his head. It was like a white line dragged through an endless catacomb of black stone halls. The image of the line grew in his mind as it carried him further onward. He knew where he had to go.

The pair turned down Maple Street. Sure enough, his earlier hunch was correct. The fat insects were clustered around the abandoned mall. The teenagers slid to a stop.

The skies were thickest with the fat hornets here. The black sky bubbled in a cauldron. The insects bobbed between the line of clouds, and swirled like a tornado over the mall. It was clearly a trap.

The news reports had failed to mention a few things. The most glaring omission was the thin and narrow streams of tornados bursting out of holes in the earth all over. They spun gusts of wind and hornets out into the sky. They reminded Teddy of pin pricks in an air mattress.

"I think we found their home, Boss."

The mall had been closed for repairs ever since an earthquake took it down. Bureaucracy had tied up repairs, which left it as much a mess now as when it first fell in on itself months ago. The windows and doors were even boarded up. However, the walls and roof appeared sturdy.

"You might be on to something, Rock. But, can we get close?"

"With our speed? Sure."

A symphony of loud buzzing cut through the wind. A small segment of the bugs detached from the funnels, and changed direction. Clusters, like flocks of birds, tore down toward the teenagers.

Rock sucked his teeth. "Looks like I spoke too soon."

The bugs were even fatter up close. They bared their stingers, and plummeted downward toward their prey. There were dozens of them. There were much too many to fight off.

Teddy wrinkled his brow for an idea. He couldn't risk a transformation, not yet. There was no guarantee his armor would hold, for one. For another, he couldn't spare the power he might need on the master of the bugs. The two would just have to run for it.

A hornet drew its stinger toward Rock's head. He punched it off, and ducked a second hornet.

"Keep moving!" Teddy yelled. A stinger jabbed for his face. He kicked it out of the air. "Head for the mall! It's our best bet!"

"I hate the mall."

"Join the club."

Teddy sidestepped the swarm, and fired off across the street toward the parking lot. Rock followed after him.

The pair tore through the bushes on the opposite side of the road. Hornets passed overhead. The parking lot was their last obstacle. The bugs were gaining on the pair.

"Shouldn't we transform?" Rock asked.

"No," Teddy said. "We're out in the open. Anyone could see us change. Wait until we get inside."

"I ain't shy."

"That's not the point. It's too late to stop now."

It was a hard call. If this was a trap, and they were being lured, it would be best to wait until they were alone to transform. The Order couldn't know who he was. It was the same reason he didn't transform at home. The last thing he wanted was to be tracked back to his home.

"Watch out, Boss!"

Teddy ducked. A punch soared over his head. There was a crunch, and a hornet was knocked away from him. Rock had punched the bug out of the air. Teddy scratched his head.

They kept moving.

"Cool!" Rock said. "I punched that one across the parking lot!"

The buzzing was directly overhead. The bugs were only inches away. The pair could not afford slowing down.

"Good hit." Teddy chuckled. "Might as well have some fun if you're gonna die, right?"

"I knew there was a reason I followed you."

The building was up ahead. Only thirty feet.

Twenty feet. Sixteen feet. Eleven feet.

"Oh, no," Teddy mumbled. He hadn't practiced slowing down yet.

His arms swung sideways in a propeller, and his legs wouldn't stop moving. He crossed himself as he slammed through the front door ahead of him.

Teddy's shoulder plunged into the boarded up front door, almost knocking it from its hinges. He tripped over his feet, and fell to the floor. Face first, he skidded forward. Tiles cracked underneath him. He flipped over back onto his feet in a roll. Finally, he tumbled straight into a bench. The seat broke with his momentum. Dizziness caught up to him. He finally arrived at a stop—on his head.

The door slammed, and he looked up. Rock had his back up against the broken boards.

The two of them pushed the broken bench against the door. They also used the rest of the benches strewn about for barricades. The hornets bounced off the boards around the door.

The buzzing muffled outside with the walls. Within minutes the noise faded entirely.

Rock. "I've seen some wipeouts in my time, but that one was a killer. Bet the Princess would've loved it."

"If you're gonna go down," Teddy said, "you might as well go big. Also, you were right about transforming. We should have done it. That was too close."

"I dunno. It was wide open out there. Feels like anybody could have spotted us. Anyway, forget it."

The power had been cut inside. Shops were half-demolished and forgotten, all abandoned mid-construction. Boards and plaster lay strewn about everywhere. There were even scaffoldings lying around.

"What now?" Rock asked.

"I've got an idea."

The two slid down a maintenance hall not far from the front door. They turned into a darkened bathroom.

Teddy slid his hand into the emergency panel, and

turned on the hidden light. The room shone bright red.

"How did you even know that was there?"

"The maintenance guy eats at my dad's restaurant pretty regularly. His name is Rutabaga, or Rossini, or Rutgers, or something. I should really pay more attention when he tells me these things. Anyway, no one will see us here. Transform to your heart's content."

"Then let's light it up."

Teddy placed his hands together, and made the call. The room filled with a flash.

He was the Pyre Knight again. The cracks in the red armor were not fully fixed, though at least it was more or less whole again. He was more excited that his helmet was back, even if it had seen better days.

Rock took a deep breath and copied his friend's movements. He clapped his hands together and gripped them tight. "I beg you, bestow on me the glory."

Another flash of light filled the small room. When Rock emerged, he had changed.

A dark white shade of armor encased Rock Carson. Even in the red hue of the emergency light, it shone through. Unlike Teddy, the older boy kept his normal appearance under his helmet.

Rock checked himself all over. He found two short grey swords holstered on each side. A faint trail of smoke drifted from their blades when he brought them forward. Rock swung them like they were made of papier-mâché.

"I wanted a big red sword that burns stuff. And your color is better, too!"

"I *knighted* you, remember? I don't think your armor being better than mine would make much sense."

"Yeah, but these two small swords just aren't as cool." He removed his blades and ran his armored fingers along them. The edges glinted against the red emergency light. A smile passed Rock's lips. "Okay, they're still pretty cool."

"Let's go try them out."

The mall echoed with their every step. All the abandoned stores they glanced inside were barren. It could almost be confused for a normal construction zone, if it didn't stink of ash.

Teddy hated the mall. He had a lot of memories shopping with his mother. Not to mention, Hoffman's gang would hang out there. The stores were pretty lame, too.

The place just wasn't very good in general. The mall had been built to attract customers from the neighboring towns to bolster both McLeod's economy and general popularity. Neither really ever happened. The constant earthquakes didn't help. Teddy wasn't too broken up when it fell in on itself.

"My sixth sense is guiding me to the food court," Rock said. "There aren't a whole lot of places to hide in here. Plus, I'm hungry. It's a win-win."

"We just had breakfast. Also, this place has been closed forever. Whatever food is there, you don't want."

"Give me a break, I'm a growing boy."

Teddy laughed. "Most of the quake damage was in the food court, though. You're intuition isn't that off."

The food court was in the northeast section of the mall.

It wasn't far. However, the closer they got, the less comfortable Teddy got.

The silence had given way to a low hum. It pitched louder the closer they got to the food court.

"You hear that?" Teddy asked. His sixth sense was screaming at him.

"Kinda," Rock replied. "There's so much nothing in here it's hard to know if it isn't my imagination."

The low hum eventually twisted. Teddy recognized the sound. The piercing buzz of hornets filled the hallways. The two Knights were getting close.

Eventually, they spotted the disturbance. There were lumps of mass hiding in the shadows of the boarded up stores. Giant insects slept on the ceiling and along the store windows. It was as if they were sleeping—or waiting.

The pair reached the food court, and Teddy let out a sigh of relief. He felt a nudge on his shoulder. Rock was pointing ahead of him. Teddy cursed his short-lived relief.

A green cylinder-like object suspended by sticky wires sat in the center of the food court. It stretched up to where the skylight lay. The food court was covered in the glistening wires and green gunk, and it all led back to the cocoon. The green gunk it was soaked in had been spread all over the place.

The mall had been thoroughly infested.

"Is that a cocoon?" Rock asked.

"The Manslayer is losing his touch," a voice said. "Master Jero would be so disappointed."

The Parasite sat on top of the large cocoon. He grinned and waved down at the pair.

Teddy smiled back. "I wouldn't recommend you making the same mistake the tiger did."

"Don't equate me with that relic." The monster straightened his stained tie, and wiped back a greasy strand of hair. "Once my insects have nice fertile ground to grow in, they should spread quite nicely. I won't even have to lift a finger to take this town."

Rock laughed. "You really chose a mall as your home base? The jokes almost write themselves."

"And who is this? Some clown in a Halloween costume?"

"He's a Knight of the End," Teddy interrupted. "And he's going to help me take you down."

"He's not one of the three legendary knights. He can't be. This boy is just an innocent."

The cocoon cracked below the Parasite. The crunching bounced through the empty halls like the roll of a snare drum. Inside of the darkness of the cylinder poked two giant black bug eyes. Green slime slid from the opening.

"That means he's disposable," the Parasite said.

Teddy went for his sword. "You're going to regret this."

The Parasite smiled as his pet shimmied free under him. "Regret what? I've been dying for you to get here and meet my baby for yourself. I wonder if they'll make me one of the Four Generals when I devour one of the Knights of the End?"

Chapter 15
Extermination Battle

The cocoon split open, its shell slamming against the mall floor. There was no earth-shattering explosion when the slimy fabric touched down. Green liquid splashed all over.

A creature the size of a truck with the body of a hornet, the wings of a fly, and face of a beetle, emerged from the remains. It stretched and hummed as it tossed off what was left of its former cocoon. Teddy's stomach flipped as he listened to it shimmy out of the mess.

"That ain't no dragon," he whispered to himself.

The monster tumbled free, and soared upward. Its buzzing was earsplitting. It darted across the food court, and winded back around to the Parasite. The bug man leaped on its back like a stallion.

The two knights could only watch as the giant hornet whipped all over the food court. The skylight above stretched over the whole area, with flashes of light from the storm illuminating the flying monstrosity. Teddy was beginning to appreciate lightning more and more.

Thunder rumbled above the skylight. The dancing of raindrops struck the glass. Teddy needed to act before it became too hard to see inside.

Rock glanced at the monster soaring above their heads. "So, what exactly do we do here?"

"We separate them," Teddy replied. "I'll get the Parasite, and you go at that big guy like your fists are flyswatters. Sorry to throw you in the deep end on your first day."

"No, this is my kind of plan. I can deal with it."

"Just punch it until it stops moving. If I can stop the Parasite, then maybe it'll take out the other hornets, too." He thought of his fight in the warehouse. Burning the monster to ash destroyed any remains of those insects. If the boss worked like his minions, then it was sure to work here.

"Alright," Rock said. "But how do we get them apart?"

Teddy studied the Parasite, and the enormous lapdog. The pair dipped in and out of range, slamming into whatever wall or pillar possible. Stone debris rained down on the teenagers. There would eventually be a pattern to the madness. He just had to watch for it.

The bug dipped low every ten seconds. Even if it spun sideways or struck a wall, it always dipped. Teddy had an idea.

"I'll hit 'em high, you hit 'em low," the Pyre Knight said.

One the tenth second, the creation dove low to the ground. It angled for a killing blow. Rock fell backwards into the floor's gunk. Teddy simply waited, confirming the pattern. The beast glided over them.

Eventually, it passed around again. The Pyre Knight

waited. When it swopped in, Teddy jumped forward.

"Are you serious?" Rock called out.

Teddy landed on top of the giant insect's back. He readied his balance. The Parasite flinched when he noticed the Knight in front of him. The bug man thrashed at his enemy, grabbing at Teddy's neck. Teddy grabbed on to the Parasite's face. The pair tottered as they wrestled with each other, trying to break the other's grip.

The giant flew erratically. Teddy tried to guide it with kicks to the side, as he struggled with its master. The beast spun as Teddy messed with its sense of direction. They barreled upward.

The monster crashed through the skylight. Glass rained down on Teddy, bouncing from his armor. The Parasite let the glass fall through him like a knife through butter. Neither were bloodied. Rainwater splashed against them. Rock exclaimed from down below in the mall.

When they met the outside, the beast spun. The Knight lost his balance. As they tipped, Teddy grabbed hold of the Parasites arm. They plummeted off the monster.

The two bodies struck the roof beside the broken skylight. The roof cracked under the Pyre Knight's weight. The sky was so dark that Teddy could barely see the swarms of hornets swirling above. A flash of lightning jolted over the dark clouds. Rain mercilessly beat down on the boy.

The giant hornet ignored the two of them. It squealed when it saw a lightning flash. Without pause, it flew downward back through the shattered skylight. There was a crash in the mall below.

The wind blew raindrops across Teddy's red armor. He stood back up.

A fist smashed into his face. Teddy stumbled backwards. The Parasite flailed his blackened arms toward the Knight. It was thick black hair. The fur sliced apart the air like a sword. Teddy jumped back.

"I am a Knight of the End," Teddy said. "You're going to have to do better than this."

The Parasite's skin now shone a greasy green. He paled like rotten wood under the storm's pulsing light.

"I know you were one of those kids in the school," the Parasite said. "None of the others believe me, but I know you are. There's no way you weren't one of them. You stink of it. Between you and me, which one were you?"

"I'm the one who is going to burn you to cinders."

"Give me a break, boy. You're nothing. Just a kid playing pretend. You've never fought anyone like me before."

"Ask the Manslayer how that worked out for him. You better hope you're tougher than he was."

The enemy wiped his greasy lips. "That freak wouldn't go full-out against a weaker opponent. He went easy on you, because he was gauging you. I won't."

"He didn't." Not *during* the fight, at least.

"He also goes easy on kids." The rain plastered its dirty orange hair down. It was as slimy as the rest of his ragged green body. His suit was in shreds, though he hardly noticed. "I hate kids."

"I'm pretty sure they hate you, too."

The Parasite brought his arm back, and plunged it

forward. He went for Teddy's throat. The limb cut through the rain like a hot knife. Teddy ducked. Thunder cracked. The Parasite leaned in for a backhand. The black hairs struck Teddy's armor. The screech cut through the thunder.

Teddy backhanded the enemy. The Parasite fell backwards in a roll.

His armor now had added scratch marks. It wasn't fully patched yet. One good shot would break through. The rain rapped against them.

"What's wrong, boy?" The Parasite moved in again. He went for Teddy's head. The boy weaved. "Rain no good for the fire?"

The truth was that Teddy didn't know. His fire might have dulled in the downpour. Maybe it didn't. He only needed to wait for his opening.

"Don't make this embarrassing." The Parasite sneered. "Fight back, already."

"You don't want that."

A series of loud clatters rolled out through the broken skylight. There was a yell from a teenage boy. Teddy flinched. He almost forgot Rock was down there.

The Parasite swung for his head. The boy tilted his head. Teddy's helmet screeched.

"Your pal in the costume isn't going to last long against my baby. You better make a choice, kid. Kill me, or let your friend die. You got the stomach for that?"

He did. "You want flames, ugly? You got them."

"Ugly? I happen to look distinguished with my big eyes and sharp edges. Real cut. It beats looking like a hairless ape."

Teddy moved forward. He bobbed and weaved under the enemy's strikes. The air sliced around Teddy. Armor screeched. The Parasite moved in close again, and let Teddy put his plan into action.

The Pyre Knight sidestepped the creature's charge, and kicked the Parasite in the back. The enemy was sent off balance.

Teddy went for his sword.

The Red Sword fired flames forward. The blast tore through the rain, striking the Parasite dead on. The deep crimson inferno sparkled through the downpour. The Parasite was consumed.

"Yes, that's right," the Parasite said, as he burned. "But I'm sure you can do better than this. Don't disappoint me, now!"

The Pyre Knight moved forward. The enemy wasn't fast enough to react. The Red Sword plunged into the Parasite's green chest. Flames exploded from the sword's tip, cascading through the bug man's body. The Parasite let out a squeal.

When the flames finally cleared, all that remained was a charred black shell. The husk was in the vague shape of the bug man. The remains broke up under the heavy rain drops until there was nothing left.

The Pyre Knight took a breather. The hornets still flew high above. Nothing had changed with the Parasite's death. Something was not right.

He scanned the mall below the broken glass. It was empty. No giant bug, no Rock.

The floor below was now soaked. Green gunk from the

cocoon now floated on the water. The slick mucus webs on the walls and floor lay undisturbed. Chairs and tables were broken into pieces, and chunks of marble pillars and store signs had been knocked to the floor. It was a warzone.

"Hey," Teddy called out. "Anyone down there?"

There was no response.

He leaped down. Rain clinked against the back of his armor. He tucked in like he did at the school. The ground crunched under his weight.

"Don't think that'll ever get old," he whispered to himself.

Teddy glanced around. The resulting racket of his landing should have brought everything inside running to him. But nothing happened. Only the echo of the dented floor rebounded through the empty mall.

Rotting ooze like garbage filled his nostrils. The water was making things worse. A sickness grew in Teddy's gut.

"What exactly were you doing in here, Rock?"

Teddy retraced his steps back toward the center of the mall. He found a trail of broken stone. It led from his corner of the mall and back toward the center square.

Things were different on his way back. The resting hornets had vanished from the storefronts and ceiling. Chunks of wall, floor, and ceiling, had been knocked in.

After enough running, he drew close to the center of the mall. He passed the door they first entered through earlier. He soon reached the phone outlet, and the store specializing in chocolates from around the world. This was where the kids would meet Santa in December and where public events and promotion had been, or would be, held. It was also ground zero for the earthquake.

Four paths sprouted from the mall's center like a cross. He had arrived from the north path where the food court was. There were three other hallways like the directions on a compass. This position would be the easiest to find Rock from.

The water fountain lay demolished in the center of the mall. The old statue was built like a dolphin for some reason. McLeod was nowhere near the ocean so the choice in animal was confusing. But there was something else there that wasn't right. A giant hole had been dug underneath the fountain into as if a new basement level were being dug. It looked like a tunnel.

Beside the broken hole sat Rock, still in his armor. He was slumped over toward the hole. He also wasn't moving.

Teddy moved slowly to Rock, and knelt beside his friend. The grey armor was cracked. One of the short swords looked slippery, as if covered in grease. The second sword was planted in the ground. He'd been in a real brawl.

Teddy put a hand on his friend's shoulder, and the older boy jumped.

Rock let out a breath when he saw Teddy. "You scared me. I mean, uh, I didn't see you."

"Right." Teddy let out his own breath.

"Anyway, did you get him?"

"I did, but it was too easy. Not to mention, the bugs are still outside."

"Not the ones in here." Rock gestured around the empty

ceiling and halls. "When that big thing chased me out here, the fat hornets were all gone. Disappeared. I don't know what's going on, but it ain't right."

Teddy grinned. "So, you got the big guy without my help?"

"Actually, Hornet Truck did a number on me. I cut him up, but it didn't do much. It stunk like rotting trash."

"*Hornet truck?*"

"That's what I'm calling it," Rock said. "As I was saying, I threw everything I could at it. I jumped out of its way when it charged, I hid behind pillars, I mean—it was embarrassing. The thing rammed me a few times, and was about ready to do me in. But then this smell of burnt skin and ash came out of nowhere—and I think it smelled it too, because it took off. Down here."

Teddy glanced down into the darkness. He couldn't even see the bottom. The deep darkness could have gone on forever.

"Must have been when I torched the Parasite."

"The tunnel system," Teddy said. "Looks like the Princess and our potential employer with the goofy tie was right."

"Why did Hornet Truck run away?"

Teddy paused. It finally hit him. "Because that wasn't the real Parasite."

"What wasn't?"

"Heads up!"

A hornet the size of a fat Chihuahua flew out of the giant hole. It hovered before them. Both Knights went for their weapons.

"Even kids can be something other than stupid, I guess," the hornet said.

"Like I thought." Teddy raised his sword. "That wasn't you on the roof."

"Good eye, firebug. My parasites do such a good job of imitating my eccentric beauty. If you want to see the real thing, well, I'm sorry to say that won't happen."

Teddy's sixth sense rang bells in his head. A cacophony of shattering glass and bending metal ricocheted out through the empty mall. Heavy steps bounced from all four directions leading out of the center square. The enemy was coming.

Fat hornets filled each hall, floating under the ceiling. The source of the footsteps turned out to be dozens of Parasite clones just like the one on the roof. They blocked the Knights' escape. The Parasite planned out this whole trap.

"Which will run out first, Pyre Knight? Will it be my children, or your fire?"

Rock sliced the insect in two. The remains turned to ash in the air.

"It was never going to be easy," Teddy said.

The giant hornet darted from the hole. *Hornet Truck*, as Rock had named it, circled around the open floor. It joined the gathering crowd of smaller bugs and Parasite clones. Its hideous eyes glared down at the pair of Knights.

The stench of ash encroached on Teddy and his friend. It was enough to make the Pyre Knight want to gag. But there was only one way out. They had to make it through the small army barreling down on them.

Teddy tightened his grip on his sword, and ran out to meet them.

Chapter 16
To the Surface

The Parasite clones all moved in awkward jerks. Their green faces were empty and dull, and without life. They were as soulless lemmings marching onward.

The clones weren't alone. The fat hornets swirled around the mall's ceiling, making their way toward the Knights. Their large brother, Hornet Truck, waited for its moment to strike by hovering above the gathering crowd.

Shouts echoed through the center square. The Knights cut into the monsters, returning the crowd of attackers into piles of dust. No matter how many the pair cut down, more would take their place. The bugs and clones piled into the mall endlessly.

"Some ambush!" Rock shouted. "This is starting to get fun."

Then, Hornet Truck finally moved. The giant bug screeched forward, barreling over fat hornets and clones like bowling pins. It screeched as its stinger went for the older boy's neck. It grazed Rock. He tried to dodge but tripped, falling on his rear. The giant bug swooped around for a second attack.

This time, Hornet Truck twisted toward Teddy.

"Keep your guard up," Teddy said. He ducked under Hornet Truck. "It only takes one good hit, and your armor is done."

The monsters were nothing to the Knights. Their blades cut through their forms and returned them to ash. But they weren't the problem.

Hornet Truck dove for the Pyre Knight. Teddy sidestepped. The giant barreled into a tea store.

The big one was the problem. The swarm was knock aside, as, over and over again, Hornet Truck rammed through them to get to the Knights. Rock narrowly missed slicing it, as it spun away from him.

"Hornet Truck is getting on my nerves, Boss."

"Give me a second." Teddy cut down three more shambling clones. He needed space.

"What are you gonna do?"

"Watch your eyes."

Teddy pointed his sword upwards. He remembered the sensation of flames he had in the warehouse. The rush flooded through his bloodstream, and out through the tip of the Red Sword. Flames peeked out.

The inferno burst from the blade. Pure red fire sprouted out like a flamethrower. The surrounding insects were torched. They disintegrated into dust. Fire filled the center square. The flames burned themselves out without scorching anything but his enemy. Teddy turned it off like a faucet.

He fell to one knee. Hornet Truck was still racing around the mall. It was the only survivor. It had dodged the flames by hiding down the eastern hall. The flame blast was simply not wide enough.

The monster soared through the clear. It had a clear path back toward them.

Rock followed Hornet Truck's approach. He held both short swords beside him. He breathed heavier as the monster got closer.

"Rock?" Teddy asked. They didn't have time for this. The sound of footsteps meant more enemies were on the way. "We should get moving."

The Grey Knight smiled. "I got this."

The monster picked up speed. It dove toward Rock. Its mouth filled with saliva, dripping over its beetle-like face. Rock stood still. The beast would smash him to pieces.

"What are you doing?" Teddy's energy wasn't back yet and they had to get moving.

"Hey," Rock said. "If you can do it, so can I."

Rock bent his knees, and jumped. He spun sideways in the air. The hornet passed under him. His right sword buried down into Hornet Truck's back. The monster flew off with him still hanging on.

The two of them twisted upwards. Rock turned, still holding his embedded sword. He flipped his left blade around, and jabbed it downwards into the monster's back. Hornet Truck screamed. The boy removed his right sword, and sliced off the monster's wings, stopping their ascent.

Hornet Truck flailed all the way down to the floor. Its

body skidded through tiles, and its momentum carried the monster forward. Rock perched on its back. It smashed through the phone kiosks and into a shoe shop. Teddy lost sight of it when it continued past the cashier desk, and into the back of the store.

Down the hall, the clones stirred closer. They rounded the corners, mindlessly romping forward. There were at least three dozen on the way. They were endless.

Rock jumped back through the demolished store window. Ash wafted from the opening. Rock dashed back toward his younger friend. Both his swords were at his sides, and he was laughing

"So, you beat him?" asked Teddy.

"And how. Poor Hornet Truck is nothing more than a big pile of dust." Rock glanced at the madding crowd. "Which is what we're going to be unless we get out of here."

"That's what I was saying. We need to get moving. We'll go by the tunnels. The Order built them, so they have to lead somewhere."

"Or you can put out another flamethrower so we can get out the front door. Then we can make it back to your place to regroup."

"I can't do those forever," Teddy said. He still hadn't recovered from the last one. The fire was building back up. He glanced toward the hole in the center of the mall. "If we can stop the Parasite, we should be able to stop this whole thing. I say we go through the tunnel."

"Right." Rock tapped his grey helmet. "That built in radar should also help. That's why you're the boss."

The pair turned to the pit, and leaped down. Darkness swallowed them.

Teddy lingered in the air. There was no floor underneath them. Somehow they were still dropping.

"Where's the bottom?" Rock shouted.

Before Teddy could reply, his friend got his answer. The red armor smacked the rocks underneath him. He bounced like a pinball, rolling a good ten feet, before finally arriving at a stop. His back stiffened. Rock struck the ground a moment later.

After a pause, Teddy spat dirt from his mouth. The muted light of the mall was light years away.

Rock groaned. "Well, there it is."

Even if the light was far away them now, their enemies were not. The stomping of the clones, and the buzzing hornets, were still getting closer. It wasn't impossible to imagine the enemies would fall down into the dark. They were utterly mindless.

Teddy drew his sword. A low red light shone from the blade. They were surrounded by stone walls of the tunnels. There were multiple paths ahead, at least six from left to right.

"Let's go," Teddy said. His sixth sense was kicking in. "We'll go down the furthest one on the right."

"I'm getting that feeling, too."

The path continued in a steep drop. It twisted on like the inside of a snake. The path winded this way and that, over and over. Teddy's head began to spin. Soon enough, a pattern emerged from the insanity.

"How did nobody notice this tunnel?" Rock asked. "It's huge!"

"The same reason *we* didn't notice them. We just thought they were earthquakes. It doesn't matter now."

Teddy signaled to Rock. They both stopped. There was a forty feet steep drop before them. Teddy pointed down the drop to the ground below. They couldn't afford to waste more time on a fall.

Both of them leaped down. There were several more drops to go before the path leveled out again.

Whoever dug the route was immaculate. They built a maze, and they did it without anyone being the wiser. The Order could go anywhere in town, and no one would ever know. Teddy was going to enjoy cracking some of their skulls.

The tunnel snaked onward, refusing to end. The growing buzz behind them only pitched closer, as did the steps.

They passed by so many dead ends and blind drops, that Teddy was beginning to wonder if there was a way out.

Rock groaned. "I feel like I'm in one of those maps on the kids menu at the Burger Barn. How big is this stupid thing?"

"They were at this for a long time. It can't be much linger. We've been running for a while, too. There's a chance we're not even in town anymore."

"No way."

"It's possible. I've seen longer than this in the forest."

Rock scoffed. "The jerk that made this needs a life."

Teddy didn't object to that. He wanted to meet each of

the jerks as soon as possible. There were scores to settle.

"They wanted us to come through here," Teddy said. "Be ready."

"This is why I like you, Boss. You keep it simple."

"I'm not sure if I should be flattered, or horrified."

"I prefer simple plans. We follow this path to the end, punch this bug freak through a wall, go back home, have a burger, and things go back to normal. I follow that. Easier than a day at Harding."

Teddy forced a smile. Things wouldn't ever be normal again. The Order was still out there, and the Pyre Knight would have to hunt them down. If they could do this to McLeod with only four of them, there was no telling how far they could go. Teddy shook his head.

"Ready to be a hero, Rock?"

"Like from the old comics? We better be talking about the classics here." He faked a western drawl, "We ain't stopping 'til our bones are beat and broken. Fill me with bullets, and I'll keep moving. A man never stops."

Teddy tried a hand at the accent. "You get up, you go forward. You go *through*, if you have to."

"So what do you say, fellow Knight?" Rock said, laughing. "Do we turn tail and run? Or do we continue through to the endless frontier?"

A realization hit Teddy. Both the buzzing and the heavy steps from behind them had stopped. He fell back to his thoughts.

Light began to peak out of the path before them. The pattering of raindrops caught his attention. Cold wind blew through the tunnels.

Finally, they made it to daylight. Faded daylight shone through the cavern opening.

The outside world awaited. An overcast sky with muted daylight, and a stream of trees, lay outside the cavern. The two of them were outside the city limits, near the west end of the forest. Teddy knew the forest too well to be lost in it for long.

They left the cold cave, and right away his sixth sense kicked in. Rock stopped beside him.

The air changed, blowing musty mold back at the pair. There was movement through the trees. The bugs were waiting for them.

Teddy smiled at Rock. "I'm ready, fellow Knight."

"Glad to hear it," Rock said, bringing his swords forward.

The fresh air of the forest was replaced by ash. Parasite clones fell out from behind the trees. A river of fat hornets flowed over the treetops. They had infested Teddy's forest. These monsters were determined to ruin it all: the oaks and maples, the crunching of leaves underfoot, and the scent of pine and fresh dew. All they did was destroy, and they were determined to destroy all he loved.

Rain crashed down on the two Knights. They slowly went for their blades.

A roar erupted through the trees, piercing the thunder and downpour. The world paused, and the clones ceased their march forward. The hornets hovered still. Bark crunched a few miles away.

The enemy was here. A large figure leaped across treetops, and crashed down into the forest grass. Its weight kicked up rocks and dirt as it landed by the bordering trees around the Knights. A growl escaped the monster.

Rain cascaded from the Manslayer's orange mane and chest scar. The beast man swung one meaty limb sideways into an oak tree, shattering its trunk. The tree crashed down into pooling mud. The enemy stepped from the shade of treetops toward the Knights.

"That isn't what I think it is, is it?" Rock asked.

"Yeah." Teddy bared his teeth. "A problem."

Chapter 17
Duel with a Demon

The Manslayer crossed the clearing toward the two Knights. None of the surrounding clones or hornets budged at its advance.

Teddy grimaced. These monsters didn't belong in this place. Their presence stained the woods. The open forest of pines and birches, nature trails for the curious, and the golden autumn leaves, were not meant to be soiled by invaders. The stench of ash no longer sickened Teddy—it brought his anger to a boil.

"We are here for the Parasite," Teddy said to the Manslayer. "We have no quarrel with you. Leave now, and you'll walk away unharmed."

Rock tilted his head at his friend. "Quarrel?"

"It makes me sound more knightly," Teddy whispered.

"Ah, I getcha. That's a good word, too. Very adult."

The enemy eyeballed Teddy's sword. It folded its arms and snorted under its heavy breath.

"This is between me and the Pyre Knight, little one." The

Manslayer did not even glance at Rock. "No one else may interfere. Not whatever you are. Not even the Parasite's little nuisances. Return to your sandbox, child."

Rock began to charge forward, but Teddy blocked him with an outstretched arm.

"This is good," Teddy whispered. "If it's just me and him, then I have the advantage."

"Are you sure? I saw what this thing did back to Harding. What if those bugs attack while you're fighting him?"

"They won't." Teddy glanced at the Manslayer. He didn't know everything about this monster, but he did believe Rock's earlier assessment about it was right. To the Manslayer, only the duel mattered. That was fine with Teddy. It was oddly fine. "All we gotta do is play our hand right."

"Hand?" Rock asked. "Why are you talking so weird all of a sudden? This thing wants to kill you. It doesn't even care that I shouldn't exist. He's not all there. I don't get why you're taking this thing so seriously."

Teddy ignored his friend's comments. "Thirty feet beyond the treeline to your left is a trail. Follow the path east to the park and use the payphone to call our potential employer. Make sure to not let the bugs hold you back. We're going to need backup if the Stone Eater and Phantom Maiden are also nearby. And I'm pretty sure they are. I'll give you the number."

His friend smirked, and tapped his helmet. "Don't worry about it, I thought ahead."

"You?"

"Yeah, I got a phone, but it's in my other pants. Literally. Where do our clothes go when we transform, anyway?" That was a whole subject Teddy didn't even want to think about. Rock continued, "If I can get a breather to transform back, I can use it to call out."

"I thought you didn't have a phone?"

"The suit and tie threw it to me when I ran out of the house after you. Said we'd probably need it. That guy knows his stuff. You really should think ahead next time."

Teddy laughed. "I can't believe I'm getting lectured by Rock Carson. The world must be ending."

"Yeah, I know," Rock said, shaking his head. "Anyway, the guy said he'll try to get your girlfriend back as soon as she can get free."

"She's not my girlfriend!"

"Then why are you blushing?"

"Come on, man." Teddy tried to focus on the Manslayer. "I can't deal with this stuff right now."

"Why are you doing this, at all?"

That was a good question. Teddy didn't know. He had to defeat the Manslayer on his own, or it would bother him forever. He wanted this duel as much as the tiger-man did. His blood burned for the fight.

Rock shrugged. "It's your choice. Good luck, Boss."

The older boy sprinted to the left. He brushed through the treeline toward the eastern trail. The Parasite clones and fat hornets all moved to him. He vanished through the trees, as they fell in after him.

Soon enough, only the two warriors remained.

The Pyre Knight drew his sword. The Manslayer unfolded its arms with a grin.

Lightning arched across the black clouds.

"So, big guy," Teddy said. "You heal fast."

"As do you, boy." It growled. "There will be no excuses, no matter the outcome of this battle."

"I only have two questions, if you'll do me the honor of answering them."

"Words are not my preferred method of conversation, but if you must."

"Thanks." Teddy hoped the distraction would give Rock enough time. "Why didn't you tell your friends who I am?"

"You are a teenage boy," the Manslayer said. "What does that matter? I do not care who you are. I also do not care if it matters to the Order of the Ash, or Jero. They mean little in the grand scheme of things."

"I doubt your master would approve of such carelessness."

He thought he caught the edges of a laugh burst from the Manslayer's fangs. "Do not act as if you know who my Master is, Sir Knight."

Cold wind beat against the branches of the oaks. The rain poured on. The Manslayer rotated its right shoulder, it's breathing excited.

"I think I have the answer to my second question, but I'll ask anyway. Why didn't you kill me?"

"The phantom wench," it said. "And b-because . . ." It stuttered, and shook its head. It was as if some other voice was fighting to speak. Its smile twisted to a grimace.

Teddy decided to push the subject. "Because what?"

"Nothing." Its yellow eyes clouded over. "I've never been one for massacres. I prefer duels—then we know who deserves to live and fight on."

Teddy nodded. He agreed. There would be no interference this time.

The Manslayer dropped to all fours, completing its tiger image. "And then we know who deserves to die."

"Then, bring it on."

"Yes!" The Manslayer's voice rose to a roar. "If you are finished stalling, we can finally begin."

The beast man sprinted forth on all fours. It reached Teddy within half a second. It changed direction, instead of attacking. Teddy almost lost the enemy.

It bounded straight up into the sky with its powerful legs. The Manslayer's jump remained impressive. It soared straight up, and kicked against the air like a wall. Whistling wind cut under the monster's force. The Manslayer shot off toward Teddy like a bullet.

The breeze rustled soaked leaves across Teddy's helmet. It almost blinded him. The gust was enough to distract him. Already, the Manslayer was inches from his face.

Teddy spun backwards. The Manslayer touched down with incredible velocity. Dirt and earth exploded under its weight. Its force cut against the wind itself.

Teddy leaned forward out of the dodge, stabbing his sword toward the vulnerable enemy. The Manslayer ducked back. The Red Sword cut rainwater out of the wind.

The Manslayer struck Teddy's sword hand. The blade

shook loose. It spun away into the trees, striking into a pine.

Teddy lunged forward with a right punch. His legs floated off the ground. The world flipped underneath him. He was upside down, and flying backward through the air. He landed against a birch tree, breaking through it. Bark splinters exploded into the wind. He tumbled across the wet grass, his mind reeling. He planted his knees under him, halting his momentum. He steadied himself in a kneel.

A right jab struck his helmet. A left followed. Lighting quick claw strikes rang against the red armor, as if timed to an invisible beat. He brought his arms up to guard.

A knee thudded into his armored gut, pushing him back. The Pyre Knight slid backward with the force. He rolled across soaked orange leaves and drenched grass. His back struck against an oak tree, bringing him to a stop. He fell to the mud.

Teddy glanced up. The Manslayer was already in the air.

"You've got to be kidding me," he whispered.

The Manslayer barreled down on top of him.

Teddy leaped to his feet. He caught the falling enemy. Using the Manslayer's momentum, the Knight spun. He slammed the enemy's face into the oak tree. There was a crunch. Bark sprayed everywhere. Teddy grabbed the enemy, and slammed it forward repeatedly. The tree cracked open under the jackhammer force.

The enemy mumbled, and kicked viciously against the tree. The Manslayer flipped over Teddy, breaking his grip. It fell back from the battle in short hops. The damaged oak crashed down into the mud.

Rainy winds blew over the two combatants. Neither warrior moved for an attack.

The Manslayer panted and wiped its whiskers of sweat and rain. It mumbled once again.

Teddy craned his neck. "What did you say?"

"It's a fat and happy land, this world of yours."

"It doesn't look that way to me."

"It wouldn't. Not for a child. You do not see this ball of mud and water for what it is. If they aren't robbing you blind when you're honest, they're stabbing you in the back when you're safe. Because everyone wants their share, their piece of the overcooked pie, and why?" The Manslayer panted between exhaustion and fury. It didn't wait for Teddy to answer. "Because it's the only thing they have in their miserable lives to guard from their emptiness. Being fat and happy is all that helps them escape it. They are all worthless."

"You don't look very fat, or happy."

"I am not," the Manslayer said. "If I am going to die, it's going to on the only meaningful place in this world, or any other. I will die on the battlefield where we separate the weak from the righteous. Now, let us finish it, boy."

"I will."

Teddy entered the fray. The Manslayer flashed its teeth. Rain doused them, as the mud slipped underneath their steps toward each other.

For some reason, Teddy moved faster. It was as if something inside were responding to the Manslayer's mad words. His strength increased with ever hook, straight punch, and uppercut he threw out. In contrast, the enemy slowed. It couldn't keep up with him. In its fury, the Manslayer lunged forward. Its roar cut through thunder.

The tiger bared its fangs, but it was of no use. Teddy landed a gut punch. A crunch that was certainly heard miles away reverberated out of the beast. It leaped back several feet.

The Manslayer doubled over, and coughed out a black substance.

Teddy wiped rain out of his eyes. "How many men have you slayed, exactly?"

"The count is soon to increase by one," it said, growling.

The Manslayer sprang upwards. The leap carried it high into the black sky. Its silhouette clashed against the lightning.

Teddy knew blocking wouldn't work. If he dodged, the enemy would only leap again. This left him with only one choice.

He turned on his heel and ran.

The monster laughed. It crashed into the grass, kicking up gravel, leaves, and dirt. It leaped back into the air, following after Teddy.

It laughed again and again as it leaped up and down.

"Run, brave Knight, run!"

Teddy kept his pace. The impacts were getting closer to him. He did not stop. It would only be a few more feet until Teddy reached his target.

Running forward, Teddy put his shoulder first. He tackled the pine tree in his path, hitting it at just the right angle. It split near the bottom, and tipped back on him. He slid under the crashing tree. The resulting thud and crumpling branches blocked his enemy from advancing. The Manslayer yelled a curse, as it landed on the broken branches.

The enemy roared, glancing back and forth. It had lost sight of its prey.

"Do you see what I mean?" the Manslayer's voice boomed into the storm. "Run away and hide. Flee and cower! All you humans can do is run. This is why the battlefield is the truth, the real test—it shows you what you are. And you are a coward like the rest!"

Teddy slipped through the fallen brush. He held the sword that had been embedded in the trunk only seconds ago. The Manslayer didn't see his approached.

It spotted the glint of the blade, as Teddy brought his sword forward. The Red Sword pierced through the striped chest of the Manslayer. The monster's eyes widened.

A burst of crimson flame erupted from the wound. Red fire towered up into the dark skies. Loose flame sprinkled into the mud-covered grass and wet leaves, extinguishing as they touched the earth. The beast screamed.

"I wasn't running away," Teddy said. "Knights don't run away."

The Knight removed his blade. The Manslayer fell to one knee.

He brought his sword down and on the enemy. A bright red flame gushed from the blade, through the Manslayer's shoulder, and all the way down its crumpling body.

Chapter 18
Pale Lightning

Red flames burst out of the Manslayer. Orange and black fur became entirely engulfed. Its roars echoed across the rain-soaked forest.

The beast was pulled apart by the inferno. It separated into two figures, just as it had in the warehouse and the school.

Before Teddy, fell the young man in the suit from the assembly. He had buzz cut blonde hair, and an old tiny scar under his left eye. It looked as if he hadn't had a good meal in months. He wore sunglasses to hide black circles under his eyes, and his sickly face.

The second figure was far less human.

In the flames, was a bony black tiger with thin orange stripes across its lean frame. Its beady eyes leaked blackness like tears. A thin white veil covered it over, as if it were the only thing holding its physical form together. The monster shook from the force of the heat.

"It hurts," the monster said, "but it will not silence me, Pyre Knight."

The young man before Teddy slowly crawled up. He glanced away from Teddy and saw the Manslayer. His pupils widened. It sent him sideways toward a tall oak. He fell back against it as he tried to flee, staring between the two warriors before him.

"It's alright," Teddy said to the famished man. "It has no more control over you."

The Manslayer laughed. "He asked for power, and I delivered what he wanted. He was nothing but a lowly criminal, trapped in his pathetic vitriol, when I found him. I never controlled him."

"You were in my head," the young man said. Sweat ran down his thin face.

"But my presence was quenching, wasn't it? No one could betray you. No one could tear you to pieces. You were a predator. Only I can make you strong."

The thin man stared on through his cracked sunglasses. The scar under his left eye twitched. He wiped his hair free of rain, as if it were crawling with bugs. He did not reply to the monster.

"I've heard enough." Teddy put himself between them. "You do not belong here, Manslayer."

"Have you learned nothing, puppet of the Light? You do not have the power to destroy me."

"I'll dig a good grave for you," Teddy said. "You're done."

The blazing shadow-like creature lunged forward, its dark teeth flashing against the red flames. It dove toward the knight, stinking of something darker than ash. Then, a white flash across the dark skies. The monster skidded to a stop on the wet grass.

Teddy recognized the lightning from above. He shielded his eyes from the impact.

The lighting bent through the overcast sky and down into the woods. It blew through the Manslayer, shooting through the beast's skull and firing out through the tail. The beast wailed.

The Manslayer dropped. Red flames ate away into it as it hit the earth. The remains burst into a pure white bonfire. Its empty eyes flashed toward Teddy. Then it blinked into ash.

The flames tapered off into the wind.

Only the storm remained.

Behind him, the man named Felix had vanished. He had disappeared during the lightning strike. He decided against giving chase. There were more important things to deal with right now.

Caitlyn West, the Lightning Maiden, landed before Teddy. She was transformed, though looked half-dead. Her robe-like brown dress with the white edges had tear marks as if from a claw. The black circles under her eyes were masked by the shadow of her hood.

"You alright, Caitlyn?" Teddy asked.

"Don't use my real name in public," she said, breathing rather hard. "I'm alright."

She stepped past him. A crystal vial like the one Mrs. Sands had sat on the grass where the Manslayer's remains were only moments before. Caitlyn fired a lightning bolt into the vial, incinerating it.

"You don't look alright," he noted.

"I'm fine." She leaned up against a nearby birch, regaining her breath.

He knew better, but let it go. "Have you seen Rock? He was off trying to call your cousin."

"He's fine. When I was flying over here, I saw him running back this way from down the trail."

Teddy glanced back to the tree the Manslayer's host had been up against. Teddy had finally recognized the name of the man. Felix Barfield was one of the escaped prisoners who completely vanished. He had a different hair style and some elaborate makeup on his cheekbones, but it was the same face from the mug shot the internet loved to post. The Order was involved in that escape after all.

"You shouldn't worry about that man," Caitlyn said. "The Manslayer was the real threat. But the fire made short work of it. Anyway, we really should try to combine lightning and fire like that more often. If it's that incredible, then I bet even Jero wouldn't stand up against us."

He licked his dry lips, and turned back to her. "What did the Manslayer mean when it said Barfield was trapped?"

"It really doesn't matter. He accepted the deal, he escaped from prison, and he helped the Order achieve their goals. He made his choices, and now he has to live up to them regardless of what he *thought* he signed up for. I'd consider going after him if we didn't have much more important things to worry about."

"Can I ask you something?"

"You *could.* Will you?"

He rolled his eyes. Girls were always so pointlessly pedantic.

"What is the Order of the Ash?" he asked. "What is it *really?*"

"What are they?" She glanced up at the sky for a moment. "Bad guys."

"That's it? That's very simple coming from you. I thought you hated stories. Since when do you believe in bad guys?"

"I believe in objective reality. It is what it is. The Order wants us all to die; I don't want to die. They are obviously not good."

"That's why they did a number on you." He looked her over again. "These guys are evil and they need to be stopped. I get that. But what I don't get is why you don't seem so fazed by what happened to Barfield. Do you know something about these guys you aren't telling me?"

"Does this face look familiar to you?" She stared Teddy in the face, and pulled back her hood. He'd never seen this version of her up close. Her transformed cheek bones and narrow forehead reminded Teddy of the Phantom Maiden. However, this face was far more beautiful, glowing warmth even as Caitlyn frowned. "Well?"

"So this has something to do with the Phantom Maiden."

She shrugged. "So, you get it? It's my business."

"Your secrets mean nothing," Teddy said. "You don't need to worry about them anymore."

"Don't I?"

"Hello?" He said with a grin. "Pyre Knight's here, lady! I'm on your side, remember?"

She stared at him a few moments. Then she craned her neck as if listening to the wind.

He heard it, too. Someone was coming.

White streaks of smoke billowed out of the woods. It moved toward their location as if it had legs. Teddy didn't have to guess at what it was.

Rock Carson weaved between trees before them, and slid across orange leaves and mud. He was still wearing the grey armor. Smoke steamed off of him as he skidded to a stop before them.

He panted. "That was more exercise than I was hoping to have anytime soon."

"You made the call?" asked Teddy.

"She's here, ain't she?" He nodded to Caitlyn who awkwardly waved back. "Also, I think I figured out my element."

"Smoke isn't really an element," Caitlyn said.

"I get smoke, the Boss gets fire. What a rip off."

Teddy glanced between the two of them. "Good to see you both, anyway."

"You should have heard the Princess here. She tore the phone away from the suit and asked for our location. She was nearly screaming her head off. Girl's got fire."

"Really?" Teddy blinked.

Caitlyn blushed. "I take my job seriously."

"I'm glad she came when you did," Rock said. "Most of the bugs flew off when they saw her. Although that giant bonfire from before also helped. How did you do that? That thing hit the sky. What happened to the Manslayer?"

Teddy filled Rock in on all that happened. They still needed to find out where the Parasite was. The forest was too big to bumble through without a plan.

"Unfortunately," Teddy said, "the jerk didn't give me a single clue."

"When I flew over here," Caitlyn said, "I spotted one area of trees to the northwest that had been toppled over. They were probably taken down by the Stone Eater."

"No one else would be there this time of year," Teddy said.

Rock shrugged. "You would know, Boss."

The northwest horizon did indeed look off. The sky and the clouds bent like a mirage. Teddy's blood boiled, and his fists tightened. The Order had done something to his forest.

The Knights ran on, and the Maiden flew overhead. They whipped past groves of birches and pines. Carpets of green grass were stained with wet mud from the storm. The stink intensified the further the group traveled. Teddy's sixth sense told him he was on the right path.

"Hey, Caitlyn," Teddy said, calling to the Lightning Maiden above him. "How are your bones doing?"

"My bones are strengthened when I transform. But I don't get a boost of physical power, just energy. I don't work like you guys."

Rock nodded. "Is that why you slept in this morning, while the Boss and I were up in an hour?"

"Yes," she said. "Maidens are different from Knights. We destroy shadows and purify. You slay demons and monsters. Two sides of the same coin, I guess."

"How many of you are there?" Teddy asked.

She paused. "That's a long story. I think we should concentrate on what's ahead of us."

"You ain't telling us everything," Rock said. "I know that much. If I'm gonna die, I want to know what I'm dying for, and who. I hate this town, and everyone in it, remember? I should just get my pa and leave town. I don't even know why I'm here."

"You know," Teddy said. "You're here because you're a Knight, bringer of Light. Remember the coin? If you still need to know why you're risking your life, maybe you should reconsider this line of work."

Rock paused, and then laughed. He didn't bring it up again.

"Look guys, it's just complicated," Caitlyn said. "I'm sorry if I've been obscure. I have a lot on my mind."

Teddy grunted. "The only obscure thing is the reason you came alone. What is happening in New Sun City right now?"

"A lot of Dustwalker sightings," she said, raising both hands. "And don't make me explain *those* now. That's a whole other kettle of rotten fish. Needless to say, the other four Maidens are dealing with them now. They have enough problems. I came here because, well, I have something I need to do here."

"That woman," Teddy said. The Phantom Maiden and Caitlyn had some relationship he wasn't privy to. But he wasn't just going to let the girl from his dreams have her way. "I'll let you help us on one condition."

"And that is?"

"You have to read some *Rangers of the Endless Frontier* comics with the two of us when we get back. Alright? I'm gonna give you some decent taste if it kills me."

Caitlyn did a double take. "Are you serious?"

Rock laughed.

"Yeah," Teddy said. "I am."

She shook her head, still flying onward. "Fine, I'll read your silly comics. Let's just get this done."

Teddy laughed with Rock. He thought he caught the edges of a smile from Caitlyn.

She explained where she'd been all day. Those Dustwalker creatures had popped up all over New Sun City, and the Maidens were hunting them. The girls purified them with their powers when they hunted them down. Caitlyn *slid* back to the MacIsaac household, after things were under control. She had already returned when Mr. West received Rock's call. She flew out to the woods as fast as she could.

"So they're still dealing with that stuff," Teddy said.

"The more people I slide with, the more it drains. Not to mention, they have their hands full as it is."

"Glad you're alright." Teddy grimaced. New Sun City was a puzzle. But it was one that would have to wait. "Tell me, Caitlyn, do you know anything about the knights that came before me? Well, *us*."

"There was no Grey Knight before me," Rock said. "That's why I'm the only one of us who has their real face right now."

"I don't know what you are, Rock," she said. "There are

only three Knights of the End in the legend. There is no Grey Knight among them."

"Oh boy, I'm special. I feel like I'm back in the guidance counselor's office in third grade. I showed him, though. Next Red Rover game I played, I took them *all* down hard. Detention was worth it."

Caitlyn rolled her eyes. "Think of it this way, Rock. Now you have a reason to do stupid things like that. It's good to feel like what you do, matters."

"And you don't feel that, Princess?"

"I'm too tired to feel anything most of the time."

Teddy laughed. "I'm going to make you a Rangers fan if it kills me."

"What is your obsession with that stuff?" she asked. "They're just stories."

"That's exactly why you need them," Teddy replied.

The forest was deep into autumn. The fallen orange and brown leaves and bare branches had waited everywhere. Soon they would disappear and be lost in a cleansing snowfall, leading to Teddy's least favorite season. But that didn't compare to what lay before him.

A trail of destruction led on ahead of them. Tall oaks had been ripped from their base, and birches were toppled over in heaps. Large stones under the earth had been pulled out and left strewn about everywhere. Upturned dirt and scourged trees lay on either side of their path. Eventually, the forest widened into an open field of boulders and stone. Teddy nearly swore when he saw it, his rage growing.

"What's wrong, Boss?"

"This was the deepest part of the forest." Teddy gritted his teeth. He'd been there many times in the summer season over the years. He camped out there with his father and his brothers. He'd played with friends there. "It *was* the deepest part. Now it's *this*."

The old world of Teddy's dreams had been pulled apart and defiled. This was reality. The Order wouldn't stop with McLeod, they would destroy everything else. He couldn't let that happen.

They slowed to a walk, and Caitlyn landed beside them. The wide field of destruction gave way to a sloping hill. They climbed over the top, and his blood pressure rose again.

There sat a fortress made of stone. It looked like it was made in another era, surrounded by broken rocks left thrown about where the grove of pines had been. The impossible structure was twenty stories high with plenty of windows that peeked into the darkness inside. Two spires on both sides rested against its massive height. Broken, dead trees were left crumpled against the castle walls.

This monstrosity could only have been made by the Order. It was made only to spit in his face, and to mock his town. The Order had only built it to proclaim their inevitable victory.

"Someone made this," Teddy said. He uncurled his fists and let himself cool off. "Someone destroyed everything for this garbage."

"The Stone Eater," Caitlyn said. "He can manipulate stone and rock. He's built underground bunkers all over New Sun for the Order."

Teddy nodded without looking away. It could only have been that murderer. He would really enjoy scorching that scum to ash.

"So, what do we do, Boss?"

Caitlyn put a hand on Teddy's shoulder. "The Pyre Knight leads his charge."

He glanced at them both. There was much of a decision to make.

He nodded to Rock. "We finish it."

Chapter 19
Last Attack

The castle was almost alive. Teddy wiped his gauntlet across the stone. A thick, green slime slid off his armored hand and plopped on the muddied earth. It was the same ooze from the mall.

Thunder boomed. A purple aura wafted in between the storm and the clouds. A figure flew down through the downpour.

The Phantom Maiden hovered above them. She still wore her black robes, and her fractured face was as ugly as ever. Rain doused her pale skin.

Her cracked face broke into a grin. "Well, if it isn't the Pyre Knight, the Maiden of Faith, and the help. You all look half dead."

"You are insane," Caitlyn said. "This whole campaign against McLeod has been a mess. All this just to get one knight. Jero must be so disappointed in a failure like you."

The Phantom Maiden's expression darkened. "And you would know all about failure, wouldn't you?"

"As far as I can tell, I've inherited a curse." Caitlyn pulled back her hood, revealing the transformed face. "In more ways than one."

"The World of Man is a disease," the Phantom Maiden said. She dared not glance into Caitlyn's eyes, looking instead to the knights. "They cannot save themselves from slipping into despair, tilting into madness, and falling into the abyss. You are fighting a losing war, Maiden. So just let it fall."

"Never." She spoke through gritted teeth.

Teddy decided to sidestep the argument. "Where is the Parasite?"

"You are going to die here, Pyre Knight, and your home will be razed. I've lived far too long to know that you don't measure up to the best. You're just a pale imitation of those that have come before you." She glanced at Caitlyn. "You both are."

"I never claimed to be the best," Teddy said. "I never claimed to be anything! But I promised I would stop you back at the school—and I plan on keeping that promise. A man's word—"

"—is iron clad," Rock finished.

Teddy shrugged. "Yeah, what he said."

"Is that all you have to say? This is why you refuse to back down?"

"Exactly, lady," Rock said. "We're the Knights of the End. And you're in the way."

"Heroes are the worst sort of scum. Meet us inside, and I will show you what all your meaningless resistance will amount to."

The Phantom Maiden lifted into the air, purple lightning crackling. She vanished into the storm clouds.

Thunder raged on.

Caitlyn's face fell, and she put her hood back on. Rock's mood soured. The evil woman ruined the atmosphere.

Teddy approached the castle door. The sight of the thick wood aggravated him. He didn't even bother to check which tree it was made of.

He unsheathed the Red Sword and sliced open the front door. It erupted it into a fireball, and then crumbled to ash.

"I'm going in," Teddy said.

"Me too, Boss."

"Right behind you," Caitlyn said.

"Neither of you have to come, you know."

Rock clapped him on the shoulder, and walked past him into the castle. "What part of *punching through walls* do you not understand? I'm living the dream! You ain't getting rid of me."

"It is a sweet gesture," Caitlyn said, "but silly. You have no chance in there alone, and you know it."

"Kid," Teddy said, "what I don't know could fill four hundred libraries."

"Don't call me *kid*."

"We also have to work on that attitude of yours." Teddy stretched his arms and legs. He loosened up. "My point is that things are going to get rough in there."

"Listen!" Caitlyn placed a hand on his shoulder. "The Phantom Maiden is not like the others. She's not just another Order lackey. You won't be able to beat her alone."

"Right." The Phantom Maiden had already hit Teddy with her purple lightning. He wasn't clamoring for more of it. "You know who she really is, don't you?"

"I do, but we need to get going. Lingering on the past will not help us deal with the present."

The heavy raindrops left them when they entered the castle. Rock had already been waiting halfway down the hallway, tapping his foot. They quickly joined him.

It stunk just as much inside the castle as it did outside. The walls were coated in mucus, looking oddly fragile. Wind whistled through the stone. The taste of garbage clung to Teddy's tongue.

They continued on. Stone pillars jutted up along the hall and polished granite coated the floors. The inside was at least twenty feet tall. It was impressive—at least, on the surface. It was oddly empty. There was nothing in any of the adjoining chambers. There were no paintings on the walls, no tables or chairs in the rooms, and no indication of life anywhere. It didn't feel like it was made yesterday—it looked as if it had been abandoned for centuries.

At the end of the wide hall was a winding staircase. It climbed up to what looked like the tops floor.

They traveled the stone steps. The dead silence from their enemies continued.

"The Phantom Maiden was the last Maiden of Faith," Caitlyn said. "She was the one before me. That's why we look the same."

Rock turned blank-faced. "I thought you were the Lightning Maiden?"

"My official title is the Maiden of Faith. Lightning Maiden is just the common name. Each of us Maidens of the Old World are named after both our powers and the virtue we represent at our core. At least, that's how it's traditionally worked."

"And what do you have faith in?" Teddy asked, over his shoulder.

"A few things," she said. "Purpose, life, love, God . . . but it's more than what *I* believe in. I'm the one who represents faith as a whole. My will cannot be shaken because others have to believe in what I represent—what we *all* represent. That includes you. I represent the faith that the Light will someday overtake the Dark. Whatever happens, I cannot fall."

"Well," Teddy said, "you were the one who found me. Far as I can tell, you're doing your job. But you could stand to loosen up a bit."

Rock shrugged. "That's the Princess, for you. Doesn't it get tiring carrying the world on your shoulders all the time?"

She bit her bottom lip. "Enough, you two."

"All this is fascinating," Teddy said. "Really. But we have some evil to slay."

"Right, Princess. How about getting to the point about this Phantom Maiden hag?"

"Alright. As I was saying . . ." Her voice fell dark. "She was the Maiden of Faith before I was. Not long after the Order was seemingly defeated for good, she disappeared. No one ever knew what became of her. Years later, when the Order reemerged, so did she—on their side. She was different. Dark. Her powers had also twisted with her soul, turning her into something much different. She was instrumental in killing the other Maidens, and destroying the Nameless Kingdom. And I will make sure she does not do the same here."

"Why did she turn tail and run in the first place?" Rock asked. "It feels like something's missing in this whole thing."

She shook her head. "I don't know why she did it. I just know that she betrayed both the Knights and the Maidens, and was responsible for this whole mess."

Teddy thought on it. "If she was a Maiden, then I don't get it. Wouldn't she be with that Jero guy who leads the Order? That's one powerful ally."

"That's because her powers are fading. She was once the most powerful of our enemies, and now she is past her peak. Every time we've fought, she has gotten weaker. The Order has no further use for her except to be a fly in our soup."

Rock blinked. "But they sent her after the Boss. He's a Knight. They can't think she's that useless."

"Unless they don't care if she dies," Caitlyn said, flatly.

Rock fell silent.

"That's cold," Teddy said.

"The four they sent here are only Captains. There are many more Captains where they came from. The Four Generals are the highest, with only Jero above them. The Phantom Maiden doesn't realize it yet, if she ever will, but she is a pale imitation of the Lightning Maiden. I think when I was given the Coin of Light; her powers were taken, and have been draining from her ever since."

She still didn't tell them everything. The previous war was still a mystery. The last Pyre Knight burned the world to ash, and the last Maiden of Faith was a villain. They were in the middle of something big. This was no child's game.

"Can I ask you something?" Caitlyn asked Teddy.

"Don't let me stop you."

"Do you have faith in anything? You asked me, I just thought it would be fair."

Teddy hadn't really thought about it before. Since starting High School he had turned inward, avoided everything he could, and all for a reason he didn't really understand. The world wasn't what he expected, and he wanted nothing to do with it. Now, he knew different. He thought he hated his school and everyone in it, but then he went out of his way to save them. He thought McLeod had become a worse place, but then he fought for it. He thought being a hero would change everything, make him better, but he was still untrained, sloppy, and getting by solely by the skin of his teeth. Only by pure grace was he still alive.

"When I was a kid," Teddy said, "I thought this world was a great place. It was a place I'd die to protect. At least, I thought so when I played games with my friends. But then I got older, and I screwed it up. I began to think the world in my head, the one I loved as a kid, was just a dream. High School and everyone in it confirmed it. But, it's not that simple. Now that I have the power to save both the world I loved as a kid and the one I hated as a teenager, I can see that they're both the same thing. They're both worth saving."

Caitlyn tilted her head. "So, you believe in the world?"

"No," Teddy replied. "I know that things are awful, and always will be awful, but there are also great things that will always be there. It's the same with people. Having the power to exterminate the bad, leaves you with more appreciation for the good, I guess. I have faith that the reason I was given the Coin of Light was to understand the difference. If I know what I'm protecting, I can be a hero. The Light chose me because of what I could be one day."

"Well, it's a start," she said. "You just need to stop reading those dumb stories."

"Not on your life, kid."

She rolled her eyes. "Oh, I give up."

"Hey," Rock interrupted. He was no longer in a jovial mood. The serious look on Rock's face was incredibly ill-fitting. The stink of the green slime probably didn't help. "I've been thinking about what you said earlier, Princess. About the war in that old world, and junk. I know what bothered me about your story. We lost the last war. The Order won. No matter how much we beat them back, we still lost in the end."

"We didn't win," Caitlyn answered, "but we didn't lose, either. We drove them back and decimated their forces the first time we clashed. But the years afterwards were what did us in. Overconfidence, disillusion, corruption, emptiness: we became shells of what we once were. I think that might have been what ended up turning the Phantom Maiden. She didn't think it would ever end. Then the Order attacked, and easily overtook everything. She knew which side was the better one to bet on."

There was also the world of ash. Teddy didn't bother to bring up another failed battleground. The fight never really ends. Not until the Dark has nothing left to leech on. The Rangers knew that too well.

Teddy licked his lips. "And here I thought the Order was responsible for everything."

"They got exactly what they wanted," Caitlyn said. "Kevin always says that it doesn't take much for a man to fall, but it takes a lot for him to stand back up. This war is much older than us, and we should be prepared to deal with the fact that it won't end with us, either."

Teddy's sixth sense kicked in. He cocked his ears. The slime on the stone had been bothering him for some time now. The wall itself was breathing. The stink of mold twisted into something more familiar.

Ash.

They exited the stairway into the hall on the top floor. Rock and Caitlyn went on talking. Teddy watched the walls.

More stone pillars, this time with curves like an hourglass awaited them. The dark halls, and blackened floors, were as perfectly symmetrical and expertly crafted as the entranceway. This place was built to last. Teddy tightened his fists.

"Hate to break up the history class, kids," Rock said. "But just because other people screwed up and lost, it doesn't mean we will. We're not them."

Teddy shook his head. "We're just as capable of screwing up, just like I screwed up at the school. You said it yourself— you can punch through walls. What if you decide people are better targets? Who will stop you? How much money could you get from someone who wanted to buy your abilities? Pay attention to your surroundings."

"Yeah, yeah, whatever. We're not in school, so stop trying to teach. I'm not as weak as you think I am."

A bubble moved in the right side of the hallway. Teddy watched it from the corner of his eye. He needed to make sure not to bring attention to it.

The hall led out into an open dining hall. A large wooden table at least forty feet long lay in the center of the room. There were no chairs. The dining hall was cavernous and round, like the inside of a giant badly cleaned fishbowl. It stunk just as awful. The leaking walls were almost breathing with ooze.

"The old woman who let you sleep on her couch," Teddy whispered. "Her son was killed by the Stone Eater."

Both Rock and Caitlyn flinched. Teddy kept his eye on the pulsing wall.

"Why are you telling me now, Boss?"

The bulge moved against the right wall. Teddy drew his sword, and the blaze licked off the blade. He fired a blast of flame toward the bubble, blowing a chunk of stone directly out of the wall. There was now a hole into the empty bedroom beside them.

Caitlyn and Rock jumped. They both stared at him, confused.

"Thanks, Boss. I needed those last three years scared straight out of me."

"What was that about?" Caitlyn asked.

Teddy kept his sword drawn toward the large hole. He didn't glance away. "I told you that about her son, because his killer is on the other side of that wall."

"What?" Rock glanced toward the broken stone.

An object in the darkened opening jumped back into the stone. The wall bubbled again.

Teddy followed the moving pattern pulsing against the slime. It slid up and down, getting close to the three intruders. It was coming from the right. The pattern was stupidly simple.

Teddy fired red flames from his sword once more. The blast struck the mucus covered wall. Stone exploded.

This time, a figure dove forward out of the solid rock. It skidded to a stop before the three of them as the wall was knocked out behind it. Stone covered the figure from head to toe like armor thicker than the fat of its body. The stranger regained his balance, and stood tall.

"Very good," the Stone Eater said. "How did you see me, Pyre Knight?"

"Help from a friend." Teddy was grateful to Mrs. Werner for Darryl's tip. He would have to thank her son the next time he saw him. "I have a very personal bone to pick with you, Stone Eater."

Broken rock crumpled into a smile where its ugly mouth was. "Do you?"

"You killed someone important to me."

Teddy remembered it. He thought of Darryl pulling him out of the garden one day when he was five, and Mrs. Werner apologizing to Mrs. MacIsaac for her son's laziness.

It was Teddy's fault for what happened, and yet Darryl accepted the blame. He was a good guy.

Flames spun at the end of the Red Sword. "You're going to pay for it, monster."

"You're going to have to be more specific, chief. I'm not as old as the witch, but I'm also no spring chicken. I've been at this for years. I didn't need the Order to get my foot in the door."

"If I'm going to cleanse this world of evil, I might as well start with a roach like you." Teddy pointed his blade forward. The monster might have the experience on him, but it didn't matter. "You will fall today."

"The words of an amateur. I'm going to enjoy smashing you to dust."

The Stone Eater sank into the wall behind him. He fell as if sliding through sand. The bulge disappeared in the slime-covered wall. Teddy had lost him.

"This entire fortress is my weapon," the monster said. His voice echoed around the stone.

"Hey, Boss," Rock whispered. "Did he really kill that lady's kid?"

Teddy breathed deep. "Keep your guard up."

Rock grunted. "If you say so."

Teddy stayed to the front, watching the walls. Rock and Caitlyn remained behind him. He had the point. This battle would be his.

"Look out!" Caitlyn yelled.

Teddy turned around. Rock looked down

Below Rock was an arm gripping onto his ankle. It

yanked, and pulled the boy down into the stone. The floor spread open like a sinkhole.

Caitlyn dove for his flailing arm, but he was already gone.

Cacophonous crashes like falling bricks rang out floors below. Teddy ran back toward Caitlyn, watching the cold ground. It was like a wrecking ball was slamming against the fortress pillars underneath them. The Stone Eater was on the move.

"Move forward," Teddy whispered. "We need to get out of this room. He has too much of an advantage in here."

"But what about Rock?"

"He's made of tougher stuff than us." The rattling of stone was climbing higher. Soon, it would reach their floor. "Let's move!"

They continued forward. The hallway shook. The Stone Eater chuckled throughout the castle walls. He was getting closer to the pair.

Teddy flung his fire through the halls ahead of them. The heat melted the mucus from the walls, though it also held the flames. They ran past the fire. The Stone Eater's laughs were falling further behind.

The path ahead spun into a winding maze. It was hard to tell where they were going. Behind them, the Stone Eater bounced between stone walls, floor and ceiling. He was dashing between the flames.

Caitlyn tossed lightning behind them. Rocks exploded into wet green ooze. Still, the Stone Eater advanced on them.

"What's the rush, heroes?"

Then, Teddy saw it. A large wooden door sealed off the hallway ahead in the path.

The castle walls were violently shaking. The Stone Eater was right behind them.

Teddy charged forward, shoulder first. He smashed through the wooden door, with Caitlyn just behind him. The door cracked into pieces. He slid forward on the floor, as Caitlyn spun around.

She blew the entranceway closed with her lightning. Stone rained down where the door had been. The laughing ceased.

They stared at the broken stone, catching their breaths.

"Boy," a voice said from behind them. "You are not having a good day, are you?"

The pair snapped their attention behind them. Three figures stood on a tall, fractured stone staircase leading up to the roof.

They were the Stone Eater, the Phantom Maiden, and the Parasite.

Chapter 20
Knock-Down Drag-Out

The Parasite stood at the top of the stairs, hands outstretched. His green skin cracked and broke around his palms. The pieces shattered and slid down to the stone steps. In the center of his palms were holes that continued up through his arms. Darkness stared out from the openings.

Small drops of greed blood sizzled in the monster's hands. Buzzing hummed from the holes, and small hornets streamed outward. They tumbled out in wide funnels, pouring out like water streams. The insects covered the ceiling of the twentieth floor, and were spilling out the open windows. The Parasite smiled, euphorically.

Teddy's stomach churned. He smelled death.

The hornets consumed stone on their way up, growing twice their side as they did so. They'd been doing it for some time. Patches of the outside storm poked through the openings in the top floor. The insects whirled out into the storm.

The Parasite blew strands of orange hair out of his green

face. "I see we're missing one of our guests."

"I sent him down a few floors," the Stone Eater said. He had been crouching near the bottom step, the Phantom Maiden standing beside him. "Some idiot in a knight costume. No idea what he was doing here."

The Parasite nodded. "I have a job to do. You two can handle the cleanup."

"Just what I like to hear."

The Stone Eater approached first, with the woman behind. The pair was grinning wide. They were as a pair of mountain lions cornering two gazelles.

Teddy and Caitlyn lined up side by side. Teddy raised his sword, and Caitlyn lifted her sparking hands. They glanced sideways at each other and nodded.

Teddy grinned. "Let's mix it up."

Caitlyn knelt, and shot lightning from her hands. Teddy waved his sword over her head as she ducked. Flame shot from the blade into the chest of the Phantom Maiden, just as Lightning leaped into the Stone Eater's stomach. The impact blew both enemies backwards.

The Phantom Maiden crashed back into the stairs, breaking stone out from behind her. The Stone Eater was thrown sideways through the wall on the left side of the room. They'd been knocked senseless.

Teddy and Caitlyn switched places again. Teddy jumped through the hole in the wall into the adjoining room. Caitlyn dashed toward the stairs.

The Pyre Knight brought his sword down on the fallen Stone Eater. The Lightning Maiden charged into the

Phantom Maiden with her hands flashing. Stone shattered all over the room.

The Stone Eater took the hit from Teddy's sword. Fire leapt out over him. He jumped backwards and sunk into the floor of the fortress. Teddy watched for movements in the castle walls. The slime on the walls caught ablaze as the enemy moved.

"Show yourself, murderer!" Teddy shouted.

The Stone Eater growled. "Fire is not enough to stop me, fool."

"I'll scorch you to dust," Teddy said. "What did you do to my friend?"

"You want to see him?"

An arm burst through the floor. Fire spurted off a stone limb. It took hold of Teddy's ankle. It pulled him downward with a jerk, through the fortress floor.

"Here you go!" the Stone Eater shouted.

The floors passed under Teddy as if they were intangible. Wind whipped against his armor instead of hard stone. The enemy fell below him as if swimming through the air between floors. He still gripped Teddy's ankle. The Stone Eater flowed through the stone. Then, as if bored, the Stone Eater whipped Teddy loose.

Teddy struck the floor. Stone crunched under him. Armor cracked. Before he could get up, he spotted the enemy. A stone hand gripped his leg once more. He sunk into the stone.

The stone castle spun. The enemy released him again. The boy again felt the stone floor underneath him as he landed. Armor cracked again. Once more, he was grabbed.

Teddy fell into one wall, and then another. Before he knew it he was already in the air again. He hit the floor. Rinse and repeat. The Stone Eater continued to toss him about the castle.

"Almost there," the Stone Eater said, laughing.

Teddy held back a groan. "You have a sick sense of humor."

The Pyre Knight landed again. He flipped over to his knees. Armor creaked as he stood up. The stone wall was streaked by burn marks all over, the slime crisping up. The red flames had still gripped onto the Stone Eater, and followed him about the fortress.

In the distance, the castle rumbled. A support beam or pillar must have been knocked loose somewhere.

Teddy raised his sword upward. He thought of the battle in the mall, and concentrated. He had enough power left to end this.

"Don't take this too personally," Teddy said. Darryl would be able to rest in peace soon enough.

Light illuminated from the Red Sword. Fire spurted from the tip. It shot across the room like a twister, tearing stone. Mucus on the walls and ceiling burst apart. The crimson blaze spread out and filled the destroyed room. The Stone Eater flew backwards with the impact. He skidded across the floor.

All the walls had been blown out. He could see the hallways surrounding the destroyed room.

The castle quaked yet again.

"Your flames sting, Knight," the Stone Eater said. He slid up through the floor. The enemy had been charred, his solid skin stained black. "But you will not be able to pierce my stone."

"Flames don't pierce, genius. They burn, and they mark."

The Stone Eater checked over his body. His stone was smoking. The black scorch would not rub clean anytime soon. There would be no more running away.

"This isn't permanent." The monster swore under his breath. "You haven't won."

"No, but it does stop you from what you love to do." Teddy flipped his sword onto his shoulders. "No more hiding from me."

The ceiling broke, and began to crumble. Whatever was shaking the fortress was getting closer.

"This is nothing!" the Stone Eater shouted. "You are only an amateur!"

The wall behind the Stone Eater burst open. A figure stepped through the hole, panting heavily. The Stone Eater turned to face it, and swore again.

Out of the opening stepped the Grey Knight, panting. His breathing was strained, and his armor was crumbling with the fortress. His anger overwhelmed exhaustion. The boy growled underneath his cracked grey helmet. His glare stabbed the Stone Eater. The Knight sprinted forward.

"You threw me down five floors." Rock's voice leaked malice. He raised his fists, since he had somehow lost his swords. He bolted straight to the Stone Eater. "Now I'm going to throw you through ten!"

The agitated youth delivered a straight punch to the Stone Eater's jaw. A chunk of rock the size of a golf ball broke off in the hit. The enemy stumbled backwards.

"He's a real Knight?" the Stone Eater yelled, pebbles bursting from his mouth. "That isn't possible!"

"The Light works in mysterious ways." Rock charged forward. He slugged the Stone Eater once more in the face. "So sad for you."

Yelling a garbled mess, the Stone Eater threw an uppercut. The first swing whiffed. Rock had sidestepped. He wasn't lucky enough to avoid the second hit. The body blow crushed armor on Rock's right breastbone. A follow-up strike smashed into Rock's gut. He coughed saliva as armor broke off. But the boy wouldn't be deterred. He delivered a straight left to the shoulder of the enemy. The hit broke off yet more stone.

"I'll smash you into dust!" the Stone Eater screamed. "You are just a pretender! You're nothing!"

Swings flew back and forth between them. Rock laughed as they exchanged blows. The castle continued to fall in on them as they remained oblivious.

Teddy needed to end this quick. Rock was too frenzied. Unfortunately, there was no opening to take advantage of. The floor crumbled under him. The Pyre Knight jumped to the left. He was running out of opportunities.

Then, Teddy spotted something. It shone out of the wall beside him. He felt along the charred slime-covered wall. A flash of white lightning poked through a tiny hole the size of a pen tip. They were at the edge of the fortress.

The two behind Teddy battled on. He only had one idea left.

He placed his sword into the small opening, and pried into it. It was like digging for treasure. The hardened gunk easily peeled and chipped off the stone. The more he dug; the more muted light from the storm fell through.

After he broke the last rock, Teddy scanned it. They were fifteen floors up from the muddy earth and jagged stones of the overturned forest below. The fortress was still shaking. The crumbling stone was seconds from sealing them in to their deaths. He had one shot left to end it.

"Hey, Boss!" Teddy called out to his friend. Rock glanced at him. Faded light cascaded through the opening across smashed stone. "Remember what happened to Hoffman?"

Rock furrowed his brow. He circled around the enemy, leaving the Stone Eater's back to the storm. The enemy kicked him. A piece of armor broke off from his stomach. Rock kneeled before the enemy, clutching the new opening.

"Is this it, little man?" The Stone Eater chuckled. He swayed in place. "You might be wearing armor, but you're still a meat puppet. Gonna enjoy cracking you open."

Rock sneered. "It must be hard to talk with a broken jaw."

"What are you babbling about?" the enemy asked.

Rock charged forward, shoulder first. He lifted the enemy in the impact. The Stone Eater flailed. Rock charged in a straight line toward the light. Then, he tripped, letting the momentum carry the monster the rest of the way.

The enemy would have gone pale if his skin wasn't blackened stone. His eyes widened when he saw Teddy. The enemy fell backwards, unable to defend.

Teddy spun around, sword in hand. The swing of the sword shattered the monster's chest. Flames leaped all over the Stone Eater. The enemy stumbled back toward the opening, red flames consuming him whole.

The Stone Eater let out a howl. White lightning arched in the outside storm. The enemy's shadow flashed across the rubble of the castle.

"How do you think you'll like eating through a straw?" Rock asked.

A flurry of steps erupted behind Teddy. Rock shot out before him. A grey gauntlet slammed into the monster's face. The force sent the monster backwards, his eyes rolling in his head. The Stone Eater soared out of the opening into the storm, still ablaze.

"You'll burn nicely where you're going," Teddy said.

Screams sputtered out of the Stone Eater. Wind whistled against the red flames clinging to him. Chunks of his skin broke off in the downpour. The enemy plummeted fifteen stories, flailing uselessly. He struck down against upturned rocks. His body exploded in a shower of stone and rubble. Lastly, the flame flickered out with the Stone Eater's life.

Rain tapped against the remains down below. Nothing would get up from that.

A weight lifted from Teddy's shoulders. Darryl would rest easy now.

Rock spat on the floor, rubbing his bruised face. His

helmet was almost entirely gone. "I told him he should watch his jaw. That's what he gets for making someone's mom cry."

"Don't celebrate yet," Teddy said. A piece of stone ceiling fell down beside them. Rock jumped sideways. He narrowly avoided it crushing his head.

"What was that?" Rock asked, eyes darting around the room.

"We're going down!"

The creaks and groans of the castle roared louder. Around them, the walls and ceilings gave in. Stone shattered and cracked all around the open floor. There were only seconds left until it was rubble. The fortress was finished.

Then the ceiling fell in on them.

Chapter 21
Knight of Flames

The two Knights leaped into the storm. The castle rubble fell in behind them. They plummeted like falling boulders toward the ground.

The fifteenth floor crushed in on itself, and the fortress crumbled in. A symphony of crumbling stone played behind them.

"Tuck in!" Teddy yelled to Rock. "The armor will absorb most of the impact."

"Right!"

Teddy remembered his fall back at the school. If they landed just right, they would be okay. He brought his limbs close together, and balled himself up.

The pair struck the earth, indenting it. The ground shook. Their boots sunk into the soaked earth. The pressure cracked Teddy's armor all over. Beside him, Rock looked much the same as he did. Teddy's body cried out and his legs wobbled, but he forced himself forward. There was no time to think on it.

"Don't stop!" Teddy shouted. "Keep going!"

The pair charged forward. Heaps of stone landed around them. Mud pulled loose from the rain-soaked earth as they struggled forward. The fortress rained down upon them.

Green mucus and broken rocks crumbled behind them. Loose stones cracked down onto the earth. They ran past where the Stone Eater had been dashed into pieces on the jutting rocks. They made it several feet, until they were out of range.

Finally, it was finished. There was nothing left but rubble. Mist kicked up with the rain.

Rock laughed. He elbowed Teddy in the ribs. "Man, we just survived a fall from a castle ten stories up. Not even the stone guy did that. That's insane."

"I think it was fifteen." Teddy glanced at Rock's armor. There were deep fissures all over. It would break at any moment.

"Even better!" Rock wobbled.

"You're about to collapse, aren't you?"

Rock's armor flashed white, and Teddy shielded his eyes. When the brightness cleared, Rock was no longer transformed, but a normal teenager once again. He still had his cuts and bruises, though his clothes were untouched.

"I lost my swords in there," Rock said, sleepily.

"They'll return the next time you transform. For now, let's get you to safety and I'll go find Caitlyn."

"Up there, Boss." Rock pointed to the overcast sky.

Two women flew about the darkened skies. Flashes of white and purple light flowed from their wrists toward each other. It sounded like the air was being ripped apart. The pair dipped and soared through the skies.

"She can take the ugly chick, right?" Rock asked, his grin weakening. "I mean, do we need to jump in?"

"I thought you were raring to go?"

"I was, but for some reason I kind of want to take a nap." Rock fell sideways. Teddy grabbed him by the shoulder before he hit the mud. "Thanks, Boss."

Teddy led Rock by the shoulder. In the rubble was a particularly large overturned stone. It was still sturdy despite the collapse of the fortress. It was in an oblong shape, blocking the rain from pouring underneath. Rock leaned back against the stone in the center, and slid to the dry earth. His eyes drooped.

"Your armor doesn't look too good," Rock said. He let out a yawn. "There are more cracks than a sidewalk. You might be in trouble."

"It's always a pleasure talking with you, Rockhead."

"I know. I'm a half-full glass of sour milk."

"Stay put. I'll be back before you know it."

"I just need a few seconds." Rock fell limp against the stone. He breathed smoothly as he slept.

The Pyre Knight left the shelter behind for the battlefield. Rain clanged off his fractured armor. He wouldn't be able to take many more hits. The day's events were catching up to him. He couldn't afford to run dry like Rock.

Teddy scanned the remains of the fortress. The Parasite was nowhere to be found. There were no new hornets being sent into the sky. He peered around the castle rubble. Small rocks and pebbles crumbled under Teddy's boot steps.

He caught a glimmer in the sky. A purple lightning bolt struck the broken stone before him, spraying pebbles everywhere. Teddy slid forward against broken remains. More chunks of stone exploded where he had stood.

"Phantom Maiden," Teddy said under his breath. "Just what I needed."

The stone guarded him from the bolts. The dark clouds made it hard to find her. He cringed as a purple spark jumped off broken stone. Getting hit by her was not an option.

Another bolt fired through his shelter, splitting open the stone wall. It scorched the side of his helmet. He fell down. Finally, he spotted her above the trees to the east. She was aiming another shot.

Caitlyn was nowhere to be seen.

"Where are you, kid?" Teddy whispered.

A white bolt arched up from the forest. It narrowly missed the Phantom Maiden. Caitlyn flew up out of the forest and back toward her enemy. Her robe-like dress smoked. The two Maidens clashed in the sky.

Teddy breathed a sigh of relief. "That was a close one."

"Not close enough," someone said.

The Parasite emerged from a pile of debris behind Teddy. Rain streaked the bug man's unkempt hair. Rubble slid off him. The bug man limped a few steps down the melting green mucus in the wreckage. His smirk was nowhere to be seen.

"Didn't make it out in time, did you?" Teddy asked.

The villain smiled without humor. "Don't worry; I have enough left to finish you off."

"You're just as beat up as I am." Teddy gripped the handle of his sword tight. "If you think I'm going to let you walk out of this, you're just as crazy as you are ugly."

"Speaking of crazy . . ." The Parasite's scowl betrayed his attempt at control. "Who was that Grey Knight? Where did he come from?"

"The same place all the Knights of the End came from."

"What are you babbling about? That's not an answer."

"You'll get your answer when you're dead." Teddy readied his blade.

"You managed to destroy countless members of my children and clones, the Manslayer, and the Stone Eater. You are one lucky idiot. If it wasn't for the sword in your hands, you'd be dead twenty times over."

"I am the Pyre Knight," Teddy replied. "I obliterate evil, and you're standing in my way."

The Parasite laughed, wheezing. "This is why I hate kids. Idealistic idiots. There are no such things as heroes, boy. They're all liars. They're snake-oil salesman selling phony hope to a bunch of rubes out in the sticks. There is nothing special about you, punk."

He stumbled as he stepped forward. Teddy laughed back at the clueless monster.

"Want some more? You must like losing."

"No, I just enjoy a good slaughter. And that's what this is." The enemy pointed to the sky. "That woman up there is one of the five Maidens of the Old World. You and your grey lackey make seven in total."

"And you are part of a group of four freaks that attacked my town. I can do math, too! So, what's your point?"

"Four? Are you really that short-sighted? We're not even Generals, boy. You're three of seven—we're four of hundreds. We're insects. If you step on us, there will be far more to take our place. Meanwhile there are only a handful of you. You went through all this for what basically amounts to nothing. Don't you get it? This town will fall whether we're the ones to do it or not!"

"Are you going to fight, or are you going to brag? I already promised that I'd wipe you out. You know what they say about a man's promise, don't you?"

"Enough!" The Parasite lifted his right hand and jerked two fingers upwards. An earthquake of mud shook around him. Stone broke under the rubble of the castle. Two dozen Parasite clones emerged, covered in dirt and grime. They all were as beat up worn down as the original.

"This again?" Teddy asked.

The orange-eyed freak smiled, and cracked his knuckles. "You're almost out of juice."

The monster wasn't wrong. Teddy's vision had been blurring since Rock passed out. Muscles ached. He only had one good shot of flames left in him.

"Look who's talking," Teddy replied. His muscles twitched and grinded.

The sky burst more lightning. Holes appeared where clouds had been pierced. Flashes of white and purple lightning struck the tops of trees and the rubble of the fortress.

Teddy straightened up. Caitlyn had been using her powers most of the day. If she could tough it out, then Teddy could do the same.

The clones shambled toward him.

"This is going to end the same way as last time," Teddy said, holding his sword forward. He could still cut them down, but he couldn't risk using his flames.

"Don't get cocky just because of your tremendous luck. You're out of power, and time." The Parasite snapped his fingers. His puppets darted in a full run. "Now just stand still, and I'll try to make it quick."

The clones sloppily dove upon the Pyre Knight. Their blows scraped against his armor. He parried and thrust back. Every slash hurt his muscles, but he fought through it, cutting them apart.

Screams erupted from the clones. Teddy let out a hard breath as he cut through the last one. The shells of the Parasite returned to dust in the rain. Two dozen down.

Teddy stared at his sword. Even without flame, it was still a sight to behold.

"I hate kids so very much," the Parasite said, growling.

"Murderers don't get to complain," Teddy said. "I've got one good flame blast I've been saving for you."

The Parasite shook with fury. Then, a smile fell over his greasy lips. "You have no idea how this world is about to change, or how much it already has. Even if you defeat me— everything is going to be different tomorrow. The old world is gone. It's not coming back."

"Right." Teddy knew that. He might have been wrong about the world, but it was still worth defending. "This is the world I live in. It might not be what I wanted it to be, but it's still my world. You're not welcome in it."

The Parasite spread his arms, and shook his head. "I should have leveled that whole gymnasium myself.

The sky flashed white, blinding Teddy. A scream choked from of the sky, as a figure fell. The Phantom Maiden slammed into the mud ten feet beside the Parasite. Her black robes smoked. She stood beside the Parasite, clutching her ribs.

The Lightning Maiden landed beside Teddy. Her robes faintly glowed purple, and she was cut all over. She dropped to one knee, breathing heavily.

"You couldn't even beat one Maiden on your own?" the Parasite asked his ally. "No wonder Master Jero sent you out here."

"Shut up," the Phantom Maiden said. "The whelp only got lucky."

"Well," the Parasite said, with an awkward pause. "Time for Plan B."

The Phantom Maiden stood before the Parasite. They stared into each other's eyes, their breaths stiff. They grabbed something around each other's necks and pulled back. Caitlyn called out, but it was too late. The vial on the chain around their necks shattered. Darkness swam over both enemies.

The Phantom Maiden and Parasite shouted. The black slick consumed them whole like a black ball of oil. Popping noises filled the air around the darkness until the screams died out. Black electricity crackled around the ball of darkness.

Teddy knelt down beside Caitlyn and took her arm. He lifted her up, and she let out a yell. Her left foot dragged.

"Can you stand?" Teddy asked.

"I can fly." She hovered half a foot from the mud. "We have something far worse to worry about."

"You looked like you knew what they were doing. What was that?"

"You'll see."

As if on cue, the ball of black tar burst like a balloon. Sparks lashed out around it. It took a second before both the darkness and electricity vanished in the downpour.

The two looked upon the new terror before them. Caitlyn let out a shiver, and hovered back a foot. Teddy instinctively tightened the grip on his sword.

A single monster, straight from Hell, stared back at them.

Chapter 22
Deep Darkness

A single creature emerged from darkness, instead of two. It towered over the Pyre Knight at twelve feet tall, with long black hair covering every inch of its pale white body. It hunched like an ape with thickness in its limbs to match. Stiff joints and jerking shoulders followed its every erratic movement. Its face was as a warthog's—only smashed in with a hammer.

It let out a pathetic, watery roar. Its beady, fogged eyes, large as marbles, glanced toward the Knight and Maiden standing in the rain-soaked remains. The creature made one step forward.

Teddy felt the urge to take a step back, but resisted. He brought his sword behind his back. The heat built up in the blade.

The boy gathered as much energy in the sword as he could. He needed to scrape deep inside for the last of his fire.

The beast took another step forward. Teddy threw out his red flames. The creature was struck in the face. It did not even attempt to dodge.

He already knew the result before the smoke cleared. There was not even a burn mark to be seen. The beast took another slow step forward.

"Where's Rock?" Caitlyn asked. Her face paled sheet white. "We could really use him now."

"He's out of energy, and sleeping. I could go wake him up, but he won't be able to do anything."

"Beautiful."

"Watch out!" Teddy shouted.

The monster leaped forward, black fur blurring in the rain. Its claws crashed down. The blow landed upon Caitlyn's shoulders. Teddy moved in. He shoved Caitlyn aside, and met the attack. The beast landed on him, claws out.

The Red Sword guarded against the razor-sharp nails. The monster's full weight bore down on him. Armor creaked. Teddy slid backwards in the mud. Thankfully, the blade held strong.

Teddy's muscles throbbed. The ground underneath him sank and twisted. He pushed back against the chimera, his armor cracking under the pressure. If it wasn't for the Red Sword, he would have been smashed into dust.

The creature howled in his face. The stench of mucus and ash wafted out of its mouth. It leaned in closer.

A bolt of lightning grazed the side of Teddy's helmet. The white flash struck the monster in its open mouth. It flipped backwards in the mud onto its bare, hoofed feet, and leaped away into the downpour.

The beast landed on top of a nearby oak, cracking it

underneath its weight. There were no marks where the lightning struck. It glanced down with a vacant, confused stare.

"Well, this ain't good," Teddy said. His breaths were falling harder. "What is that thing?"

"I was expecting something . . . else. The Dark consumed them both. I've never seen it do this before."

The chimera made one more arching jump into the storm, landing in the remains of the fortress where the Stone Eater had landed in pieces. The creature hopped around the wreckage. It moaned mindlessly and hoisted chunks of broken stone roof onto its shoulders with no effort. The creature spun in a circle, and let the large hunk out of its claws. The stone slab soared into the stormy sky. After flying over half of the forest, the remains finally descended. Stone and trees rumbled where the projectile. The forest shook.

"Teddy," Caitlyn whispered. "I think we're in trouble."

Sweat rolled into his eyes after that understatement of the century. "Tell me you know how to beat this."

"I'm sure Kevin has told you about how Jero and the Order learned how to twist Life Force."

"Yeah, they turned it into Dark Energy. It gives them incredible power with a risk. That's why these guys we fought were so ugly looking."

"There's a cost in using the Dark Energy," she said. "You can bend it to your will to give you tremendous strength, but it can turn on you at the drop of a hat."

"Breaking that vial gave them an overdose?"

The beast threw more giant rocks into the air, and

danced about. It moaned mindlessly as it picked up more stone. The monster was trying to fight the sky.

"This is what happens when the Dark Energy takes control," Caitlyn said. "There's no more free will. There's no more consciousness. That is a risk of using it. But I didn't think *this* would happen."

The monster went on thrashing the wreckage.

Teddy shook his head. "You still haven't told me how I beat it."

"I've never seen one of these things before. The Phantom Maiden's powers must have warped the transformation. I don't think they planned for this to happen. I can't imagine they would."

"I've got no fire left." He tightened the grip on his sword. "But I can cut it until it stops moving."

"It doesn't even remember we're here. We could probably walk away and it wouldn't even notice."

"Until it eventually gets into town," Teddy said. "I'm not letting these things touch McLeod."

She forced a smile. "I won't have to read your comics if we die, you know."

He gave her a grin in return. "All the more reason to finish this thing."

Sword drawn, the Pyre Knight charged. Teddy brought his blade back, and jumped. He brought his sword down just as the monster turned around.

His helmet crunched. A backhand struck him. Teddy slid across the muddy ground. He flipped over himself, his helmeted head striking the mud and stone. A large boulder met his back, finally stopping him. The rock split in two.

Pain seared into his skull. The world faded for a second. He pushed himself up and his body fought him. The remains of his helmet tumbled into the mud. He watched the pieces of his broken helmet fade away.

"Teddy!" Caitlyn caught up with him.

Purple lightning surged from the monster. It sparked out from the mucus dripping down the monster's tree trunk arms. If it hit like a truck, then Teddy needed to hit like a train.

Teddy spat liquid from his mouth. He hoped it wasn't blood.

"We need a new approach," he said.

"I could have told you that, *Rockhead*."

"Very funny," Teddy replied.

She sighed. "Its weak point is probably its heart. Whenever you strike one on a Dustwalker, it usually destroys them. Only problem is that this is nothing like a Dustwalker. They aren't this strong, or fast."

He didn't bother to ask what those were. "Then we just need to cut through it without getting backhanded all the way to New Sun City. Sounds like fun."

The creature's flesh stirred. Its white skin twisted and shifted underneath the black fur slick. The chimera went back to smashing the stone. It had already forgotten the pair's presence. Teddy shook his head as he looked it over. If it had a heart, or anything close to one, they would still need to get through that skin.

"I do have a trump card," Caitlyn said.

He kept watching the chimera. "Then use it."

"I'm going to have to trust you, Teddy."

"It's nice to have people believe in you."

"I didn't want to have to do this." She glanced down at her hands. White lightning cracked. "I'm going to use the Blind Lightning. It's our best shot. Please don't lose yourself."

"What are you talking about?" he asked. "Stop waffling around and say what you mean. We need to beat this thing, kid. So whatever you're going to do—just do it!"

A small tornado of wind swirled around the Maiden of Faith. Her hands blew white sparks into the gust, and her eyes pulsed light. She caught his stare, and, for some reason, he knew exactly what she was going to do. It was a bad idea.

A bolt of terrific white lightning fired into his chest. Pain shot through him. Electric currents spun inside.

"Caitlyn, what are you doing?"

"We can't do this separately." She staggered, and bit her lip. "My Blind Lightning and your fire together should give you what you need."

Searing lightning whipped through his bones. Words choked in his throat. He was being filled over capacity and his glass soul was starting to crack. But somewhere inside, he heard an ember of flame begin to flicker.

The lightning ran out, and she stumbled over. Her robes faded into the wind with her powers. Teddy dashed over. His speed was insane. She fell into his arms with a dead weight. No longer was she the Lightning Maiden.

Now she was back to her usual self. Her blonde hair

flapped in the breeze. She gazed up at him, her blue eyes narrowing.

"Hold yourself together," she whispered.

"That's what I was going to say. What did you do?"

"Don't worry about me. I'm just drained, not dead."

"What did you do to me?" White lightning rolled across his fractured armor and into his skin. It lashed out against his heart and lungs. White sparks fell from his skin like electric sweat. "It feels like I'm being grinded into paste."

"It's an ancient technique." She groaned. "I can use my lightning to charge a Knight past his limit. It was what helped to defeat the Order the first time. But there is a catch."

"Yeah, you have no power left."

She shook her head. "But you have more now. The problem is that you have to control it. You have to hold together to beat this thing. I'm sorry I put all my chips on you like this."

"I don't know what you're talking about," he said, teeth chattering through the surge flowing inside him. "But I'll do what I can. My family, Mrs. Werner, Rock, you, even Stieg . . . I can't let them down."

"Good." Her eyes slowly shut, and her voice faded. "Then, get moving."

The beast thrashed around the rubble, mindlessly. It still had no interest in them.

Teddy jumped back, Caitlyn in his arms. White electricity burst from his boots. His height easily eclipsed that of the Manslayer—and it took no effort. He grinned over the twisting pain.

He brought the girl to where Rock lay sleeping. The shelter held strong from the rain, and it was far from the battle. He placed Caitlyn against the stone. The pair slept soundly.

"Wish me luck, guys," he said.

The Pyre Knight jumped back to the battle. A snap of power surged through his legs. The air whipped around him. He could do anything. An ecstasy grew inside of him. The white lightning told him that he could crack the world in two. He believed it.

Teddy landed in the mud thirty feet from the monster. He stepped through the rainstorm like a blur. For the first time since it emerged, the chimera deliberately faced him. It backed away as he approached.

It knew the truth. He wasn't just a Knight—he was a god now.

The monster took a step back.

"That's right," Teddy said. He laughed. "You know what I am now, don't you? Even something like you feels fear."

The Pyre Knight lifted his blade, and white lightning rolled off him. The tiny spark of flame inside of him caught light like gasoline on a bonfire. White, crisp flames gushed like a geyser. He would burn the world down.

Black was white, and white was black. It hit Teddy like a wrecking ball. Pain for pleasure. The world made perfect sense.

"I am a Knight of the End!" he shouted into the storm. Flames spilled from the Red Sword. Lightning bounced off his every step forward in the mud. "We are Agents of the

Light come to extinguish the Dark. You will be sent back to the abyss you crawled from. Cry and gnash your teeth. It will make no difference."

The chimera barely kept up with his approach. It flinched when it noticed him standing before it.

He cut into the beast. The slash tore through its chest in a single swing. White sparks rolled along the black fur. The monster didn't bleed, or flinch, though it caught ablaze in the white fire.

The chimera swung a claw down. Teddy sidestepped. Another swipe went for his head, striking air. Teddy was already standing behind the creature.

The boy laughed. The beast spun around, its left arm bared. It struck into Teddy's ribs. A crack reverberated through the woods.

"Good one," Teddy said, grinning.

The beast howled in pain. Its left arm hung limply at its side at a wrong angle. It warbled around, clutching its shattered appendage. Another watery roar escaped its throat. It backed away from the Pyre Knight, whimpering.

"No lie," the Pyre Knight said. "This will probably hurt a lot."

The Red Sword stabbed through the chest opening Teddy had made. White lightning leaped off of him as if he were too fast to contain the energy.

The monster froze in its tracks, its whines silenced.

A voice rang in Teddy's head. *"Focus, Theodore MacIsaac. Cleanse, and purify."*

"This is everything I have," Teddy said, gritting his teeth. The world would soon turn red.

Fire exploded out of the beast. A geyser of white flame spun up into the sky. An iron feeling tightened in Teddy's gut as the beast shrieked.

This flame was different. The Red Sword soaked in white lightning, was far beyond him. Purified waves of light flowed out into the beast and out into the forest behind it. Unsteady trees were knocked down, and cracked boulders in the battlefield shattered. The white flames consumed everything, including Teddy.

"*It is done.*"

The lightning that had once filled him with passion, overturned. Familiar warmth fought its way through the cracks in his fracturing mind, and gripped his soul tight. Fear overrode his pleasure, as his armor shattered into a thousand pieces in the burning white flames. He begged them to burn out as he fell.

The world glowed pitch white before him.

And then it turned black.

Chapter 23
Knights of the End

"Open your eyes, Theodore MacIsaac."

The warm voice took Teddy out of his slumber. He blinked. An ocean of starlight twinkled above him.

"Am I dead?" he asked.

"It is time to wake up, Elder MacIsaac."

Teddy sat up, and found no solid ground under him. He spun in the air. His arms and legs were bent back behind him, his chest pointed to the death drop below. An intangible wind blew through him.

Finally, the world came into focus. Far down below lay a scorched land of ash. The stench of death throttled him. It was the dead world from his dream.

"Did I die?" he asked again.

Only wind answered. It blew ash across the empty world below.

For a second, fear shot through Teddy. He rubbed his eyes and slapped his cheeks. "Did I do this?"

"No, this is not your home," the voice said. "You do not have the power to do this yet."

"But I wanted to."

"No. You pulled yourself back. Remember and assess, Elder MacIsaac."

Teddy let himself think back to the battle. He had asked them to stop in a final moment of clarity. "But does that mean I can do this," he pointed to the black desert, "someday?"

"Eventually you will have enough to destroy everything you hate, and love."

"The white flames overtook me. I don't know how I pulled back at the end."

"That is because you have a good conscience. Having tremendous power, and knowing how to use it, are two separate qualities. The Coin of Light chose its bearer right."

A weight clamped on Teddy's chest. He still wanted the lightning. He needed it. It wasn't true, but he still believed it regardless.

"If I'm not dead," Teddy asked, "why am I back here?"

"You are here because your first obstacle has been overcome. A crossroads now awaits you."

"I just want to go home. I don't want to choose anything."

"That is not how it works. You always have to make a choice. Look to the land below you. What do you see?"

Teddy squinted. "I can't see anything except a big drop that will break every bone in my body if I fall. How did I get here?"

"I invited you to this place."

"Then you can take me down. I have to get back to my

friends, and my town. I don't have time for this."

"Calm yourself and close your eyes, then you will see." The voice waited for Teddy to do so before it continued. "Do you know who I am?"

Puzzle pieces slid together in Teddy's mind. They slid into a bigger picture. Teddy had seen this voice before. Then the shape appeared in his mind's eye. It was a man wearing red armor.

"Yeah," Teddy said. "I know who you are."

"My name is Tola," the Pyre Knight said. "I am the previous Knight of Flames."

"That is totally freaky. I look like you when I transform."

"For now. As you learn, and your flame grows brighter, you will shed my shadow. You will become your own Knight. Your flame is still weak."

"I noticed. Luck is the only reason I'm not worm chow."

"But you did not waver in battle. That is the mark of a True Knight. You will succeed where I failed, Elder MacIsaac."

"Fail?" A flash of lightning ran across his brain. His eyes shut tight. The pain inside had been growing for some time now. His wounds were catching up with him. "How did you fail?"

"See for yourself."

Rolling fire tumbled across the empty sky in his mind. His eyes snapped open.

There the figure of Tola appeared, covered in sparks of red flame. The old knight wore the same armor that Teddy wore. He floated in the infinite space above the dead lands, staring up at the boy. The fire red eyes of Tola betrayed a deep sadness that went deeper than the boy knew.

"You shouldn't be here anymore," Teddy said.

"You are correct." Tola nodded. "But I am not here. I speak from your sword and not from this world. Even in death, my mission is not yet finished. I still have . . . sins to atone for."

"You mean this world. You killed all these people. You burned the world into ash."

"I did. My allies fell honorably in battle, but I did not. I fell to my despair in defeat and let wrath be my guide. But you are not me. I spoke to you in that battle with the demon to remind you of your path. This is not the path of a hero." He waved down to the world below. "You had almost forgotten that."

"It was the lightning." The blinding surge cracked in his skull. He bit his lip. "It still hurts."

"The Blind Lightning of the Maiden of Faith is dangerous, Elder MacIsaac. Do not rely on it."

"Will this craving ever go away?"

"Abstain. You must turn from it. It offers tremendous power, but it will tear your soul apart."

Teddy noted that Tola did not answer his question. He shrugged off the pain. "Does the Blind Lightning have to do with what you did here? You wouldn't willingly destroy everything like this."

"My family," Tola said. His tone stiffened. "They were betrayed by the Maiden of Faith, Elena. Not long before, I watched villages and towns fall to Jero's puppets, unable to stop them. I let despair grip my heart, and let my rage flow unto these lands. Now, there is nothing left. The Blind Lightning is not why I fell. I was weaker than that."

"But what about Jero, and the Phantom Maiden?" Teddy asked. "Shouldn't that have killed them?"

"They had already escaped to your world. Elena used her power to take the pair away from this fallen place. Jero abandoned his men to the flames."

"But why did he come here? Why did the last Maiden of Faith betray you?"

"I can only speak of what I knew when alive, Theodore MacIsaac. You will find your answers. Questions were made to be answered, in time."

"Then you can tell me who the Order is."

"I can," Tola said. "But you were already told most of it by, what did your friend call him—your *potential employer*."

Teddy nodded. Kevin did tell him most of it. The Nameless Kingdom, scorched of even its name, after years of complacency and malaise, was wiped out. The Order of the Ash had won. Tola unwittingly finished their job for them. Jero the Boundless, General of the Order, was a man who came out of nowhere to see control of the kingdom and all the lands. He was a man obsessed with the Dark.

The old knight continued without pause. "But never mind the past. It matters what you do now. Your choices are the key. There are good ones, and bad ones. Simply wearing the armor of a Knight of the End is not enough to be on the side of the angels. I am proof of that. You must hold strong. Never waver from the path of a True Knight, Elder

MacIsaac. The battle never ends as long as we breathe."

"I still don't get it. You defeated monsters, gained incredible power, saved the world, and then you destroyed it? I'm just finding it difficult to process. I thought Knights were supposed to be heroes."

"A hero?" Tola laughed. "It takes more than the ability to crush your foes to be a hero. You should know that by now. My lack of humility and faith lead me to where I am now. It led to the dead world below you. But you are not who I am. Where will your decisions leave you in the future?"

Teddy swallowed his pride. "If you brought me here to warn me, then I get it. But I have to get back. I was in the middle of a battle, you know? Not to mention, I have to find Caitlyn and Rock."

The previous Pyre Knight glanced down at the ashes far below them. His expression steadied.

"Your friends are safe," Tola said. "Your enemies are gone. They will not return to further trouble you. There are many tasks I cannot complete—or interfere with, but these words I can readily give you." He appeared to anticipate Teddy's next question. "You did not kill them. But you will never see them walk the streets of your cities ever again."

"What did those white flames do?" Now his headache was flaring.

"That is a discussion for another day. All things in their time. For now, you must worry about the road ahead."

"The Order of the Ash and Jero are still out there. I know."

"What are you planning to do next, Pyre Knight?" Tola asked. "This fight is not over."

"But I'm not trained in this. I made it through by luck and only luck."

"No one said it would be easy. I will show you how to use the flames when you have need of it. You only need to ask. The Red Sword will remain by your side." The former knight glanced into the endless swirling stars shining above. "My time is nearly at an end. I can guide you on a path away from my own, but only if you allow it. If you wish to be a hero, there may be hope for you yet!"

Teddy's headache slammed inside his skull. "I can't deal with all this now."

"You will need to. This is no game."

"If I keep this up, people are eventually going to figure out who I am. My family already knows. People could get hurt because of that. My parents, my friends, or strangers."

"Then you will have to ponder on your path as a Knight, and a hero. You did not believe this was going to be easy, did you?"

Teddy thought to himself, staring at the empty world far below. His head was reaching critical mass. "If this is a path I can choose, then why bother choosing at all?"

"Those are the questions you must ask yourself. Ponder, pray, and muse, Elder MacIsaac. There is still much to do. A hero always gets up again."

Flames rolled across the vision of Tola. The red twisted into an orange sunset hue, and then settled on blinding white. The heat enveloped Teddy MacIsaac whole, soothing his open wounds and burning muscles. His headache was crushed into pieces. The cleansing fire tumbled through him like a breeze.

When the world arrived back into focus, everything had changed. He was no longer suspended in the space above the dead world. He tasted dew on the tip of his tongue, and caught scent of a smoke from an extinguished campfire. He was standing on the edge of an unfamiliar forest. A sky as blue as it was bright shone down.

A warrior in red armor stared off the edge of a cliff ahead of him. Standing beside the Pyre Knight was a second warrior in dark blue armor. This stranger had a bull-dog like face, and eyes as blue as the endless sky above, and as deep as the ocean. He glanced from the cliff to the forest. He looked directly at Teddy.

"Did you hear something, Tola?" the Knight asked.

"No," Tola replied. "Nothing."

They did not see him. Teddy approached the cliff side, beside the two warriors.

Beyond the cliff lay a new world that spread out for hundreds of miles. Ancient towns, wild forests, and clean lakes, could be spotted stretching out to a mountain range. Tall houses, stone streets, trees he had never seen before, and rock formations carved from the tools of men much older and wiser than him, were spread all over the land below. It was magnificent. He wanted to be impressed, but creeping horror prevented him. They were all destroyed, broken, and left in tatters.

He glanced away. His stomach couldn't take it. The two Knights did not look away.

The Pyre Knight was Tola. He had the same full cheeks, black hair, and fire-brown eyes which stared out over the land as he did in the dream. His eyes were not as fierce as one would expect from a warrior. His fists were clenched tight.

"The Order has invaded the South Country, according to our scouts," the blue warrior said. "Are you sure you must go? I would much rather die with a friend by my side."

"I am weak, Juss," Tola said. "The words Elena, spoke still haunt me. I must go and discover the truth for myself."

"If you believe your family is at risk, then I will not stop you, my friend. Elena is a traitor, and will suffer for it soon enough. But I fear we are at a disadvantage. We have lost Morgant, and the western lands."

"We have lost, yes. But it is not yet done. If you and the remaining warriors can hold the ground, then I can slay Jero and bring this Order of the Ash to an end. It may take some time to reach his castle in the outterlands, but I can do it. I just need time." He paused, and closed his eyes. It was obviously not their first choice of action. "Unless, of course, you have a better plan?"

"What else can we do? "Juss growled, and punched his gauntlets together. "We can only fight until the end. The king is gone, as are most of our allies. But they all went down in battle. We can't be expected to do less than that."

"Of course not," Tola said, smiling. "I would have been proud to die by your side, old friend."

"This is not the wisest course of action, but I dare not stop you." The Ocean Knight stuck out his hand, and Tola glanced at it. Juss grabbed his friend's hand and shook it vigorously. "Farewell, Pyre Knight Tola."

"It has been a pleasure, Ocean Knight Juss."

Juss gave a wry smile. "Until we meet where the Dark has no sway."

The Pyre Knight drew the Red Sword and held it forward. He cut the air before him. The blade sheened white, and a red flare swirled into the wind.

"Goodbye, old friend," Tola said. He did not look back.

The Pyre Knight jumped, his leap carrying him high into the sky. He then fell like a boulder down the cliff.

Tola struck the ground, kicking up earth and stone, and bolted onward without pause. The previous Pyre Knight whipped forward through empty fields and forests to the mountain range off in the distance. He was already a blur in the horizon. This power was easily beyond Teddy's capabilities.

"Goodbye, Tola," the Ocean Knight said. "Do not lose your way home."

The Ocean Knight stood staring at the horizon for a few extra moments. Finally, he turned down the trail Teddy had been watching from. The Knight's deep blue eyes were somehow empty, beaten. The warrior forgotten by the fog of time and space walked right though Teddy as if the boy was invisible. Despite his impending defeat, Juss marched onward to where some soldiers waited down the trail. The Knight, and the world, faded away in fog.

The vision flashed white, and Teddy left the world behind.

Though the dream had ended, the world he knew did not return. Instead of the overcast skies of the forest, there was darkness surrounding him. He tried to speak, and found his mouth covered over. Sweat rolled down his back. Wherever he was, it was not home.

Chapter 24
Into the Night

Teddy wasn't dead, but he couldn't imagine feeling any worse. His muscles cried out, and his legs pulled against him, heavier than two tons of lead. Cold stone lay under him.

A warm, soft object wrapped itself tight over his lips, blocking him from speaking. It took him a moment to realize it was a hand.

The world fell back into focus. He was in a cave of some sort. Faint outlines of light passed through stone cracks in the rock bed. A long fissure split the darkness open. A flash rolled through the crack over and over again. It reminded him of headlights shining out in the night.

When the light disappeared, so did the palm silencing him. He gazed up at the outline of Caitlyn West sitting beside him in the dark. She nodded toward the fissure, a finger over her lips. A figure stood by the cave opening.

"Boss, you awake yet?" Rock whispered.

Teddy sat up. Everything inside screamed at his bad idea.

Sleep was calling him back to dreamland. He tried to ignore the pain. He leaned forward.

Then his back let out a crack. Stabbing needles fired through his spine.

He let out a short yell. Caitlyn cupped his mouth once again.

"Quiet!" she said, her voice low. "They're out there searching for us."

Teddy nodded, and looked them over. They were as bad as he was with cuts and bruises all over. Then the realization hit him. Nobody had enough energy to transform.

He slid her hand from his mouth, scowling at his pain. "The Order?"

"No," Rock said, peering through the fissure. "We got all four of them, and the bugs are all gone. They were destroyed when you took out the Parasite. But I guess you missed that. More dust than a desert, man."

Caitlyn coughed. "There's something else out there."

"They look like mercenaries, or military of some kind. They're crawling all over the woods, Boss."

"They showed up around sunset," Caitlyn said. "Or so I'm told."

A sharp stabbing sensation rang out from behind Teddy's right eye. He gripped his temples, thoughts jumbling. Though he slept for hours, he didn't feel rested at all. Everything still ached and the hollowness from the lightning remained.

"What happened after the fire killed it?" Teddy asked, still holding his head.

Rock told him everything. The older boy woke from his slumber when a voice spoke in his ear. It was as if he were being shaken awake by someone who wasn't there. He stepped out into the downpour in time to see the white flames extinguish instantly. He saw Teddy fall to the ground, his armor shattered. The chimera was incinerated. The rain stopped soon after.

He pulled Teddy and Caitlyn along with him looking for a more hidden resting place. He found the cave, and laid the two of them down. All he could do was wait for them to awaken.

Hours later, when the sun had set, he started to hear the trucks arriving. Men in uniforms were patrolling all over the forest. There were nearby boulders, left over by the Stone Eater, and Rock used them to block the entrance. No one had stumbled upon them yet, but they were getting closer.

Eventually, Caitlyn woke and they went over their options. Rock only managed a single phone call from Mr. West's cracked phone, before he destroyed it. She had been annoyed with him since.

"You've seen the movies, kids," Rock said. "They track phone numbers to precise locations and imprison their targets in mysterious underground prisons—if they're not aliens, anyway. That's when they dissect them."

"What is wrong with you, Rockhead?" Caitlyn sighed, grimacing when she tried to stand. "If you ask me, you watch too many dumb movies. What is with you two and this type of thing?"

"Well," Rock said, slanting his head, "where's *your* phone, Princess?"

"Right here!" She reached into her pocket and removed the phone. She tried turning it on.

Rock chuckled. "Dead, huh?"

Caitlyn's face shone beet red in the dark. "It was a busy day! Not like I had time to check."

"It doesn't matter, Princess. I wouldn't risk another call out here, anyway."

"How do we know these people aren't on our side?" Teddy asked, his throat dry.

"We don't know how much they know." Rock leaned back out into the dark. "They could know how we can use Coins of Light to transform and are here to help; they might be in the Order's pocket and are here to clean up. Who knows? I don't, and neither do the two of you."

"You ever see them before?" Teddy asked Caitlyn.

"No, never. I don't think they're really military, but I don't know who they are."

"In that case . . ." Teddy forced himself up after many failed attempted. "In that case, I agree with Rock."

"You're finally making sense, Boss!" He reached over and clapped his friend on the shoulder. Teddy stumbled. "Uh, sorry."

Caitlyn leaned against the cave wall, arms folded. "You think he's right about the aliens? You can't be serious. Is this a boy thing?"

"No," Teddy said. "I agree with him that we don't know whose side those guys outside are on. The bit about the aliens is a bit out there even for me."

"You throw fire from a magical sword, and you don't

think alien hunters could be out there, ready to dissect us?"

"That's only because I'm not crazy, Rock."

Caitlyn giggled. It was always a treat seeing a pretty girl laughing. She wiped a tear from her eye.

"See?" Teddy gloated. "It's not so bad having an imagination, is it? You look much better with a smile."

She glanced away and rolled her eyes. "Yeah, yeah."

"By the way, I was thinking about teaching you how to make shrimp with tomatoes and olives." His throat hurt as he laughed. "It's pretty easy to make, and I think you can handle it. What do you think?"

Rock glanced between them. "Huh?"

"Okay, okay, it's a deal" she said. "You sure can be a pest. But first, let's make it out of here in one piece."

"Enough, kids," Rock said. He raised both hand. "Listen up. I got through to our potential employer on the phone before I smashed it to save us from the aliens. He said he's going to be waiting at the Riverview diner, on the highway. He's going to be with your dad, Boss. That was hours ago, but I'm pretty sure they're still there. They know it won't be a cakewalk for us."

Caitlyn tilted a blonde eyebrow. "Potential employer?"

"In-joke," Teddy replied.

Caitlyn went on, "Since we all seem to be out of juice and lost in the middle of the woods—at night, no less—what do you boys propose we do to get out of here?"

Rock grinned. "Improvise."

"The last time you two improvised," she said, "you ended

up falling about ten stories out of a crumbling castle. Yeah, I saw that."

"It was fifteen," Teddy corrected.

"Well, Princess, at least, I didn't need help to get over a fence."

She turned to cough. "Yeah, well . . ."

"Alright, guys," Teddy said. "I've got a better idea." He peeked out into the night. Streaks of light pierced the darkness like spears through prey. "I know these woods pretty well. Once I get my bearings, I should be able to find the way out, no problem. Just follow my lead."

"You got it, Boss."

"Lead on," Caitlyn said.

Teddy and Rock pushed against the boulders as gently as possible. The stones lightly slid aside into the soaked tallgrass. The boys covered the entrance again when the trio left.

Cold night wind whipped Teddy's face. Autumn at its worst slipped into his aching bones. Before he gathered himself together, there was a tug at his arm. He found himself being pulled sideways.

Rock dragged the younger boy by the collar behind a nearby warped oak tree. Caitlyn fell in beside them.

Rings of light flashed over where they had just been standing. They followed along the treeline toward the group, and spread out over the brush. The three teenagers crouched lower. Four figures passed the warped oak and kept walking. The circles of light fell away with the four of them.

Boots kicked against leaves and pebbles nearby.

Flashlights slid through waves of leaves. Shuffling branches rustled all over the forest. Teddy waited for an opening.

The younger boy signaled to the two of them, and they moved. A light glided across their path and the trio steadied, Teddy raising a hand. A second later it vanished. The trio stayed low to the ground and hobbled onward.

Teddy recognized their location. The cave was several miles from where the battle had taken place earlier. Rock had traveled for about an hour and a half lugging the two of them to safety. Teddy would have to thank his friend later. Unfortunately, this meant using the cave back to the mall was no longer an option. For now, he had to worry about finding another path.

If they traveled west they would reach an old wooden bridge strewn over a small river. A bit further and they would reach the small backwoods town of Riverview. After that they could get through the dirt roads and make a straight dash for the highway. The diner was not far from there.

It sounded much easier than it would be. But he couldn't let his friends know that. He needed to keep them calm.

"Okay," Teddy whispered. "We need to go west. Avoid the open meadows, and stick to the trees. Try not to step on too many leaves, and follow me close behind. Any objections?"

"Not a one, Boss."

Caitlyn shook her head.

Chatter burst from the south where the majority of lights were flashing. There were strangely hollow voices, but no radio static or echo to them. That shouldn't have been possible. Maybe Rock's alien theory had merit.

Bushes shuffled. The noise centered on the broad rock bed to the west. Lights shone with no coherent direction.

Teddy waved a hand to his companions. The two followed behind him through the forest maze. A flashlight scanned over their heads. Two men were chattering on the side of the dirt road.

Teddy craned his neck to hear anything from them. All he could make out were the words "*rock*" and "*man*" above the whistling night wind. The hairs on the back of his neck stiffened.

Rock elbowed him in the ribs, and nodded to the talkers. These people were not using a ninth grader's nickname, but there was no point telling Rock that. These people were obviously looking for a monster that should be dead. Teddy shrugged it off, and moved on.

They reached the end of the brush, and he held out his arm to stop the group. A wide dirt road like a river crossing awaited them. Blowing dust fell across the darkened path. If they made it past here, it would be a clear run along the rock trail toward the bridge. After that, they would be in Riverview.

Teddy explained their predicament to his companions. They all nodded, and filed in behind him, still crouching. He knelt forward and counted to three. Then, a flashlight beam passed two inches from his face.

Boots crunched leaves to his right on the road. Teddy and his friends fell silent. Nobody moved.

More heavy steps approached, voices attached. Two figures emerged from the dark, marching side by side. They were wearing camouflage uniforms to match the forest, just as Rock said.

The shorter one was complaining. "This is insane, Fields."

"It's still happening," the well-built one said. "We have to find that thing before it gets out of the forest."

"What do you think happened here, anyway? Strange stuff like this rarely happens outside New Sun."

Fields stopped two feet from Teddy's hiding place. The boy held his breath. Fields turned and stared into the bush above Teddy's head. He didn't appear to notice the three teenagers.

They had no equipment except flashlights. But they weren't armed with any weapons. How exactly could they take on something like the Stone Eater? They couldn't. That is, unless they had abilities of their own.

"I'll worry about that later," Fields said. "Right now, we should worry about McLeod. Swarms of insects covering the sky and then vanishing into dust. Reports of crazies in knights costumes running around town. Just like in New Sun, there's no footage, either. Then there were all those earthquakes, the mall, and that crater a few miles back. If the freaks in New Sun are leaving, we have to cut them off before they get any breathing room."

"And what do we do if *it* gets away?"

Fields opened his mouth to respond, but froze. Silence fell as both uniformed men stood still. There was a faint trace of a voice speaking somewhere beyond the night. Both men nodded and spoke as one.

"Roger."

Teddy glanced at Rock. His friend gave him a cheesy thumbs up and a grin in return. Caitlyn shrugged, as confused as the boys were. Neither of Teddy's friends noticed that the strangers didn't have any equipment on them for communication. They had no phones, no earpieces, no radios, and nothing distinct at all. All they had were flashlights.

The uniformed man opposite Fields continued down the path. He contemplated to his ally. "We better hurry before the military gets here."

"Then we should get moving."

The possible aliens disappeared down the road. Their whispers fell further and further away. Teddy waited for their voices to trail off before he moved again.

He leaned out of the brush. Cool air blew across the dirt road. A sweet pine scent tickled his nostrils. Silence reigned in the forest again. He moved out, keeping low.

Rock followed, tripping slightly on the gravel. Caitlyn slowed down in the rear. Her breathing was growing heavier, and her skin was getting paler. Exhaustion was hitting her the hardest. Eventually she reached the opposite side of the trail, and filed in behind the boys. Teddy let them have a breather.

There was only one more road to go. The bridge was just ahead. But he needed to exercise caution. These people weren't even military, and they didn't know what the Order was. This was no game.

"Guys," Teddy said. "We're going down the riverbank instead of crossing the bridge."

"I'm not sure if I can make it," Caitlyn said. She fell against a rotting birch tree. "I'm shutting down."

Rock glanced at her and grunted. Teddy tightened his brow in thought. Caitlyn had her physical condition to worry about, and Rock was the best rested of the group. If they were going to get out, they had to work together.

"Rock, carry her on your back." The older boy looked at him with a slanted head. "I know you're tired, but you have the most strength left, and I have to lead the way. We still have Riverview to get through, and we can't do it this way."

"Hey," she said to Rock, "this isn't exactly my idea of a picnic in the woods, either."

Rock sighed, and rolled his eyes. He lifted Caitlyn onto his back, and grunted. He had more energy than the pair, but not much.

They turned off the road, and down a steep hill of thin birches and pale orange leaves on the grass. Teddy slid down the bank, arms outstretched, slipping between the gauntlet of trees. Rock stumbled down after him, grunting the whole way. A running creak awaited them at the bottom.

His intuition was right. The bridge was well guarded. One uniformed man lay on each end of the thin span, watching the pathway. They wore the same garb as the others Teddy had seen. They also had no weapons or equipment other than flashlights.

Teddy knew the woods like his backyard. He'd walked the trails, taken bike trips, and camped, wherever he could or was allowed to. Crossing the creek would be easy. He nodded to his friends, and led the way. He skipped across the creek's stones. Rock followed after him, grunting heavier with every jump.

The forest rolled into the backwoods ahead of them. Riverview's rural community packed itself into the ocean of trees. There was much cover. He paused, peeking over the bank. Flashlight beams brightened the woods ahead. Riverview was even more of a minefield than the forest trails were.

Caitlyn and Rock fell down on the slope. They lay sprawled out, catching their breaths.

"You two take a breather," Teddy said. "I'm going to scout ahead for some help."

"Wait, Teddy," Caitlyn rasped. "Before you go, just let me say that . . . Uh . . . I want to apologize."

"For what?"

"For using my lightning on you without even explaining it. The Maiden of Faith is supposed to believe in her allies. I passed the buck to you because I was scared. I shouldn't have done that."

"No." Teddy shook his head. "You gave me the lightning because you believed I could beat him. You had plenty of faith. And now you're going to need to have some more. Rest up. I'll be back soon."

Teddy ran up the bank. His friends watched him go, unable to stop him.

A thick line of birches covered both sides of the dirt road into Riverview. Shadows of light were cast across the roads outside the trees. Uniforms were coming. They would cross his path in seconds.

Teddy pushed onward. He decided to cut through the trees and across a rarely traveled path he knew well. Only the darkness stood in his way of finding the right way.

He plunged into the curtains of birches and picked up the pace. He smacked branches out of the way. The grass-carpeted meadow was up ahead. From here, it would be straightforward.

He tripped over a loose stone and cracked his head against a low hanging branch. His body jerked, and twisted. He fell on his back. The ringing in his skull stewed his brains. Teddy rolled over to his knees, stifling a groan.

Never before was he more grateful to be alone.

He paused on his right knee, letting the world spin back into view. His left eye began to seal shut, a result of having no energy left. His muscles burned.

A voice spoke from the shadows. He froze. The whisper cut through the trees ahead. Teddy slowly rose.

He edged toward the source, slipping between thin trees. Up ahead was his shortcut—the secret field he knew so well. No one knew about it. He stopped by the field's edge and peered through the branches. There in the center were two figures chatting away. Teddy held back a deep breath and clutched the bruise above his forehead that his low energy rewarded him with.

One of the voices was that of the Stone Eater.

Chapter 25
The Black Sword

Teddy stayed behind the shelter of the tree. There were two people in his hidden field. One was standing, and the other appeared to be sitting against a tree. Teddy cursed his luck at having hit his head on the branch.

"Did you hear that?" the standing figure asked. It was hard to see either of the men in the field, but the one walking around sounded young. "It's probably nothing."

Thunder roared off in the distance. Teddy tried to ignore it, hoping the storm wasn't coming his way. There were more pressing concerns.

Moonlight slipped through the dark night, allowing Teddy a glimpse of the speaker. He wore a black hoodie to hide his face, and casual blue jeans. He was a teenager.

At the same moment, the moonlight allowed Teddy a glimpse of the second party. Where the other person should have been sat nothing but a pile of rocks stacked beside the tree. There was no second human. Teddy almost dismissed the stones—until they spoke.

"Who cares if there's anything out there?" the stone pile mumbled. The stack of pebbles slid against itself to form a vague human shape. Something prevented it from reforming and becoming the Stone Eater. "Just kill them and be done with it. General Snow is waiting for me."

The monster was still alive! Rage choked Teddy. Darryl's murderer wasn't dead at all. But his fear for Caitlyn and Rock held him back from exposing himself to the enemy. Now wasn't the time to play a hero.

The unfamiliar teenager paced the field. "If you would just hurry and reform yourself, you would already be back in New Sun. It's not like I want to be in this stupid forest listening to bumps in the night. I'm only here because I was asked. If it was up to me, I'd let those uniforms have you."

"I didn't ask you to come get me, boy."

"No, the Captain asked me to come get you. Jero told *him*, and *he* sent me. I wouldn't be here for you, scumbag. I never approved of coming here in the first place. As far as I'm concerned you all deserved what you got. The chick and the dimwit have bitten the dust, and the Manslayer is missing, but Jero still wants a full report, so you get to live. You're lucky he's so merciful."

"So you say," the Stone Eater said. "Let's get going, then."

"I've told you like three times now, but you refuse to get it through your thick stone skull, or whatever that thing is on your shoulders. I can't bring you unless you're whole, or else you'll break up in motion. If you lose pieces in the void, you will never find them again. Either hurry up and pull your pebbles back in place, or whatever it is you do, or we continue waiting here until we're found. Your choice."

"Yeah, right," the Stone Eater said, growling. "Let's see you go up against two Knights and get thrown out of a twentieth story castle floor, and walk away from it. Not to mention dealing with incompetents that can't even control their own abilities. It's a miracle I've gotten this far with so much against me. Lord Jero will understand."

The two continued going at it for some time. More thunder boomed closer. Teddy's head throbbed as he waited.

"Just send me now," the Stone Eater said. "If I have to grow new pieces later, I'll deal with it then."

"That's assuming Jero lets you leave this *meeting* in one piece. But, if you insist."

The teenager threw a hand forward, and the world split open before him. A ball of darkness consumed the empty air between the boy and his target. The mass was twice as tall as the teenager and triple the width. A cold sense of death reeked from the void.

Teddy's hair stood on end. This place in the opening was impossibly barren. There were no ceilings or floors.

The world bent around the pulsing black ball. Everything stopped around the void. The wind stopped with the thunder, and the leaves ceased falling, sticking in the air above the darkness. Time itself ceased around the orb. The teenager brought his opposite hand down, and a hole in existence tore open. It was like a door into the infinite pit of space.

The boy reached down, and lifted the Stone Eater's shabby body with one arm. Teddy marveled at the hooded figure's strength. The teenager sighed.

"Good luck, scumbag," the boy said. "Hopefully Jero and your General Snow will be more forgiving of your uselessness than I would be."

"There's a reason no one trusts you," the Stone Eater replied.

"Keep your trust, murderer."

The teenager tossed the broken Stone Eater into the invisible void, and the emptiness sealed itself shut. The breeze and distant rumbles of thunder returned to where the opening once was. The teenager turned, his boots crunching fallen leaves, toward Teddy's position. He stared toward the tree Teddy hid behind.. A chill ran through his sore eye.

The teenager clapped his hands together, and said the phrase Teddy knew by heart.

"I beg you," the strange boy said, "bestow on me the glory."

A flash of light overtook the night. It sent Teddy stumbling backwards. When the light cleared, there was a new figure standing where the teenager had been—a Knight wearing black armor. Just like a darkened version of the Pyre Knight, this one stood above the teenager's height as a new man. Instead of a weapon licked with flames, the sword the Black Knight held was a slab of darkness battered into the shape of a blade. Its sheen was colder than the forest.

The Black Knight kept his stare in Teddy's direction. The boy remained in the brush, keeping his breaths quiet. It felt like hours passed as he waited.

Finally, the Knight drove his sword into the earth. The dirt rumbled around the black blade. The Black Knight laughed to himself.

"How long are you going to wait in the bushes, kid?" the Knight said, his voice completely changed from the teenager's. "If I was going to hurt you, I would have already done it. Come on out."

Teddy's legs were as jelly. He thought through his options.

The Knight called louder. "I heard you hit the branch before. Sounded nasty. The faster you come out, the faster I let you go home and get it looked at."

That was a tell. This guy thought Teddy was just a kid. It was his best chance. Teddy steeled his nerves.

"You got me," Teddy said, pitching his voice slightly higher. His hands raised, he stepped out the bushes into the field. "I'm just trying to get home. Those scary guys in uniforms almost caught me while I was spying on them."

The Knight raised a gauntlet to his helmet, and his eye. "You've got some bark on your eyebrows. And a nice shiner."

Teddy wiped his brow. "Thanks. I'm surprised you heard that."

"I have sharp ears. Comes with the Knight thing. What are you doing out so late? In case you can't tell, those guys in the uniforms aren't nice guys."

Teddy scratched the back of his neck, and thought quickly. He was fortunate the Manslayer, or Felix Barfield, had a sense of honor. The Order still did not know what he looked like. "My friends and me were just sneaking around. We like to play games about killing dragons and stuff. We thought it would be fun to do it at night with those weird guys hanging around. It got a bit scary, though. Are you the one they were looking for, or is it your weird pal from before?"

"He ain't my friend," the Black Knight said, his voice a shard of glass.

"I've never seen anything like you before." It wasn't as if that was a lie. "Who are you?"

The Knight looked him over, but said nothing.

However, it was the Black Sword that caught Teddy's attention. The blade didn't catch the reflection of light from the moon like the black armor did. The sword was darker than midnight, a sharpened slab made out of eternity itself. Teddy could hardly keep his eyes off of it. The Red Sword was completely different, being that it didn't bring his soul on edge.

"I wouldn't stare at it too long," the Knight said, still watching the boy. "It brings unpleasant thoughts out into the open."

Teddy took a hard swallow, trying to sound uncertain. "Are you going to kill me?"

"It's not part of the job." The Black Knight pulled his sword from the ground. His matter-of-fact tone grated. "I'm not even going to tell you to keep quiet about seeing me, because it really won't make a difference soon enough. No one will be able to stop what's coming."

"You were with those guys that attacked McLeod."

Teddy widened his eyes, and let his mouth fall open. "Those weren't just stories?"

A smile peeked under the black helmet. "You're a smart one. I am the Black Knight, but not like that one from the stories you've heard. I'm a *real* Knight. But it doesn't matter. I have much bigger problems than a kid with a bruised face. Get moving."

"Yes, sir." He forced out a relieved breath. "The guys aren't going to believe this. They think you're just a story."

"The stories are true. You'd be surprised at how many are."

"No kidding."

The Black Knight swiped his sword forward. The slash cut through the air like his hand did earlier. The atmosphere stilled, and existence itself cut open. Teddy's skin crawled with the cold.

"Go get some rest," the strange Knight said. He stepped through the empty space. "The world will be a much different place soon enough."

Then, the Knight was gone. The void closed behind him. The autumn breeze blew across the field.

Teddy's knees shook. A sharp stab split inside his brain. He fell to one knee. Fatigue was catching up. He wasn't quite sure how he got out of that mess, but he also didn't have time to think about it. He'd wasted enough time.

He glanced up to meet a strange sight. White flakes from the sky.

It had begun to snow.

He didn't know whether to take it as a sign, or an omen,

but he did laugh. Life could be weird sometimes.

"You've got to be kidding me." He stretched out his right hand and caught a snowflake. It melted in the warmth of his hand.

He laughed again, and stood back up. The snow ceased as soon as it had started. He smiled to himself.

Thankfully, there wasn't much further to go. He sprinted through two dirt roads and another small field. After that was a thin creek. He hopped stones to get to the other side, panting under his breath.

Finally, he made it. The grass on the lawn had been freshly cut and raked, and the windows on the house were dusted and scrubbed vigorously. The Fishers had always kept things clean, but he always wondered how they made things so immaculate every time he visited. The older generation had a thing for cleanliness. He walked around to the back.

The Fishers had spent their retired years there. His parents met them on a camping trip years back. They had grown to be friends of the family. Teddy hoped they weren't sleeping early.

He rapped his knuckles on the backdoor, and waited. His brain played a drum solo for him. He leaned against the doorframe.

Mr. Fisher answered the door after a second. He was wearing red-framed reading glasses. Mr. Fisher was a thin balding man at average height, and he always dressed in fancy sweaters or turtlenecks. Today was no different. He wore a two tone sweater with black slacks.

"Theodore MacIsaac," he said, squinting out the screen

door. "What in the world are you doing out at this hour? The military told everyone to wait inside. Do you have any idea what is going on out there?"

"More than you think, sir."

"Well, come on in. Get out of the cold for a bit, and me and the wife will take you home. We'll think up an excuse if we're seen. Don't want folks getting a strange idea about you."

Mrs. Fisher arrived beside her husband. She was a slightly plump woman with curled white hair. Today she wore a green blouse with matching pants. It looked as if they had been out on an errand not too long before he showed up.

She looked Teddy up and down. "Now is not a good time to be playing in the woods, honey."

"I know, ma'am. But this isn't a game. I need a favor. I'll explain everything later, but I have two friends that really need some help. They're waiting for me. Can one of you drive me to River Road to get them?"

Mr. Fisher folded his glasses into his hand. "Did something happen?"

Teddy chose his words carefully. "One of my friends is suffering from exhaustion, and the other is carrying her. I told them to wait by cover until I got back. I don't know who those guys in the uniforms out there are, but I don't want to risk my friends being found. Can you please help me?"

Mr. Fisher leaned behind the door and emerged with car keys in hand. "We should hurry, then."

The couple closed the door behind them. Mr. Fisher and

his wife ran ahead of Teddy toward the car. It was an old blue number that had been washed recently. The couple sat in the front with Mr. Fisher driving. Teddy crawled into the back. His eye was still throbbing.

He gave them directions while his head swam. Sleep and confusion swirled from the situation. It was as if the day's events were finally catching up with him. He wasn't just Teddy MacIsaac anymore—he was the Pyre Knight from now on. He couldn't afford to run way anymore. Things were going to be very different tomorrow. They had to be.

"Just heading home, sir," Mr. Fisher said. Teddy nearly jumped at the voice. The car had been stopped, and a man in uniform was asking them questions.

The stranger eyed Teddy suspiciously. "And who is this little guy? He looks a bit roughed up, huh?"

"My grandson." Mrs. Fisher reached over the seat and patted Teddy's tangled strawberry blonde hair. "He likes to play outside when it gets dark. Sometimes he doesn't see where he's going. His mother gets fed up with him when he does these things."

"Looks like he took quite the hit," the uniform said, pointing his flashlight at Teddy's swollen eye. "You going to be alright, son?"

"I've felt worse." Teddy ignored his blurring vision and grinned sheepishly. "I'll be just fine, sir."

"I'll bet," he answered with a laugh. "Alright, folks, you can go on now."

The car pulled back out onto the road. No one followed after them. There were fewer uniforms on the road than there had been earlier. Teddy hoped it was because they were packing it up, and not because they found Caitlyn or Rock. It was getting darker out.

Eventually, they pulled over to the shoulder of the road. Teddy hopped out the back door, and slid down the embankment before him. His muscles tore into him as he sprinted down. He hoped and prayed he wasn't late.

Halfway down the embankment he met Rock walking toward him. The older boy was carrying Caitlyn, who was half asleep. The two boys stopped face to face and stared at each other for a moment. There was a slight pause between them. Smiles dawned and morphed into laughter.

"I knew it was you, Boss. Where you been?"

"A bit lost," Teddy said. "Ready to go home?"

Chapter 26

Going Home

Rock was still blabbering long after the car pulled back onto the road. He finally got around telling Teddy what happened while they were separated.

There wasn't much to tell. The creeps in the uniforms passed above the embankment. Rock and Caitlyn ducked low to avoid any flashlights that shone their way. Nobody spotted the pair.

"When I heard the car pull over," Rock said, "I just knew it was you, Boss. Something told me to head up the bank and I did. It was so crazy. It felt like a voice speaking directly into my brain."

The three kids were stuffed in the back seat. Teddy sat behind Mr. Fisher, Rock behind the older woman, and Caitlyn between the two boys, drifting in and out of sleep. The girl told Teddy that all Rock did while they waited was talk about old fights he had. She half-begged for sleep to take her.

"I met someone weird," Teddy said, thinking of the

Black Knight. "But I'll tell you guys about it later."

He wasn't going to get the Fishers involved. To their credit, they didn't ask any questions. Teddy thanked them once more for their patience. They smiled back at him like only the old and wise can.

The Fishers listened to Teddy's directions, bringing them out onto the highway past the open hills. They left the backwoods of Riverview behind.

Soon enough, they arrived at the parking lot and filed out of the car. Teddy spotted his father's empty truck parked by the entranceway. The lot was otherwise empty.

"You did well, son," Mr. Fisher said. He shook Teddy's hand. "You did well finding help when you needed it. You're not that same quiet kid that Jonas went on about. It's good to see you with good friends. I hope this means you're starting to grow up a little. Never go it alone unless you have no choice."

"Yes, sir," Teddy replied. "Thank you, again."

"You listen to Mr. Fisher, Teddy," his wife agreed. "You still have a ways to go. If we hadn't been there, what might have happened? You have to be better prepared in the future."

Mr. Fisher shook Rock's hand and turned back to Teddy. "Tell Bethany and Jonas we give our regards."

"Yes, please do," Mrs. Fisher said. "We should be getting back now. Good night, everyone."

The Fishers climbed back into their old blue car and drove out of the parking lot. They were long gone before Teddy realized how lucky he was to have known them. Adults really weren't all that bad.

The three kids stared at each other under the lone parking lot streetlamp. Teddy nodded, and they moved toward the diner.

Caitlyn failed to stifle a yawn. "Whoops."

"It's alright," Rock said, rotating his left shoulder. "I feel the same way."

"Then let's not waste any more time," Teddy chimed in.

"I'll try not to collapse on you boys again. It feels like it's been one embarrassing moment after another around you two. It's been a weird few days. I could use a good shower after all this."

"By the way, Caitlyn," Teddy interrupted. "Do you know anything about a Black Sword?"

"A Black Sword?" She scratched a blonde lock out of her blue eyes. "You mean a sword like yours?"

"Yeah, I guess."

Rock swung open the door to the diner. He scanned the booths and tables while Caitlyn thought Teddy's words over. The place was nearly as empty as the parking lot outside. No one would disturb them here.

"There is nothing about a Black Sword that I know of. Why?"

Teddy paused, staring after Rock into the diner. "I'll tell you later. It's a bit complicated. First, we have people to meet."

At the back of the diner two men peeked over their seats in a booth. They stood up from the table when they spotted the teenagers. The younger well-dressed one was smiling and laughing away as he approached, and the older wore a flannel shirt and jeans with his familiar frown. Teddy's father and Kevin Scott West met them in the middle of the floor.

Quiet whispers burst from the five of them. They packed in close. None of the few restaurant patrons or staff paid them any mind.

"Hi, dad," Teddy said.

His father nodded. "Come here."

Mr. MacIsaac squeezed his son in a hug so tight that Teddy thought his wounds would pop open. It was embarrassing, but it could have been worse. If his mother was there, he probably would have been beaten into the ground. He'd had enough pain for one day.

"Glad to see you, Caitlyn," Mr. West said, steadying her. He nodded to the boys. "You, too, Teddy. Rock."

"No problem, professor." Rock glanced away from Teddy and his father. "Just happy to be alive."

Mr. West helped his cousin back to the booth the adults were sitting at. Rock followed and sat across from her. Mr. West said a few words to them before joining Teddy and his father again. The smile never left his face.

"Rock and I have thought about your offer, Mr. West. I think we're ready to accept."

"Call me Kevin." Kevin Scott West placed a hand on both father and son's shoulders, and nodded. "But we're getting ahead of ourselves. I'll be waiting outside when you all are ready to go back. It's been a long day, and I think we could all use a bit of rest. Also, I think your dad wants to say a few words to you first."

"Well, okay."

"Good to see you're okay, Teddy. Really."

The college youth bowed slightly, and exited the restaurant.

The two MacIsaac men sat on stools by the counter. They made sure they were alone. His father took a moment to speak. He rarely ever took this long to choose his words. The waitress arrived behind the bar, and his father smiled. He asked her for two cans of root beer, and waited for her to leave.

"So, Theodore," he said, laughing low. "Do you think the next time you decide to go off on your own that you could do me and your mother a favor, and take a phone with you?"

The waitress returned and left their cans before them. She returned to the kitchen and left them alone.

Teddy thought about his father's words. He was too tired to make a bad joke, and he knew he owed his father more than that. Instead of replying, he nodded and took a sip from his drink.

"Good to hear," Mr. MacIsaac said.

"I'm going away for a while."

"I know. I had a long talk with Mr. West—who you will not be calling *Kevin*, by the way. Anyway, I had a long talk with him, and considering what has happened to McLeod, we won't have many other options but to accept his offer. It's a mess back home."

Teddy downed the rest of his soda. It gave him a solid kick. "I can only imagine what they think we were doing in the mall and out in the woods."

"We'll talk about *that* later." He clapped his son on the back and stood from the stool. The old man stifled a laugh. He passed his root beer to Teddy, untouched. "Right now, we've got to get you home. I'll be waiting outside when you three are done."

Jonas MacIsaac called the waitress over. He handed her money for the drinks, and turned and left. Teddy grabbed his father's root beer and brought it to the table in the back.

He sat down beside Caitlyn in the booth. Rock sat across from her, munching on a burger and some fries. The older boy was eating like he hadn't eaten in years.

"Where did you get that?" Teddy asked.

"Our new employer ordered it about an hour ago while waiting for us. Said he couldn't eat it, and it's already paid for. Sure it's cold, but it's still food and I'm still gonna eat it."

Teddy shrugged. "Don't let me stop you. They're waiting outside, so pick up the pace."

"Could you teach me how to make that?" Caitlyn asked.

"Hamburger and fries?" Teddy blinked. He'd almost forgotten his promise to her. "Sure. Anything you want. It's not very difficult, but it's a good choice."

"It's a promise, then."

Teddy glanced at the television by the bar. The volume was off, but the newswoman was reporting from New Sun City. It was a report about sightings of monsters, and sketches of women dressed in strange robes were shown off. He wondered just why the news was talking about these rumors at all. The story then changed to one about the mayor and his fight against crime.

Caitlyn leaned on her elbow, and stared at Teddy. "You were talking about a Black Sword before."

"I met a teenager out in Riverview," he said. "He transformed into a Black Knight. He had a sword that could rip a void in the world. It was like a portal or something. He sent the Stone Eater through it."

"He's not dead?" Rock asked. He spat food from his teeth as he spoke. "That's crazy!"

"For crying out loud, Rock!" Caitlyn whispered. "Keep your voice down, and your mouth closed, when you eat." She turned back to Teddy. "Now, what happened?"

He told them about his trek through the woods. He started with leaving them behind and went through everything up to meeting the Fishers. Rock was more upset about the fact the Stone Eater was still alive than he was about the Black Knight, and Caitlyn listened in silence. When he wrapped it up, Rock had finished with his food.

"He didn't know who I was," Teddy continued. "The Manslayer really must have not told them who I was." Teddy glanced around at the others. His sullen friends were staring down at the table. "Well, he had to have some positive qualities! Not even psychopathic monsters can be evil twenty-four hours a day, right? Maybe I'll thank Felix Barfield if I ever see him again. Well, if he isn't already in a padded cell."

"Why do you always have to make stupid jokes like that?" Caitlyn asked. "Don't you understand the implications of what you just said? There's a Knight that we've never heard of, working with the enemy. The Phantom Maiden was one thing, but this is a whole other problem. And here you are treating it like it's funny!"

Teddy's eye twitched. "Why are you always so serious? Don't you understand that it changes nothing at all whether I make a joke or not? Get a sense of humor, already. They could have an army of Knights and it wouldn't change what we have to do. We fight, and we beat them. That's what we're gonna do. It's what every hero worth his salt would do."

"Again with the hero thing."

"Okay, then tell me. What is wrong with being a hero?"

"I am the Maiden of Faith, Teddy. I have faith in a loving God. I have faith that good will eventually win over this decaying world. I believe that that we were given these abilities for a reason. What I don't have faith in, is a hero. We live in a world of greys and blacks that are shading darker every day. Heroes are inventions. They're stories. There are no heroes in this world, just people who do the right thing at the right time. Even if there were heroes—we wouldn't be them. Do you know what the last Maiden of Faith and Pyre Knight did? We are one step away from being like them. They are not heroes."

"We can be." Teddy tightened his right hand, and lightly struck the tabletop with his knuckle. "That's what I believe. They gave up. They were knocked down and stayed there. Theodore MacIsaac doesn't stay down."

"And neither does Rock Carson," Rock added. "I ain't using my full name, by the way. Full disclosure, here."

"I've met the last Pyre Knight, Caitlyn. I know what he

did. I've also met Rock, and you. And I've seen what the power of the Coin of Light is capable of. I've seen what the Darkness can do. Heroes are not goody-two shoes who never screw up. They're not fairy tales. They are people who get up after being knocked down, and never stop even when they have the odds stacked against them. I've already met a few. Heck, you should have seen Rock against Hornet Truck. He went all out, and he had no idea what he was doing. Then there was how you came to help us after being run ragged in New Sun City. You think that is grey or black?"

"Hornet Truck?" she muttered.

"You also gave me that coin, Boss." Rock's stare was surprisingly tough. "I won't forget that."

"But that's all so childish," Caitlyn said, ignoring Rock. "How old are you?"

Teddy laughed, and placed his right hand flat in the center of the table. Caitlyn stared at it, confused.

"We're going to be a team from now on," the younger boy said. "If one of us falls, there are others to make the stand. You can have faith in all those great things, Caitlyn. Heck, I do, too. But you do need some faith in people."

She looked down at the table, and mumbled under her breath. "I have faith."

"Then let's make it official," he stated.

Teddy grabbed her right hand and placed it on top of his. She stared at him, wild-eyed. Rock put his hand down on top of the stack. Caitlyn glanced at him next.

The boys counted to three, and lifted their hands up.

"Hoo-rah!" they shouted. Then, the people in the restaurant stared at them. The boys high-fived each other as Caitlyn sank in her seat, her face red.

"Are you two for real?" she asked, her hands over her face.

"I dunno." Rock shrugged. "This sounds like a lot of work. What's the pay like in this organization of yours, Princess?"

"Almost certain death," she said. Her seriousness was undercut by the fact that her face was still covered.

The boys laughed.

She sat up and shook her head. As they laughed, her lips twisted into a grin, before bursting into a laugh of her own. Teddy preferred seeing her smile.

"You look better like that," he said.

She smiled back at him, letting her laughter level off.

"So, what is New Sun City like, Princess?"

"It's probably the safest place you can be. We watch over it every night, despite the Order trying to make it as difficult as possible. The Maidens of the Old World are a real thorn in their side, and now they're about to get another one." She put her hand back in the center of the table, and winked at the pair. "Are you boys in, or not?"

Teddy threw his hand on top of hers, and Rock paused for a second before placing his on top of the pile. He grinned at Teddy.

Once more after a count of three, the group cheered. For a third time, the handful of patrons stared at them. It was worth it to hear Caitlyn laugh again.

"Then we agree," she confirmed.

"Hoo-rah," Rock said.

Teddy nodded.

The younger boy finished up his father's drink, and the three left the diner. They piled into his father's truck, and finally began to make their way home.

Everything had changed in only a few days. Teddy's hometown had been attacked, Harding had been destroyed, and he was now a Knight of the End. He wasn't a kid anymore.

The darkened world whipped by his window as they chattered on. He had told Caitlyn heroes were real, but he never claimed he *was* one. No, that was the goal. One day he would return to McLeod a real hero.

He still felt the hilt of the Red Sword in his hands. It was a sword that could slay any enemy. It could light the world on fire. And now it was his to use as he saw fit. If he had been chosen to wield it of all people, someone had a bad sense of humor.

But he was still chosen, and he wouldn't let that choice be a mistake.

They reached the turn back into McLeod. For now, the road was looking much too dark and long. He merely smiled.

"So," he said, laughing. "School on Monday should be quite interesting. Wherever that might be!"

Epilogue

Three figures sat in the park outside the hospital. It was remarkably bright outside, the afternoon sun beaming columns of light through the few clouds there were. For autumn, it was surprisingly warm.

Teddy and Rock sat on a park bench. The older boy's father sat in a wheelchair. Rock had told his father he was leaving McLeod, and Teddy was there to explain it. It went over as well as expected.

Mr. Carson scowled at the afternoon sky. Rock's father wore his hospital gown outside, though he hated wearing it, since his burly frame, broad shoulders, and brown beard worked against it. Teddy was starting to understand just where his friend had come from.

"You're supposed to be staying with Uncle Marty, Rochester. You're still in trouble for not telling him, or me, anything about what you were doing that night in Riverview. Did you forget? What makes you think I would agree to let a moron like you go off to New Sun City, and leave your family behind?"

Rock laughed. "Uncle Marty's never liked having me around, Pa. I can do far more good in a place like New Sun than I could here. Other than you, there's nothing keeping me here."

"You hate the city."

"Not as much as I hate sitting around waiting for something to happen."

Mr. Carson leaned forward, his expression hard. "Is this about your mother?"

Rock's lip twitched. "Look, Pa, you get transferred to New Sun and I'll still come to visit. What's wrong with that? We both get what we want. It works out great. I'm in ninth grade. I'm not some little kid."

"I know." His father paused. After a moment, he whipped his attention to Teddy.

The younger boy smiled his best. He didn't understand why Rock had to drag him into this. They hadn't even been acquaintances before recent events, making this even more awkward. But he made a promise, and he would help Rock out. Teddy locked eyes with Mr. Carson.

"Theodore," the older man said. "You haven't known my son very long."

"No, sir."

"Do you think he's got a head on his shoulders? Do you think he has what it takes to help you all in, whatever it is that's going on out there? Don't look surprised, I've heard the rumors. Why else would you go to New Sun City? So, do you trust him? Did he not take money to beat you up?"

"That's not what happened, Pa!" Rock scowled.

"Anyway, how did you even know about that?"

"Your uncle talks about you even when you forget to call or visit. Now, hush." He turned his attention back to Teddy. "Rochester is not the type of person you can pin your hopes on. He's got a head like a bowling ball. Do you think getting him involved with this mess is smart?"

Teddy scratched his tied-back hair. He was the Pyre Knight, the Knight of Flames, but he couldn't just unload this all on Mr. Carson. The previous night, Rock and Teddy had tried out their armor, and the shattered pieces were whole again. This power was miraculous. Just like magic. But Mr. Carson was a hard-nosed man. It was incredible enough that Teddy could describe this to his own parents. All he could do was be honest.

"I don't really know, Mr. Carson."

"Call me Donny."

Teddy flinched. "You have the same name as my brother, sir."

"Donald Roderick Carson. It's a good name. Does your brother have the same sense as you, son?"

"My brother was a lot like me before this whole thing started. Quiet kid. I spent most of my time in the woods, or on the trails, waiting for anything to happen. High School didn't give me any thrill. I wanted something more than normal teenage life. I think Rock was the same way."

The older man shook his head. "That was your first mistake. Rochester is just an idiot."

"Pa!"

Teddy laughed. "Then something did happen, something I

thought was impossible. I could be a hero. For real! But I wasn't ready to deal with it, and I screwed up over and over. That all changed when your son showed up. He had my back. He was there for me in a way no one else could be, and we saved the town. Rock is my friend. I've had them before, but you know how kids can be. I can't imagine not having him by my side in a fight. Rock may be rough, but he is a good guy. I would trust him with my life."

Mr. Carson's expression changed. "That is something I never thought I would hear."

"It is the truth," Teddy said. He felt heat in his cheeks. Now it was starting to feel embarrassing.

"You missed it, Pa." Rock giggled like a nine-year-old. "I punched this guy made of stone through a castle wall. It was just like out of the comics! He fell twenty stories and broke into pebbles when he hit the ground."

Teddy chuckled under his breath. Tomorrow it would be thirty stories.

"So you were those Knights, after all," Mr. Carson said, still watching Teddy. "That's hard to believe."

Rock sighed. "Come on, Pa. He ain't lying."

"I never said he was. Look, this is a hard thing for a father to say to a son, but I can't just make this decision at the drop of a hat. I have to think it over." He pushed himself forward in the wheelchair and grunted. Before Rock could stand up he put an arm out to stop him. "The truth is that you haven't had it easy. Your mother disappearing and how I dealt with it was hard on you. And despite all the stupid things your uncle and the school tell me about you, I know there's a good man somewhere in that thick skull. Theodore here is your friend, and he told me so himself. That has to count for something."

Teddy coughed and leaned back against the bench. He couldn't escape the feeling that he shouldn't be listening to this. He tried glancing away from the conversation. He remembered he forgot his root beer in Mr. Carson's room. That would be his chance to slip away.

"Keep this up and you might even have a girlfriend by the end of the week." The old man smiled at his son. "You're becoming a man so fast. Just do something about that hair."

Rock blushed. "Pa! I told you, I'm waiting for the right girl. And my hair is slicked back like the old rockabilly guys. It's cool!"

Teddy shook his head. Rock's old fashioned tastes were so very weird.

Mr. Carson laughed. "Anyway, I do think you should go, if only so that you realize what it is you're leaving here in McLeod. Sometimes we have to leave home to truly appreciate it."

"I don't think I'll be coming back here. This place is nothing but bad news."

"You think that now," Mr. Carson said, "but just wait. Time has a way of changing everything."

Teddy excused himself from the conversation. He used the excuse of getting his drink from the room. They hardly noticed he left.

The hospital halls were remarkably quiet. Most of McLeod was these days. Everyone was leaving, the military having shut the town down, and they would probably not come back. Soon enough, Teddy's family would also be leaving McLeod behind. The old days were gone forever.

He leaned on the windowsill at the end of the hall, and stared out into the town. The afternoon's red sun draped the world in a thick curtain. Those men in the uniforms back in Riverview were definitely not military, but there was nothing he could do about it now. New Sun City would hopefully have the answers he needed. There was much more going on than he knew.

"MacIsaac?"

Teddy looked up. Stieg Johns stood several feet beside him.

"Stieg?"

"You're still here?" Stieg had his hair cut short, and wore normal jeans and a black shirt. It was odd seeing him dressed normal. "I thought you would have left by now. I was just visiting my grandma with my folks. We're getting ready for the move. How about you? Where are you going?"

Nobody would be staying in McLeod, but neither were they all going to the same place. Their homes had been taken from them, and now they had to find new ones. If this was the worst thing Teddy lost in his battle against the Order, he would cope. But things would never be the same.

"I'm going to New Sun City," Teddy replied. "You?"

"Clermont, out west. We were just getting my grandmother ready for the move. You remember her, right?"

Teddy nodded. "I remember everyone."

Stieg slid in beside him, and stared out the window. He

was silent for a little bit, simply letting the quiet rule. It was like things were as they used to be.

"How does it feel to swing a giant sword?" Stieg asked.

Teddy shrugged. "You remember when we slayed that giant golem on the riverbank six years ago?"

"Barely. That was back when we were midgets. We held it down, and you smashed it into bits."

"Right," Teddy said, nodding. "It was cooler than that."

"Oh." Stieg smiled slightly. "Sounds pretty amazing."

Time had a way of changing things. But in this moment things felt like they always did. This was how Teddy wanted to leave his home.

He outstretched a hand. "Goodbye, Stieg."

His old friend paused and let out a sigh. "Not such a dumb little kid anymore, huh?"

"Nope."

"Things are going to be different." Stieg gripped Teddy's hand, and shook it. "My dad says it's a hard world and getting harder. So, don't trip, alright? Be well out there."

"You got it."

They broke their shake. Teddy leaned back on the windowsill. Stieg backed up a few steps before he turned away.

"Goodbye, Teddy. Slay some monsters for me."

Teddy waved to him. "Be well, Stieg."

Stieg Johns disappeared down the hall. Teddy turned back to the red sun. He felt the heat through the window.

The coin in the center of his palm itched. He felt it shining still. He would feel it for the rest of his life.

Mr. Carson was right about missing home. Teddy already missed the trails and the woods, but he missed Mrs. Werner, his house, the people, and even Harding, just as much. McLeod would always be home.

That was the past. It was time to do what was needed, and he was needed elsewhere. That's what heroes are supposed to do.

Teddy clutched his right hand. The coin still pressed itself inside his palm. He glanced back once to where Stieg had been, and then left the hospital to find Rock.

The new world was not all that different from the old one.

About J.D. Cowan

Former anime and video game junkie, J.D. Cowan has instead turned his attention to writing the sorts of stories that inspired him in the first place. He has strange taste, so they'll be just as odd as this one.

He lives somewhere in the wastelands of the North, and can probably be reached by looking around wooded areas where there is a lot of moss. We don't recommend bothering to search for him. He's pretty good at hiding.

He posts at wastelandandsky.blogspot.ca for those interested.